Cruel Justice

M. A. COMLEY

OTHER BOOKS BY
NEW YORK TIMES BEST SELLING AUTHOR
M. A. COMLEY

Cruel Justice

Impeding Justice

Final Justice

Foul Justice

Guaranteed Justice

Ultimate Justice

Virtual Justice

Hostile Justice

Tortured Justice

Rough Justice (coming Jan 2015)

Blind Justice (A Justice novella)

Evil In Disguise (Based on true events)

Forever Watching You (#1 D I Miranda Carr Thrillers)

Torn Apart (Hero Series #1)

End Result (Hero Series #2)

Sole Intention (Intention Series #1)

Grave Intention (Intention Series #2)

It's A Dog's Life (A Lorne Simpkins short story)

ACKNOWLEDGMENTS

As always love and best wishes to my wonderful Mum for the role she plays in my career. Special thanks to my superb editor Stefanie, and my wonderful cover artist Karri. Thanks also to Joseph my amazing proof reader.

Licence Notes.

Prologue

August 30, 2007

The pain intensified from the welts on her naked back. The woman had no concept of time, no idea how long she'd been tied up. Her hands, tightly bound to an old wooden chair, had lost all feeling.

Was this how her life would end?

She had finally grown used to the vile stench permeating her temporary cell.

Time, all she had was time. Time to think, time to ask herself the same questions, over and over. Who was her captor? And why was he holding her captive? What unspeakable thing had she done in her life to make a complete stranger treat her that way? *I'm a kind and caring person, aren't I?*

What type of person keeps a woman locked up in a hellhole like this?

He tortured her with silence when he brought her food, if she could call week-old bread *food*. She had tried different ways to get a reaction out of him, shouting, reasoning—even her pitiful attempt at begging had fallen on deaf ears. His sneer, and the way his dark eyes roamed her naked body, made her skin crawl.

Her own thoughts had started torturing her. Her aching limbs cried out for warm lavender oil–filled baths, if only to wash away the urine stinging her legs and the faeces clinging to her behind. She felt utterly degraded, a far cry from her usual opulent lifestyle.

Every waking minute dragged into agonisingly long hours. *Please, when will this nightmare end? How will this nightmare end?* she repeatedly asked her Maker.

Water dripped constantly in the corner, adding to her torment. She blocked out the noise by reminiscing about happier moments, hoping the memories would help drive away the insanity threatening to seep into her mind. Fearing her life would soon come to an end, she prayed endlessly that her dead husband would be there to greet her when she finally passed over. *How wonderful it would be to feel his arms comforting me now.*

Her heart leapt into her throat when the hatch door swung open. The sudden rush of daylight hurt her eyes, causing them to water. She winced and was swiftly reminded that her right eye had doubled in size from the beating received a few days earlier.

The man gingerly made his way down the precarious ladder, followed by another person.

Her pulse accelerated, furiously gathering momentum. The man crossed the stone floor and stopped in front of her, while the other person disappeared into the shadows to her side.

"Please, please let me go," she pleaded.

The man stared at her for a moment before the vilest of laughs escaped his lips. "Why? Tell me why I should let you go?"

"I beg of you, please, tell me what I have done?"

He smirked and circled her chair. "Ah, ignorance is a blissful thing."

Bile rose in her throat, and she swallowed it back down. "Please, I'm begging you. Please tell me what I've done wrong?"

Through clenched teeth, he said, "If only you *had* done something, helped in some way; but you didn't, did you? It was far easier to just leave us there, to let us rot in that shithole for years. Well, now you know how it feels."

The venom in his voice made her flinch. "I'm sorry, but I have no idea what you mean. Do I know you?"

"You're all the same. You avoid helping those who cry for help. Your kind makes me sick." He jerked his head and spat on her face. "You and your ilk think you're all so mighty. But you're no better than the shite you're sitting on. You're all full of it!"

She cried as he ranted at her.

"You're a filthy, whimpering bitch! What are you?"

She bowed her head.

"*Look* at me when I'm talking to you."

She picked up her head.

"Now what are you?"

"I'm a filthy..."

"Yes? You're a filthy what?"

Snot ran into her mouth as she said, "I...I'm a filthy...whimpering, bitch..." Her throat tightened.

His laughter filled the room.

"Please, could I have a drink of water?"

"Oh, madam would like to quench her thirst?"

"Please?"

"And how about something to eat? You must be hungry. No?"

"Yes."

The man pulled a pair of rubber gloves from his jacket pocket and slipped his hands into them. He then moved to the back of the chair.

She couldn't figure out what he was doing, but when he came to stand in front of her again, he smiled. She gulped at what he had in his hand. Her heart pounded.

"Open your mouth."

"Please don't..."

"But you're hungry. Right? You said you were hungry. Now open your *mouth*. Wide."

Eyes stinging, she opened her mouth, and the wider she did, the more her already-chapped lips cracked.

"Yes, your kind are full of it." He moved closer and shoved a handful of faeces into her mouth. "Now chew and swallow it!"

Between gagging and sobbing, she consumed her own filth.

He looked down towards her pubic area. "You really are a filthy bitch." He removed the gloves and tossed them on the floor.

Between bouts of hysterical laughter, he continued shouting obscenities, but his words seemed jumbled to her already confused mind.

Still very much amused, he turned and walked towards the ladder.

Oh, thank God, they're leaving. She closed her tired eyes for a second, but when she opened them, he was on his way back. Then she noticed the metal bar in his right hand.

Oh, God. Is this the end?

He shuffled closer. "You disgust me!"

Covered in goose bumps, and teeth chattering, she peered up into the evil black eyes angrily eating through her flesh.

"Did you hear me?"

"I—I don't understand. What have I done to deserve this?" she mumbled.

"I have had *enough*, you stuttering, smelly bitch." He raised the bar.

The woman's terrified scream pierced the tiny room, but her terror was lost in his madness. The bar crashed down, and in one blow, he smashed her skull wide open. Her life's blood ebbed away.

He continued hitting her as images of his childhood ran through his crazed mind. Strike after strike, he punished her, unaware that her last breath had left her body five minutes before.

Satisfaction overwhelmed him.

A large saw lay in the cellar corner, and as though about to reach an orgasm, he grabbed it and positioned it on the woman's lifeless neck. Back and forth, back and forth, he pushed it—faster, faster— and as he cut through the tendons and bones, he clenched his teeth until her head fell onto the floor.

The other person stepped out from the shadows from whence she'd silently observed the proceedings.

He turned to face her. He could tell, by the way her face lit up, she was pleased with the precision and the eagerness of his actions.

"The first part of the puzzle is now in place," said the man.

"Yes, and we both know there's no turning back, now."

"Yes. This is just the beginning…"

Chapter One

September 30, 2007

Lorne pulled the large scatter cushions off the sofa and onto the floor while Tom threw another log on the open fire. They both sighed with satisfaction as they sank into the cushions.

So far, the evening had gone according to plan. It had been months since they'd shared a meal together, and even longer since they'd shared any form of intimacy. She poured two glasses of the wine on the side table next to the sofa and felt excitement build inside.

Tom pulled her back and hooked an arm around her shoulders.

"We miss not having you around," he whispered in her ear.

Sighing contentedly, Lorne swung her legs over his lap and nestled her head into his shoulder. "I know. I miss Charlie and you, too. I also miss sharing romantic evenings with the man of my dreams. It feels like years since we've done anything like this." She touched the cold wine glass against her cheek to cool it. Was she really blushing, or was that heat from the crackling fire? "I kinda feel like a naughty teenager."

"Do you remember what we used to get up to as naughty teenagers?" Tom asked seductively, his hand playfully stroking its way up her slim thigh.

His long-awaited touch sent thrills shooting through her usually tense body. "We didn't know each other when we were teenagers, you idiot. You mean before Charlie came along?"

"Point taken. Do you regret having her?"

Shocked by his unexpected question, she sat up and frowned. "Of course not. Do you?"

Tom had been in a funny mood with her for months—she had put it down to her working more overtime than usual. But maybe she was wrong, and their problems ran deeper than that.

In thirteen years of marriage, they had never really discussed how their lives had panned out since having their daughter, who was away for the night on a sleepover at a friend's house. Now Lorne couldn't help wondering where the conversation was leading.

He reached up and gently repositioned her head on his chest before saying, "No, I don't, but…"

And that one simple word appeared to linger dangerously between them like high-voltage electricity.

Again Lorne tried to sit up, but Tom's hand clamped her head like a vice. "Tom, let go of me."

She exhaled a frustrated sigh and tried to suppress the uncertainty bubbling inside. With one forceful kick, she sat upright and glared down at him, shifting position slightly to prevent him from pulling her back into a cuddle. "What the hell does that mean? *'But…'*?"

His arms formed a blockade across his broad chest, his lips pressed firmly together as he refused to answer her.

Sucking in a deep breath, she bolstered herself to demand, "Tom, if you have something you want to get off your chest, let's have it."

Oh God, please don't spoil things and fly off the handle. At the moment, I can't cope with a week of your sulking.

"Come on, sweetheart. You obviously have something on your mind," she coaxed, smiling.

"Okay, I'll tell you what's going on with me. But remember, you asked," he replied, reaching for his drink. He downed the contents of his glass in one noisy swallow and looked as if he was trying to summon up the courage to continue.

She nodded. She'd never seen Tom like this. His chocolate brown eyes showed signs of worry that unsettled her stomach.

Clinging onto the now empty glass, he stood up and paced round the room. "It's not easy to say this."

His hesitation annoyed her. "Just spit it out, Tom."

He ran a shaking hand through his thick black hair. She could see how painful it was for him to find the right words. *He's going to confess to having an affair.* She braced herself as his lips opened and the words tumbled out.

"I'm fed up with being taken for granted. Your job means more to you than we do. I'm fed up making excuses when Charlie asks what's keeping you at work. Which you have to admit, happens frequently, lately."

Tears sprang to her eyes as relief overwhelmed her; he wasn't having an affair after all. "Oh, Tom. Honey, we knew how much our lives would change when I accepted this promotion. We discussed it—"

"I seem to remember it being a one-sided discussion that began with, 'I've been offered promotion,' and ended with 'I've accepted it.' What choice did I have in the matter? None, zilch, nothing, fuck all. Some discussion *that* turned out to be."

"That's not fair. What was I supposed to do? Turn down the promotion? Do you realise how the force would have reacted to that? I would've remained a sergeant for the rest of my career," Lorne said, scrambling to her feet, ready for further confrontation.

"At least Charlie would know who her mother was," he childishly snapped back.

"I don't see you complaining when you're spending my hard-earned money," she mumbled.

"Oh, it's *your* money, is it?" he retaliated, his eyes wide with anger.

"You know I didn't mean that," she said, frustrated, beating a clenched hand against her thigh. "I appreciate what you've given up to look after Charlie, but that was a decision we made *together* years ago. Or are you going to throw that one at me next?"

The long drawn-out silence was deafening.

"Perhaps I didn't bank on Charlie being so difficult to bring up," he stated quietly.

Guilt wrapped her like a tight bandage. She kicked herself for not appreciating his loneliness sooner. "Baby, I'm so sorry..." she walked towards him.

He turned his back and stood by the window. Shocked, she placed a gentle hand on his shoulder, but he shrugged it off.

"I don't *want* or *need* your sympathy, Lorne," he said, pulling back the curtain. He placed his hands on the windowsill and gazed out.

"What do you want, then?"

After a few minutes' silence, he mumbled pitifully, "I want my fucking life back."

She closed her eyes and sighed. "I'm sorry, Tom; I just don't understand what you mean by that. *You* have a life. *We* have a life. *We* have a very good life, in fact—"

"No, you're the one with a life. I'm merely existing. You leave the house at eight and get back around seven thirty—when you don't bother doing any overtime, that is. While 'good old Tom' looks after our child's needs and cleans the house. Christ, do you have any idea how bloody mundane that is, five days a week?" he said, his voice rising along with the colour in his cheeks.

Lorne could imagine the same conversation going on in thousands of households all over the country, except it was probably the wives complaining to the husbands after they came home from a long day at work.

She blew out an exasperated breath and asked, "How long have you felt like this?"

"Months. Only you've been too busy to notice."

Henry, their border collie, sat by the kitchen door, whimpering at their raised voices, and Lorne couldn't help being distracted for a moment.

"Come here, boy. It's okay." He approached her, and she patted his head reassuringly. "Go lie in your bed."

The dog trotted back to the kitchen, his head hung low. Lorne had bought him as a pup, five years before, as a present for her husband. Tom had named him after his favourite footballer, Thierry Henry. But the dog seemed to regard Lorne as his master, not Tom, which in itself had caused problems between them.

"Huh, even the dog gets more attention than I do."

"Grow up, Tom." As soon as the words left her lips, she regretted saying them.

Tom turned to face her and grabbed her by the shoulders, "So *that's* what you really think of me? That I've failed to grow up along the way? Right, you can bloody well put your resignation in at work tomorrow, because this time next week, lady, I'm going back to work. Do you hear me, Lorne? Then we'll see how long it takes you to crack looking after our angelic daughter day in, day out. Just remember one thing: It's taken *twelve years* for my sanity to diminish. We'll see how long you last, shall we?"

His grip on her shoulders had intensified during his speech, and he hadn't noticed her wincing in pain. "Tom, you're hurting me."

"Hurt? You don't know the meaning of the word," he said through gritted teeth, refusing to loosen his grip.

Oh God, he's lost it.

Lorne tried to shrug his hands off, but his grip tightened. Despite her crying out for him to stop, he refused to let go. He was like a crazed man, and she knew only one way to stop him. Her knee made contact with his groin, a slight nudge—or so she'd thought, just enough force to make him let go. To her amazement, he dropped to the floor and writhed in agony.

"Tom, I didn't mean to do it so hard. Please, let me help you up." She bent down to try to comfort him.

"Get away from me you, crazy bitch." He flung out an arm, and his clenched fist caught her just above the eye.

She flew across the room and landed in a heap on the cushions. Henry ran to her and licked the blood trickling from her brow.

"It's okay, boy. Go back to your bed," she told him, stroking his head, but the dog seemed to sense more trouble ahead and refused to leave her side. He sat down beside her and eyed Tom warily. Lorne feared what would happen if Tom laid another hand on her.

She noticed her mobile vibrating on the coffee table by the sofa.

Here we go. Lorne struggled against the softness of the cushions to retrieve her phone. She felt bone tired, weary beyond words, and it showed in her voice when she answered the phone. "Hello. DI Simpkins."

The girl on the switchboard said, "Um, sorry to disturb you, ma'am. A body's been discovered on your patch, and we wondered if—"

"Give me the details," Lorne said, as Tom staggered to his feet and headed towards the kitchen. Henry growled as Tom passed, but Lorne tugged his collar to chastise him.

"The details are a bit sketchy at the moment, ma'am. The body was found in Chelling Forest. It appears to be a few weeks old."

"Great. Protective masks at the ready when I get there, then," she muttered drolly.

"I'll take that as an affirmative then, ma'am?"

"Yes, I'll attend. Have you contacted Detective Sergeant Childs yet?"

"My colleague's on the other line with him now. She's giving me the thumbs up, ma'am. He's en route."

"Bang goes yet another romantic evening," Lorne complained half-heartedly, pretending everything was as it should've been at home.

"Yes, ma'am. Sorry, ma'am," the controller sympathised.

Lorne wasn't sorry, though; anything but. "I'll be there ASAP." She flipped her phone shut, sighed heavily, and ruffled Henry's head. Then she told him to stay while she went in search of her pissed off and pissed up husband.

Tom was sitting at the kitchen table, his hands wrapped around a glass and a half-empty bottle of whisky.

Leaning against the doorframe, anger making her blood boil, she tucked her hair behind her ears. "Tom, I've got to go to work. We'll have to finish our discussion later."

He ignored her and continued to stare at his glass.

At that moment, she hated him for the damage he was causing their marriage. After a quick change of clothes, she gathered her phone, coat, and handbag and left the house, her heart heavy.

Chapter Two

Chelling Forest was around half an hour's drive from Lorne's home. The vile weather meant that thankfully, the roads were quiet.

The storm had dispersed, but the rain was less considerate and still came down in torrents. Lorne tutted, fearing the elements would hamper their investigation. Any possible footprints would be washed away long before she got there.

Arriving at the location at ten twenty PM, Lorne saw several emergency vehicles already at the scene. A *Sky News* cameraman and reporter were set up, broadcasting a live report. Experience told Lorne that before long the area would be flooded with other reporters, both print and TV, hungrier for the grisly story than a pack of starving wolves would have been for road kill. Mercifully, the area had been cordoned off with blue and white crime tape.

She opened the glove compartment and hunted for a plaster. After wetting her finger with spittle, she wiped the trickle of blood from her brow, then applied the plaster. She moved to the trunk and swapped her low-heeled court shoes for Wellies. Pulling on her light waterproof jacket to protect her navy pinstriped suit, she set off in search of her team.

"Inspector Simpson, can you tell us what you've found?" the reporter shouted.

"Evening, Bill. See you're first on the scene, as usual. When I'm less pressed for time, perhaps we can have a chat about how you manage to get your information so quickly. And, just so you get your facts straight this time, the name is DI Simpkins, okay?"

The reporter had the decency to look embarrassed, if only for a few seconds "Oops, sorry. Didn't mean to cause offence. Are we looking at a murder enquiry?"

"Give me a break, Bill. I've only just arrived. As soon as we have any information, you'll be the first to know. You and the other gathering news teams, that is," she added with a wry smile.

The small rivers of mud squelched underfoot as she plodded through the forest. She'd already spotted her partner's car amongst the parked vehicles, which made her feel a little easier. Pete Childs would be asking all the right questions.

"Evening, ma'am. Foul evening in more ways than one." A uniformed officer, halfway up the track, acknowledged her.

She nodded in agreement and continued along the muddy pathway.

Her head pounded with every step she took. *How has my marriage got in such a state?* She knew Tom hadn't meant to strike her, but there was no getting away from the fury she'd seen in his eyes. *Is that my fault too?*

As Lorne dodged another puddle, her thoughts turned to a few years before, when she would bring Charlie and Henry to that very wood. The pair ran innocently, playing hide-and-seek among the huge oak trees.

After the night's discovery, she'd think twice before coming anywhere near that place again, even in broad daylight. *Christ, what if Henry had dug up the body, and Charlie had been the first to discover it?* She shuddered at the thought; it didn't bear thinking about.

After a few more minutes of trudging through mud and sopping wet leaves, she finally reached the scene.

The Scene of Crime Officers had erected a marquee, protecting the body from the rain seeping through the gaps in the branches overhead.

Pete Childs approached her. "What the hell happened to you?"

"I don't suppose you'd believe me if I told you I walked into a door, would you?"

"Are you saying what I think you're saying?" he said incredulously.

"It was an *accident*. Your concern is duly noted, but leave it alone, Pete."

"You're kidding me? Some bloody accident when a man's fist connects with his wife's face. When we've finished here, I'm going round to sort out your old man."

Lorne stepped forwards and rubbed her hand up his arm. "That's sweet of you, Pete, but I'm afraid I provoked him. I can handle Tom. In fact, if it hadn't been for my police combat training, it wouldn't have happened in the first place.

"Right, what have we got here?" She swiftly changed the subject as she pulled on a pair of white throwaway overalls and put plastic shoes over her feet.

With a defeated shake of the head, Pete apprised her of the situation and informed her that the two teenagers, who'd literally stumbled across the headless corpse, were being questioned down at the station.

The only significant conclusion the team had managed to gather so far was that the corpse was that of a woman.

The putrid smell of rotting flesh hit them as soon as they entered the tent. Pete coughed and gagged. It still amazed Lorne how, after seventeen years on the force, her partner hadn't grown accustomed to the fetid odour emitted from dead bodies.

Lorne groaned when she saw who the attending pathologist was. They'd had more than a few unsavoury contretemps in the past. Jacques Arnaud had a bigger ego than Mont Blanc. Lorne and Pete stood alongside the Home Office Pathologist, who appeared to be transfixed by the body lying on the ground at his feet. His thumb and forefinger were placed studiously on either side of his chin.

"What've we got, Doc?" Lorne asked the greying forty-year-old, who was rumoured to be a descendant of the French aristocracy. His sexy French accent and good looks had most of her colleagues drooling over him. Lorne, however, remained unimpressed, as she'd been on the receiving end of his sharp tongue and French arrogance far too often.

She waited patiently for his reply.

After a while, the doctor needlessly informed her, "I'm thinking, if you don't mind, Inspector."

"About what, exactly, Doctor?" Lorne persisted sardonically, her blood boiling at his tone.

"The case, of course. It's a strange one," he said.

"In what way?" Lorne asked, fighting to keep the tedium from her voice. *He's such a bloody wind-up merchant, not at all like his predecessor, Dr Thomas, who always bent over backwards to help out the officer in charge.* Word had it that no one at the station liked working with Arnaud. But his results more than made up for his crap attitude. Arnaud was considered the best in his field, with ground-breaking developments in DNA to his name.

"I suspect the victim has been dead for approximately one month," he stated thoughtfully, circling the corpse.

"And?" Lorne prompted.

"The crime was *not* committed here. At some point, the body was moved."

"Didn't you say that the girl kicked the body as she stumbled over it?" Lorne asked Pete.

"Yeah, that's right, she—"

Arnaud, his nostrils flaring, interrupted her partner. "I mean physically moved, not disturbed by a mere kick. The killer probably thought the body would likely be discovered at another site, therefore he or she decided to move it. It wouldn't be the first time I've seen that happen. A mistake that, in the end, will prove to be his or her downfall."

"How can you tell?" Lorne asked, mystified by his assumption.

"I believe I've said too much already. It's pure conjecture at this moment in time. I'll let you know after the post-mortem," Arnaud informed her offhandedly.

"Do you mind if I'm present at the post-mortem, Doctor?"

"It's your prerogative as leading investigator on the case, is it not? Now, if you don't mind, I still have quite a lot of work to do here."

Lorne and Pete stepped outside the tent.

"God, he can be such a prick at times," Pete complained.

"Yeah, a giant one, but he's the best around. Unfortunately, the arrogant git is aware of that. I suspect that's why he thinks he can treat everybody else at the scene as imbeciles. Come on. Let's get back, see what the kids have to say?"

"We've just got to make a slight detour," Pete reminded her.

"Oh no, you don't, Pete. I can sort Tom out without any outside influences. Thanks all the same. What were you doing when you got the call?"

"Nothing much. Having a couple of beers and enjoying an episode of *CSI* on the box."

"You're pathetic, you know that? You watch *CSI* and all the blood and guts that entails, but when you're faced with a real corpse you nearly pass out. You're such an idiot," she said, playfully punching his arm as they made their way back to their cars.

Pete had been blessed with a face only a mother could love, and a body most women shied away from, so girlfriends had been low down on his agenda for years. He'd recently confided in Lorne that his last date had been fifteen years before. The relationship had turned sour quickly, and he swore blind that he'd never be taken for a fool again. He had stopped short of telling her why his relationship had come to an abrupt end.

"Telly's different to real life though, ain't it?"

"You mean you can watch TV through your fingers!" She laughed at the image she'd conjured up. "You do know the cases portrayed in those programmes are all based on actual events, don't you?"

"You're pulling my wotsit. How do ya know that?"

"It's at the end in the credits. It states that *Michael Baden* is an advisor on the show." She didn't have a clue if that was true on every episode, but the ones she'd managed to catch had shown his name.

"And who the hell might this 'Michael Balden' be?"

"*Baden.* That's *B A D E N*. Doctor Michael Baden. He's only one of the world's leading forensic pathologists. But I wouldn't expect you to know that. You just watch the damn programmes and don't think about all the work and research that goes in to them."

"All right, *Mrs. Know-It-All.* Sometimes you're just too smart for words."

"And that, my dear Pete, is why I'm DI, and you're still a sergeant," she joked, knowing that if he wanted to pursue promotion, he could achieve it standing on his head. He was the type of person who couldn't be bothered to go for promotion; the force was full of them. That, plus the facts that he enjoyed being her partner and they were regarded as one of the best teams in the Met.

They left in their respective vehicles. Lorne, in her Vauxhall Vectra family car, watched and shook her head as Pete drove away in his beat-up old Lada that looked and sounded more like a

Sherman tank. His pride and joy, the Lada was the best five hundred quid he'd ever spent, he told her daily. Lorne usually retaliated by saying the salesman must have laughed like a crazed man, the day Pete Childs drove that monstrosity off his forecourt.

As Lorne pulled away from the scene, her mobile rang. She glanced at the caller ID before answering it. Not Tom—if it had been him, she would have ignored it and thought up an excuse for not answering it by the time she got home. "Hi, Sis. What's up?" she asked jovially.

"We've had Tom on the phone for the past fifteen minutes. What the hell have you done to him? The poor man's distraught—"

"Take a breath, for Christ's sake, Jade."

She heard her sister take some heavy breaths before continuing. "Why did you do it, Lorne? How could you do such a thing, and to your husband of all people?" Her tone suggested she was straining to keep calm. Jade thought the world of Tom and tended to side with him whenever Lorne and Jade argued.

Exhaling a deep breath, Lorne indicated and flashed Pete's car, letting him know she was pulling over. Pete slowed and pulled in a couple of hundred yards ahead.

"Jade, calm down. Look, I can't deal with this right now. I'm on a case. We've just discovered a body in the woods."

"Jesus, woman. Is that all that matters to you, your bloody work? What about your marriage? It's falling apart at the seams. Can't you see that?"

"Hardly, Jade. One argument, and you think we're heading for the divorce courts. Tom and I are having a few problems at the moment, granted, but we'll sort them out without any well-meaning interference from others."

"So, now you're telling me to keep my nose out. That it's none of my business you physically attacked your child's father."

"Umm… Slight exaggeration. Is that on your part or Tom's, I wonder?" Anger made Lorne's pulse quicken. *What the hell is Tom playing at? Involving Jade in our domestic dispute. What a truly selfish bastard he is.*

"What do you mean by that? God, if that man only knew what you did behind his back last year—"

"That's enough, Jade. You promised me you'd never bring that up again. No need to ask where your loyalties lie, is there? Oh, and by the way, I don't suppose Tom happened to admit, when he was busy running me down, that he hit *me* and split my eyebrow open?"

Jade gasped. Then she was silent.

Lorne spoke softly. The last thing she wanted was to fall out with her sister, whom she'd always been really close to. "Listen, sweetie, I know you mean well, but this is something Tom and I have to sort out by ourselves. Oh, I'm fine, by the way. Thanks for asking. It was an accident," she added and laughed gently.

"Oh, Lorne, can you ever forgive me?"

"What's to forgive? It's forgotten already. Just promise me that you'll get both sides of the story next time, before having a go at me. And… don't refer to that little misdemeanour again. Look, I've gotta go. I'll call you tomorrow, okay?"

"I promise. I'm sorry. Be careful out there." Her family had picked up that saying from watching *Hill Street Blues* years ago. They'd said it every day their father left the house when they were kids. He had reached DCI during his time in the Met.

After her sister had hung up, Lorne was tempted to ring Tom and give him a piece of her mind, but she knew that would only do more damage. She'd deal with him in her own time. His selfishness was really starting to annoy her. At the moment, she got the impression she had more support from her five year old bra than the husband who had promised to love, honour, and cherish her.

She flashed her lights at Pete and pulled out.

* * *

Back at the station, the desk sergeant informed them that the kids who had discovered the body were in interview rooms one and two.

"The girl's quite distraught, and she's been seen by the police doctor. He's given you the green light to question her for a few minutes," the sergeant said. Lorne wondered if the doctor realised they were dealing with a murder enquiry.

Outside room one, she told Pete, "I'll take the boy. You can have the girl."

"Cheers, boss. That's the thanks I bloody get for giving up my evening off?" he moaned under his breath.

"Stop whinging, and get on with it. Be gentle with her. And listen to what she has to say, don't make any snap judgements."

"That's like telling my grandma how to suck eggs. I ain't new to this game, ya know."

"I know that. But your interviewing techniques lately haven't exactly been by the book, have they, Pete?" She raised an eyebrow.

"Point taken. But I'm not likely to give a distraught female a clout round the ear, now am I?"

As Lorne stepped into the interview room, Todd Altman looked up. She pulled out the chair opposite him. "Hi, Todd. I'm DI Lorne Simpkins. Look, I know how difficult this must be, and I'd like to thank you for helping us with our enquiries. I've just got a few questions, and then you'll be free to go."

"I've told your *mates* everything I know. When can Zoe and me go home?" he asked, firmly gripping his cup of coffee. His hand was shaking so much that the coffee splashed out of his cup.

Lorne felt sorry for the nineteen-year-old, who appeared to be traumatised but trying hard to disguise it. His red eyes showed how much he had cried in the last hour or so.

"Soon, I promise," she said. "Now, what were you doing in the forest at that time of night?"

He glanced over at the male officer standing in the far corner for help.

Lorne followed his gaze and saw the officer shrug. "Todd?"

The teenager shuffled his feet nervously, and Lorne got the impression he was too embarrassed to confide in her. She smiled reassuringly to put him at ease.

He cleared his throat before replying, "Zoe and me go there ev'ry Thursday. It's the only place we can be alone, if you know what I mean?"

"I think I get the picture. I can think of more comfortable places to have sex though, especially in the middle of a storm. Do you still live at home, Todd?"

"Yeah, I do. So? What's that gotta do with anythin'?" he asked defensively.

"Do your parents know that you go down the woods to play? Furthermore, do *you* know that it's an offence to have sexual intercourse in a public place?" she stated, slapping the teenager down.

"I know, I'm sorry. You're not gonna arrest me for that, are ya?"

Lorne fought hard to suppress a smile. "No, we won't be arresting you this time, Todd. But in future, watch where you sow your oats, okay?"

"Yes, miss. No fear of that, miss. After finding that body, my oat-sowing days in open places are well and truly over." His relief was evident, and for the first time, Lorne noticed a sparkle in his baby blue eyes.

"How was the body when you found it?" The lad smirked, and she sensed he was going to give her a wise-arse response, so she promptly rephrased her question. "I mean, was the body buried or exposed?"

"It was covered with leaves when Zoe stumbled over it. Something spooked her. She took flight and kicked it while she was running. She said the forest had an eerie feel tonight. She doesn't usually complain." He took a sip of his coffee.

Lorne's notebook lay open in front of her but remained empty. She had a sinking feeling this interview was going to be a complete waste of time. "When was the last time you and Zoe visited the woods?"

"Last week, I think."

"I need honest answers, Todd. Was it last week or not?"

"Yeah, it was last Thursday. The weather was better then. I wish we hadn't gone down there tonight, that's for sure."

"Did you see anyone else in the woods?"

"I don't think so."

"Think, Todd. It's important. It could be vital to the case," Lorne urged the youngster and watched pain show in his expression.

"Nope, don't remember seeing anyone. Can we go now? You won't tell our parents, will you?"

Lorne let out a dissatisfied sigh. "You can go, but if you think of anything, anything at all, ring me. Okay?" She pushed back her chair and handed him one of her cards.

There was no point hanging onto the kids. She tapped on the door to the other interview room and asked Pete to join her in the corridor. He came out a few seconds later.

"Did you get anything out of the girl?"

"Not even a tadpole of a clue. She cried, then bawled, then cried some more. Total waste. How about you?" her frustrated partner asked, pulling his trousers up by the waistband.

"About the same. Let's get shot of them and grab a coffee before Doctor Arnaud summons us. You losing weight, Pete?" she asked with a teasing smile.

"Fat chance," he replied before returning to the interview room. Lorne watched from the door as he gave the girl one of his cards. Zoe burst into tears again, and Lorne sent Todd in to calm her down.

* * *

"How you feeling?" Pete tentatively asked Lorne when they reached the canteen.

"Thanks for asking, Pete, but I'm fine." She intentionally avoided his eyes. They had a good working relationship. They'd been together for four years and knew each other well. Too well, at times.

"Why did he do it?" he asked, concern showing in his voice.

She knew what Pete thought of men who lashed out at their wives and suspected Tom, a close friend of his, had ultimately gone down in his estimation. "I'd rather not talk about it, if you don't mind." She kept her head down as she absently played with her cup.

Pete held up his hands in surrender—he knew how stubborn she could be. "Okay, boss. But you know where I am if you want to unburden yourself."

"Thanks, partner." Lorne smiled. She reached across the table and patted his hand.

Lorne regarded Pete as a brother, teasing him one minute, then shouting at him the next. It also meant they had a strong relationship, one built on trust and understanding. Pete was the type to jump in feet first, whereas Lorne took two steps back and analysed cases logically. Over the years their balanced partnership had served both them and the Met well.

A couple of uniformed officers joined them, and not long after that, Lorne's mobile received the message they'd been waiting for. "Arnaud awaits, Pete. You ready for this?"

"Far from it," he mumbled, pushing back his chair.

"Come on. Let's get it over with." She shuddered at the thought of spending the next three or four hours with Doctor Arnaud.

Chapter Three

"Nice of you to come so promptly," Arnaud said, when the two detectives arrived at the spotlessly clean St Patrick's hospital mortuary.

Knowing how Pete felt about sarcasm, Lorne shot him a warning glance to not retaliate.

"Well! What are you waiting for? A number seven bus? For God's sake, go get suited and booted. Bones, show them the way."

His pathologist assistant, Bones, grudgingly showed them to the locker room. He rummaged through the tall plastic container in the corner marked "CLEAN" and withdrew two sterilised green operating gowns that had been discarded by surgeons.

The hospital deemed it a waste of funding to supply new greens for use in the pathology department, especially when, at the end of a post-mortem, the blood-soaked uniforms were disposed of in the hospital's incinerator, anyway. Booties slipped over their shoes completed their fetching ensemble; they were ready to go.

On the return journey up the long hallway to the doctor's theatre, Pete gave a small cough and said, "Well, then…"

Lorne cringed and braced herself. Her partner was about to ask one of his dumb questions.

"What's with the nickname?" Pete asked his unsuspecting victim.

The small geeky-looking assistant snapped back, "Bones isn't my *nickname*; it's my surname."

Pete smiled.

"You got a problem with that? And yeah, I've heard all the wisecracks in this universe and the next, so don't waste your time even trying to come up with a new one."

"Hey, mate, no insult intended, just trying to make conversation," Pete replied, his smile slipping.

Lorne suppressed a chuckle at how Pete seemed put out by the young man's abruptness.

Out of the corner of his mouth, Pete said to her, "Touchy, ain't he? Guess his sense of humour died a long time ago, working in a dead-end job like this."

"Give it a rest, Pete." She elbowed him in the ribs and added, "Shut that overworked mouth of yours for a change, will you?" His mistimed humour was all bravado, a sign of how uncomfortable he was in his surroundings.

Inside the post-mortem suite, Lorne approached the stainless steel table in the centre of the room. Standing approximately eighteen inches from the corpse's feet guaranteed her a bird's-eye view of the proceedings. Pete however, positioned himself alongside a chair that'd been handily placed next to the exit, ideal for a quick getaway. His pusillanimity in their environment was laughable.

Arnaud stood next to the table and snapped on his latex gloves. His tools were laid out on the waist-high trolley beside him. Eyeing the tools, Lorne thought some of them looked as though they had been purchased at the local DIY store, rather than a medical supplier. Alongside the pruning clippers and the vibrating bone saw was a knife that resembled a bread knife she used at home. There were also various-sized scalpels, probably painstakingly sharpened by his assistant, Bones, after every examination.

Bones unzipped the bag, and both men, one on either side of the table, slid the bag from under the body.

Lorne glanced over at Pete as the corpse, which had been wrapped in a white sheet at the scene, lay like a midget-mummy on the table.

After Bones and Arnaud carefully removed the sheet, Lorne hoped Pete wouldn't faint—or throw up—at the sight of the headless, rotting trunk.

Bones cautiously placed the sheet to one side, making sure any trace of evidence, no matter how small, would stay in the sheet, to be studied in depth later.

The perforated table the body now lay on would allow any excess fluids to run through it and settle in the drip tray below, and those samples would also be analysed.

Bones walked over to the recorder and switched it on.

As Arnaud made his first cut into the torso, Lorne quickly donned her surgical mask. It didn't take long for the smell of decomposing flesh to waft over to where Pete was standing. He gagged, his knees buckled, and he dropped into the chair beside him.

Darn it. Just as I thought. The post-mortem suite was where the men were sorted from the boys. For some reason, the women seemed to cope far better in the environment than their male counterparts. Lorne always thought that having to go through the ordeal of childbirth worked in a female officer's favour.

"While I dissect the body, please feel free to ask any questions," Arnaud said brusquely.

The doctor was one of the few pathologists she knew who performed a post-mortem without wearing a mask. She'd once asked him why, only for him to snap that 'a mask disguises crucial smells,' like the smell of almonds, when cyanide had been used in a homicide. Lorne had a suspicion that Arnaud got a kick out of the vile stench of rotting flesh and was too ashamed to admit he had a fetish.

"At the scene, you suspected the body had been moved. Can you tell us why, Doctor?" Lorne asked, her fascination piquing with every cut he made.

"Ah, yes. Although the body had been discovered beneath a pile of leaves, it was caked in mud. As far as I know, when a pile of leaves breaks down, it does *not* mysteriously change its natural composition. I suspect that somebody returned to the body, to remove its limbs. You see here." He pointed to the gaping hole in the right shoulder. "The arm has been *pulled* from its socket, not detached with a sharp implement. This can only be carried out with ease once the body has begun to decompose."

"Oh Jesus," Pete cried as he bolted through the heavy plastic door.

"I see your colleague appears to have lost his stomach for the job," the Frenchman said, smirking, a glint in his smouldering dark brown eyes.

A smile touched her taut lips. So this arrogant man did have a sense of humour after all.

Chapter Four

Lorne's autopilot kicked in to get her home without much effort. Before long, she had her front door open and was easing her way along her narrow Minton-tiled hallway. Leaning against the decorative dado rail, she removed the shoes that had imprisoned her aching feet for the previous five hours. Standing over a corpse in a sanitised cold environment certainly took its toll.

The post-mortem had turned out to be disappointingly inconclusive. Doctor Arnaud suspected the cause of death would *only* be determined once the missing limbs had been recovered. He'd been positive about only one thing—a homicide had been committed.

Exhausted both mentally and physically, Lorne couldn't summon up enough energy to climb the stairs to take a shower, despite the putrid smell of rotting flesh lingering uninvitingly on her clothes. Instead she wandered through to the kitchen. The newness of the wood was a welcome relief to her nostrils. Tom had recently refurbished it in a contemporary style of beech and stainless steel.

Henry approached her sleepily. "Hello, boy. How's it going?" she asked, petting his silky head. She took a crystal tumbler from the cupboard above the granite breakfast bar and filled it with the remains of the whisky.

The sharp aroma of the amber-coloured liquid transported her to pastures far away. To the sumptuous heather-clad hillsides of Scotland. To a little holiday cottage Tom and she used to visit regularly before Charlie came along. Life had been so different back then. They'd been free spirits, without a care in the world. Now they were just an ordinary married couple, trapped in the midst of time, waiting for their child to fly the nest.

With Henry close to her heels, she crept back into the lounge, switching on the lamp on the small table beside the sofa. She groaned as she settled her weary body on the cushions her husband had left strewn across the floor. The burning embers of the fire still radiated enough heat for the room to feel comfortable. Henry sidled up to her. She stroked him, and he licked her face in return.

The whisky warmed her insides as it slid gracefully down her throat. She sighed with contentment and removed the band that had kept her shoulder-length hair in place throughout the post-mortem. She ran her fingers through her locks as she reflected on her day. Eventually her coil-sprung mind cleared, and she drifted off to sleep, wrapped around her devoted four-legged friend.

Four hours later, she woke to find Tom standing over her, glaring.

She stretched and yawned noisily. Henry ran to the back door and whimpered to be let out.

"What time did you get in?" Tom asked.

"I don't know exactly. About three. Are you still in a mood?"

He turned and headed into the kitchen. Lorne shook her head in dismay. After a few minutes, she followed him. He had his back to her. She tiptoed across the room and wrapped her arms around him, her head resting on his back, she asked again, "Are you still in a mood with me?"

Untying himself from her grasp, he stepped away. "Don't you ever stop interrogating people?"

His angry words sent a chill running up her spine. He looked handsome in his burgundy silk robe that was draped open, revealing a muscular, thickly thatched chest she usually adored running her fingers through. Her heart skipped a beat as her eyes lingered on the stunning Mediterranean dark looks he'd fortunately inherited from his father. The problem was he'd also inherited other traits that weren't so charming, such as his temper and unwillingness to compromise.

"Once a policewoman, always a policewoman, I guess." She shrugged an apology.

"You stink. The least you could have done was had a shower."

Lorne shook her head. "Tom, I was buggered when I got home. Give me a break, will you?"

"I don't doubt that. You're always buggered lately," he snapped back at her.

Without realising it, she rolled her eyes—which set him off again.

"Don't bloody do that! You know I'm right. You're always too tired to do anything when you get home from that place, but that doesn't excuse you from not having a shower. You should've had one at work. What gives you the right to bring the smell of death into our home?"

"Are you finished?" She folded her arms defiantly. "For your information, I was at the mortuary last night—"

"That much is evident," he retaliated, eyes narrowed.

"As I was saying, I was at the mortuary, and it was quicker to come home rather than go back to the station. I've never done that before, have I?"

Tom shrugged and had the grace to look ashamed at his uncalled-for outburst. He bent down and took a couple of cereal bowls out of the cupboard. "Do you want some breakfast?" he asked, his tone much softer.

"I'll grab a shower first and then have some, thanks."

As she turned to leave the room, she heard him mumble an apology.

"No problem," she called back over her shoulder and headed up the stairs.

Half an hour later, she found him at the hob frying bacon and eggs. "Not for me, hon. I'll just grab a bowl of cornflakes and head off. Sorry, but I have to be at the station for a nine o'clock meeting with my team."

That was it. The storm clouds gathered again. He threw the frying pan in the sink and stomped out of the room like a five-year-old.

Why do I bother? Her appetite suddenly gone, she left the house moments later. She was tired of fighting. Tired of stepping on eggshells. Tired of saying the wrong thing.

When did it all change?

The happiness they'd once held so dear now seemed light-years away. She didn't have a clue how—or if—they would be able to sort things out. Was their marriage really at breaking point, or was her imagination working overtime?

Chapter Five

"Morning, ma'am," the balding desk sergeant greeted her as she marched through reception.

"Morning, Burt. Anything I should know about?"

"All quiet around here, ma'am, but Chalmers asked me to tell you he'd like a word ASAP."

"What kind of mood is he in?" she asked the sergeant.

"The usual, I guess," he replied vaguely.

DCI Chalmers was an unknown quantity to her team, but Lorne had been with him for many years and understood his quirky ways. He was her mentor. It hadn't taken him long to figure out her potential. He had pushed her to the limit, knew she'd have to work harder than any male under him. He had showed continued faith in her when others obstinately neglected to see her strengths.

Without his guidance, she wouldn't have been half the detective she was, and she would've probably been driven from the force years ago, like most of the female colleagues she had trained with at Hendon. The force, unfortunately, still lived in the Dark Ages, where female recruits were concerned—something that Lorne fought hard to combat daily.

"So, Burt, retirement won't be long now."

"Yep, looking forward to it, after forty years on the job."

"And exemplary service, it's been."

"Nice of you to say so, ma'am."

"And knowing you, you'll enjoy every minute of your retirement, eh?"

He threw her one of his broad smiles that she would miss when he left.

"I'd better see what the chief wants, then. Can you contact the incident room for me? Let the team know the meeting will be delayed a few minutes?"

"Roger that, ma'am," he replied, reaching for the phone.

Lorne poked her head around the chief's door. "You wanted to see me, sir?"

"Come in. Take a seat, Lorne. I shan't be a moment." He didn't look up from the pile of documents he was signing and handing back to his secretary. He dismissed the older woman, who scurried from the room.

"What happened to you?" he asked, indicating the plaster over her eye.

Lorne hesitated, wondering if she should confide in him, but decided against it when she noticed how pale he looked. "Oh, it's nothing. The dog tripped me up last night, and I head-butted the door," she told him, avoiding eye contact.

He eyed her suspiciously, knew she was lying, but Lorne could tell he wasn't willing to press her further. He sighed. "Fill me in on the body discovered last night, will you?"

"Nothing much to tell yet, sir. There was no form of identification found at the scene. Dental records are a no-go, as the head was missing. Someone did everything they could to hinder us. The victim's right arm is missing, and the fingers on the left hand were chopped off at the knuckles."

He bounced back and forth in his chair as Lorne gave him her report. "You couldn't have got much sleep last night, Lorne."

That's strange. He's never been concerned about my sleep before.

"About four hours, I guess—average for this job, I suppose. I'll be fine once I've had my first six cups of coffee." She laughed, but his brow remained furrowed.

"I'm worried about you. That last case you solved must have taken a lot out of you. Going undercover is never easy, especially when you have to deal with scum like that. You look a bit peaky. I can arrange for you to talk to someone, if you like."

There was no denying that her last case had taken its toll on her. She'd been asked by The Serious Crime Squad to pose as a *madame* of a newly opened massage parlour. All the regular girls had been WPCs. They'd had intelligence that a gang headed by Gripper Jones, a notorious dirtbag in the community and business partner of her long-time nemesis The Unicorn, was demanding protection money from the other parlours in the area.

Once the protection commenced, they forced the owners to employ illegal immigrant girls, supplied by the gangs. The girls' families back home were badly beaten if the girls refused to work for the gang. Lorne's world had been turned upside-down—even Tom didn't have a clue what she had been involved in.

Although they caught Jones and his gang, Lorne had been roughed up a little before reinforcements had arrived. Just a few bruises here and there, but mentally her scars ran deep, which was why she needed Tom's support. Perhaps she had been wrong to not tell him about the case, and maybe her decision was backfiring.

"I'm fine. What's going on, boss? This isn't like you." She knew seeing a shrink would only add to her problems, but his concern puzzled her.

He shuffled a few papers on the desk before him—it was his turn to avoid eye contact. She feared the worst. "What I'm about to tell you goes no further."

"Of course. That goes without saying, boss."

"I'm leaving."

A ten-tonne truck couldn't have hit her harder. Her mouth flew open. "You're *what?*" she whispered.

"My, what a lot of fillings you have, my dear," Jeff Chalmers joked, trying to make light of the situation. "I'm taking early retirement. I wanted you to be the first to know."

Lorne shook her head in disbelief. "Excuse my ignorance, sir, but forty-eight isn't considered *that* old, is it?" She was babbling, didn't know what else to say.

Reluctantly he admitted, "Ill health, I'm afraid—something I'd rather not discuss. You understand, don't you, Lorne?"

His gaze switched to the family photo proudly standing on his desk. In it was his beautiful wife Anne, whom he described as having a red-hot temper to match the colour of her hair. Alongside her sat their two strapping sons, who had both graduated from law school over the past few years. He proudly called them 'the oxygen in my life.'

She watched him closely, saw the changing expressions in his face as his finger traced his family, one by one. Lorne feared the worst. She wanted to ask him what was wrong, but there was a tiny part of her that couldn't bear to hear the truth.

No, no, I don't bloody understand. She was losing the best boss she'd ever had the privilege of working with. His departure meant she'd have to spend years proving her worth again. Shit and double shit, as if her life wasn't hard enough at the moment.

You selfish bitch! she reprimanded herself. *Jeff has just told you he's ill, seriously ill, and all you can think about is your own misfortune.* "I don't know what to say, sir. When are you leaving?"

"Two weeks."

"*Two weeks,*" she screeched, like a frustrated parrot. "Can I ask who the new chief will be?"

He glanced down at his desk. "It hasn't been decided yet. I doubt they'll consider promoting anyone around here," he told her, no doubt with little satisfaction.

There was nothing left for either of them to say. With a heavy heart, Lorne left the room. She threw herself dejectedly against the wall outside his office, which was where Pete found her minutes later.

"Fiver for your thoughts? That's inflation for ya," he said buoyantly, mimicking her position against the wall.

"You could pay me all the money in the world, and it still wouldn't be worth me telling you what I'm thinking, Pete ..."

"Time's getting on, boss. We've got a killer to find."

"What are you holding me up for, then? I haven't got time for idle chitchat, man." She propelled herself away from the wall, and Pete broke into stride beside her as they marched down the long grey corridor towards the incident room.

Chapter Six

The team, more boisterous than normal, failed to notice Lorne and Pete's arrival.

Mitch was bragging about his latest conquest, "So I said to her, 'How would you like your eggs in the morning, darlin'? And get this, she replied, 'Fertilised will do.' Jesus, can you believe that? And I thought I had an answer for everything. I can tell you she certainly floored me with that one."

"If you've quite finished, DS Mitchell," Lorne warned.

Mitchell looked embarrassed. If it had been any other day, Lorne would have been the first to rib him about his male prowess not being up to much. But not that day. With all she'd encountered already that morning, her sense of humour had gone AWOL.

"You're probably all aware that Pete and I were called out to a suspected homicide last night."

Pete handed her an envelope containing the crime scene photos. She passed the set of ten-by-eight-inch photos around as she spoke. "Tracy, I want you and Mitch to carry out the door-to-doors. Specifically around the entrance to the forest, a few hundred yards either way. Someone must've seen or heard something. The teenage lovers, the only witnesses we have at the moment, were down there last week and are sure the body wasn't there then."

The photos returned to her one by one, and she passed them to Pete, who pinned them up on the notice board.

"Was there any form of ID, ma'am?" asked Sergeant Tracy Cox, the newest member of the team.

"Nothing. The search teams are out there now. The pathologist's early assumption is that the crime was committed elsewhere; therefore I don't hold out much hope of finding anything substantial at the scene."

"How did the victim die? Obviously, we can all see her head was cut off, but—I mean, was that the actual COD?" Mitch asked, his frivolity forgotten.

"Again, waiting on the path's report. It appears the torso suffered several blows with a blunt instrument. It's anyone's guess what condition the head will be in, *if* or when we find it."

"Do we know when the crime occurred?" DS John Fox queried.

Lorne shook her head. "Until it's substantiated by the report, we can't give a definite answer, but the doc suspected it happened approximately a month ago. John, I'd like you and Molly to trawl through the missing persons' database. Widen the area to, say, a fifty-mile radius of the forest."

"That could take hours," Molly moaned, pulling a face as if she was about to get a bikini wax.

At thirty-five, Molly Cornell was the one member of the team Lorne found hard to tolerate—she suspected envy often got in the way of the woman's work. Lorne had confronted her numerous times about her lousy attitude disrupting the team. But Molly had always insisted there was nothing intentional in her attitude.

"It'll take as long as necessary, Molly," Lorne snapped.

Pete took over before anything escalated between the two women. "Molly, leads are thin on the ground at this stage of the enquiry. So we have to make a start somewhere, right?"

Molly smiled sarcastically and turned back to her computer.

Lorne's eyes blazed with fury as she stared at the back of Molly's head. She could do without another confrontation. Pete was the master at dealing with Molly's obdurate behaviour, and Lorne was happy for him to step in. "Pete, get in touch with neighbouring forces. See if any body parts have turned up. That includes the river police."

"Sure thing, boss."

Lorne left the group to get on with their tasks and walked through to her office. She rang Arnaud's secretary, who informed her that the post-mortem report wouldn't be finalised until late afternoon.

After she completed hours of mindless paperwork, Pete came to rescue her. His suggestion of grabbing a bite to eat was just the tonic she needed. Her head was pounding, and her stomach felt empty after missing out on breakfast.

They decided to eat at a little Italian restaurant on the edge of town.

The waiter placed a bowl of penne pasta topped with a tomato and basil sauce in front of Lorne. "Did Molly find anything of use?"

Pete delayed answering until the waiter had served him his lasagne and side order of chips. "We've got three missing women to follow up on. They all disappeared about a month ago. A twenty-two-year-old—looks as though she's run off with an old boyfriend. Next, a forty-six-year-old bank assistant who suspiciously vanished along with ten grand from the safe—she's a possible. Finally, we have a woman in her sixties who should've turned up for a family christening. Her family listed her as missing a week later."

"Why the delay?"

"It's a regular occurrence—her taking off and forgetting to tell the family, I mean." Between large mouthfuls of lasagne, he rattled off the details of possible victims.

Lorne listened but kept her eyes focused on her meal; she found her partner's eating habits disgusting. A sandwich from the local deli was usually a far less messy option. "We haven't got a definite age from Arnaud yet, so until we do, we better check out the two older likely candidates. There's no way that was a body of a twenty-two-year-old."

Lorne finished her meal and washed it down with a glass of iced water. "While we're on the subject of Molly, what the fuck is her problem? Next time you see her, remind her she's on a final warning for her bad attitude, will you? Because if I have to put up with any more of her unnecessary crap…"

"Yeah, she knows she's on a final warning. She just takes pleasure in winding you up, boss. I'll have a word when I can. The only thing I can say in her defence is that she comes up with the goods. Without her, we wouldn't have these names to go on. Leave her to me; I'll sort her."

Lorne glanced out the window then back at him and asked, "Have you brought the details of the missing women with you?"

"Yup. I guessed you'd want to start chasing things up straight away. I thought we'd start with Sharron Fishland. She works—or worked, I should say—at the DFL bank in Castleway, about twenty minutes from here."

Chapter Seven

Lorne drove, much to the 'Sherman tank' driver's annoyance.

"You might want to wipe the remains of your dinner off your chin before we begin questioning people, Pete," Lorne suggested before they got out of the car.

"I was saving that bit for Ron." The puzzled look on her face forced him to explain the joke. "Later on, 'Ron—get it? I despair of you at times, boss. Your sense of humour—or lack of it—can be so embarrassing."

"Oh. Sorry, Pete, was that supposed to be funny?" She shook her head and rolled her eyes as they both got out of the car.

They entered the busy bank and joined the long queue.

"If there's one thing we Brits love to do more than talk about the weather, it's bloody stand in queues all day," Pete grumbled, shuffling nervously from one foot to the other.

"Stop complaining, and stop fidgeting. You seem damn suspicious. One of the girls will probably push the panic button soon," Lorne told him, voice hushed.

Finally, the computerised announcer invited them to make their way to cashier number three. Lorne produced her ID card and asked the attractive blonde if the manager was free to see them.

"I'll just check for you. One moment, please." The cashier wriggled off her high stool and made her way to the rear of the bank, swaying her oversized rear as she went.

"Jesus, it's like watching two Pitbull terriers having a fight in her knickers. I bet she has to wear those extra large ones like *Bridget Jones*," Pete crudely observed.

Lorne fought hard not to smirk but failed miserably.

The blonde returned moments later, her ample bosom fighting against the half cups of a bra that were obviously a few sizes too small.

"The manager won't be long. If you'd like to take a seat at the other end of the counter, he'll come through that door." The girl aimed her husky reply and dazzling smile at Pete, totally disregarding Lorne.

They headed for the place the woman had indicated. "It would appear you have an admirer."

"Huh, some catch. She's the type that turns a man gay. I bet most of the unfortunate guys she tangles in her web probably end up pleading for someone to cut their dicks off, before she wears them out," he replied, surprisingly straight-faced, as they waited by the door.

Lorne wondered if Pete was speaking from experience.

A well-dressed man in his early forties came to collect them a few minutes later. As he approached, his right hand shook when he slicked back his greying hair, before the same hand straightened the large knot in his pink tie. "I'm Charles Timmins, the manager. How can I help you?" he asked, from the other side of the secured door.

"DI Simpkins, and this is DS Childs. Is there somewhere more private where we can talk, Mr. Timmins?" Lorne flashed her warrant card.

"My office. Unfortunately, I can only spare you five minutes, as I have an appointment with a customer. Can't be late for that; the bank prides itself on punctuality." Timmins opened the door, let the two officers in, and bolted it after Pete.

"That's generous of him," Pete whispered sarcastically, as they followed Timmins up the corridor to his office.

Timmins's office was much grander than Lorne anticipated. A large cherrywood desk dominated the room, and matching filing cabinets lined one wall. As Lorne glanced around, she noticed several framed certificates for 'Manager of the Month' proudly arranged on the wall behind his big leather chair.

"What can I do for you, Inspector?" Timmins smiled and motioned for them to take a seat.

"We're here about Miss Fishland. We wondered if she's turned up yet?" Lorne asked, notebook at the ready.

"You mean you haven't found her?" Timmins snapped back unexpectedly.

"Not yet. We'd like a few more details, to further our enquiries."

"Like what? I told the fraud squad everything I know. The bitch ran off with ten grand. What other information do you need, for Christ's sake?"

Lorne's suspicion grew along with his aggression. "Personal details, like her height and weight. Do you happen to have a staff photo of her?"

"Surely, you should be asking her family questions like that?" Timmins appeared bemused.

"I'm asking you, Mr. Timmins. We haven't managed to locate any of her family yet," she lied convincingly. "So, do you have one?"

He pointed to a group staff photo hanging on the wall. "That's her in the middle."

"It's not very clear. Do you have another one?" Lorne's patience was beginning to falter.

Timmins wandered over to the filing cabinet, retrieved a key from his waistcoat pocket, and opened the third drawer down. After locating the missing woman's personnel file, he relocked the drawer and returned to his desk, file in hand.

Pete and Lorne exchanged a knowing glance. The photo he showed them bore no resemblance to the body lying in the mortuary. This woman was much taller and stockier. Lorne asked for a copy of the photo, despite knowing it would be of no use to their enquiries.

"I want that bitch *caught*, Inspector."

"Do you always speak of your staff so highly, Mr. Timmins?"

"*She* stole from this bank, and guess what? It's *me* who's left with the tarnished record. The quicker you find her and that money, the quicker I can return this bank to where it belongs—top. Before this happened, this branch was number one in the region. Since the bad publicity in the local press, the customers are departing in droves, and it's all thanks to Miss Fishland."

"It looked pretty busy out there to me," Lorne said.

"Yes... Well, you happened to catch us on a busy day." Timmins's face coloured up.

"Well, we won't hold you up any longer. Thank you for your assistance, Mr. Timmins. We'll be in touch, should Miss Fishland pop up anytime in the near future."

As Timmins showed them out, Pete whispered to Lorne, "He probably misses his Friday night bonking session in the storeroom with her. He's shagging her. It's a dead cert—that's why he's so pissed at her."

The same thought had occurred to Lorne, but she would have never voiced such an opinion. Especially when the person she was gossiping about was fewer than ten feet away, but that was Pete.

"That, I believe, leaves us with just one option, unless the person hasn't been logged as missing," stated Lorne as they headed towards her car.

"Yup, Belinda Greenaway. She's a widow. Her sister informed us of her disappearance. She has a son who lives about two hundred miles away."

"Does the sister live nearby? Perhaps we've got time to drop in on her before we have to swing by Arnaud's office for the PM report."

"About half an hour away." Pete glanced at his watch.

"You can fill me in on the way. It'll take your mind off my driving." She poked his chubby midriff.

"With respect, boss, as long as I'm in the passenger seat of your car, *nothing* will take my mind off your driving." He opened the door and squeezed his large frame in. "Apparently, Belinda was due to attend her niece's daughter's christening. There was no family dispute or anything like that, and the family has grown more anxious, the longer she's been gone. It was her favourite niece, you see; there was no way she would have missed it."

"What's the woman's background?" Lorne asked as they ground to a halt in a traffic jam.

"Widowed four years ago; husband, Jack, died in a crash. Nothing else showed up on file, except that she was a housewife." Pete slammed his notebook shut.

"That's not very PC of you, Pete," she teased as she crunched through the gears.

Pete cringed. "PC? What the heck is that?"

"Political correctness. Nowadays, there is no such thing as a housewife. I believe the term is 'domestic engineer'."

"Housewives, domestic engineers," he grumbled, watching the green, wide-open spaces of the countryside whiz past his window.

"It all amounts to the same thing, don't it? They all sit on their arses, watching daytime TV all day long, and then twenty minutes before the old man is due home, they rustle up a meal that they've just been watching on *Ready Steady Cook* and pretend it took them three hours to prepare. While the breadwinner is out some twelve to fourteen hours, five days a week, busting a gut so *they* can have a cushy lifestyle."

"God, you bloody MCP, you can be so infuriating at times. You missed your vocation—you should've been a caveman. You're forgetting one thing, though." She took her eyes off the road momentarily to meet his glance her way. "What about Tom? You've just insinuated he sits around all day, doing nothing. I'd like to be there when you ran through that little scenario with him. You wouldn't leave my house in one piece, mate."

"Shit, I forgot about your Tom." He looked suitably embarrassed.

"Oh, I get it—it's different for men. They can find something useful to do with their time, is that it?" *Here comes another battle of the sexes.*

"He's just finished putting in a brand new kitchen for you, hasn't he? Not that you use it much," he added disrespectfully, under his breath.

"There're plenty of women out there who enjoy DIY—in fact, they probably get most of their tips off daytime TV. And no, I don't use my kitchen much, because like *you,* I work twelve, fourteen, sometimes even sixteen hours a day. But unlike you, I don't have to rely on take-aways, as I have a loving husband at home who thinks enough of me to ensure I eat healthily every day." *Stick that in your caveman pipe and smoke it.*

"All right, all right, boss. You've made your point," Pete admitted, holding up his hands.

Lorne smiled smugly and mentally stroked the air with a finger. *Another strike to me.* Poor Pete—he always started arguments about equality but rarely won them. She constantly reminded him not to jump to conclusions, especially where people's status in life was concerned. One day, he just might listen to her.

She chuckled at the mental image of him in a loincloth, dragging a woman by her hair, wooden club in hand, ready to ward off predators after *his woman.*

"Do you want to share the joke with me?"

"Not really," she said, as they pulled up at their destination.

Chapter Eight

The cul-de-sac was made up of immaculately cared-for retirement bungalows, each with its own miniature Chelsea garden at the front. It thrilled Lorne to see all the rose bushes engorged with buds even at that late time of year.

The sight made her feel ashamed of her own shabby garden that bore the scars of a near-teenager and a dog rampaging through it. Her lawn regularly looked as if a Premiership football team had kicked nine months of shit out of it. She and Tom had decided a while back that the quaint country cottage garden they yearned for would have to be put on hold for a few years, until Charlie was much older.

"What's the woman's name, Pete?" she asked ringing the bell.

"Doreen Nicholls."

He's still in a huff. She wanted to tell him to grow up.

They listened as three dead bolts were slid back, and a safety chain was put on. The door opened six inches, and a frail voice asked, "Who is it?"

"Mrs. Nicholls, I'm DI Lorne Simpkins, and this is my partner, DS Pete Childs. Do you mind if we come in and ask you a few questions about your sister?" As she spoke, Lorne thrust her ID through the gap in the door. The woman took it, studied it, and handed it back before opening the door fully to let them in.

"You'll have to excuse the mess, dears. I've not long come out of hospital. Come through to the sitting room." The smell of Vicks menthol greeted them as they followed the woman, who leaned heavily on a stick as she slowly made her way up the hallway.

It was as if they had just gone through a time warp. Weaving its way through the bungalow was a brown swirly patterned carpet that must have been en vogue sometime back in the early seventies. Lorne guessed the home hadn't seen a paintbrush or roller in years.

The focal point of the lounge was a 1940's tiled fireplace, complete with what was most likely an original gas fire from the same era. The brown carpet clashed horribly with the bold red pattern of the threadbare velour sofas. The thick chunky wooden arms dated the furniture to thirty years or more back.

"Would you care for some tea and scones? I've just this minute taken them out of the oven," the old lady asked, her voice high and squeaky. "Even a busted hip can't prevent me from baking."

Lorne declined, but Pete jumped at the chance to make his belly bigger. The woman trundled off to the kitchen, leaving them to wander around the room.

"This must be the daughter," Lorne said quietly, picking up the photo standing proudly on top of the TV.

"Can't see the sister on show anywhere," Pete said.

The woman returned with a tray, the contents rattling precariously in her thin, weak arm. Pete gallantly rushed to rescue the tray and placed it on the coffee table in front of one of the sofas.

"I brought in a cup for you too, dear, just in case you changed your mind." Mrs. Nicholls lifted the china teapot and poured the oak-coloured liquid into two cups.

The temptation proved too much for Lorne. A nice cup of English tea, perfectly stewed and poured from a bone china teapot into fine bone china cups, was her idea of heaven. "I'd love a cup, Mrs. Nicholls. Thank you."

"Do call me, Doreen, please. Now, you mentioned something about my poor sister? Have you found her?" The woman asked, handing a cup and saucer to Pete.

His eyes lit up when she also handed him a small plate with a scone spread thickly with butter and strawberry jam.

Pete peered at the cup and saucer as if they had come from outer space, but he took them without saying a word.

"Not yet. We wondered if you had any idea why she might have gone missing the way she did?" Lorne asked, before sipping her tea.

Doreen Nicholls' withered hands nervously scrunched up her flowered apron. "She often goes off gallivanting, but she's never been gone this long before. She usually contacts someone in the family if she's delayed on a trip."

"Forgive me for asking, Doreen, but did she have any enemies?"

The woman laughed. "Belinda, enemies? You must be joking. She was well-liked in her community. Even when Jack died four years ago, her social life never dwindled. Most women curl up in a shell when they lose their partner, but not my Belinda." Sadness filled her eyes as she spoke.

Lorne suspected Doreen was also a widow and her heart went out to her. "What sort of work did her husband do?"

"He was a high flyer. Chairman of an oil company—travelled the world, he did. But Belinda never minded, as long as the money kept coming in. It didn't bother her that he was never around. That's why their marriage lasted as long as it did. He died in a helicopter crash. Terrible accident. It was taking off one of the rigs in a storm with gale force winds and went crashing into the sea. Poor things. They didn't stand a chance. Four men died that day. Belinda was well-cared for, mind, if you know what I mean."

"Insurance?"

"That's right, dear. Two million pounds. That's why she's able to go off at a moment's notice."

"Does that bother you, Doreen?"

"Not in the way you mean, dear. I'm not envious of her money, although it upset me when I had to wait for over a year to have a hip replacement operation on the NHS. No, I suppose I'm envious of her zest for life, the fact that she's able to go all around the world at the drop of a hat. Surely, all siblings find themselves envious at one time or another. Even twins. I suppose it's worse, when they're identical like us…"

Chapter Nine

"You're twins!" Pete said.

"That's right. I have a photo somewhere. Now, where did I put it? The memory takes a little longer to engage at my time of life." Doreen got up and rifled through the drawers of the 1970's oak bureau.

After locating the scruffy obviously well-loved family album, Doreen returned to her seat on the sofa alongside Lorne. Pete stood behind them, rudely looking over their shoulders, much to Lorne's annoyance.

The resemblance was startling. From babes in arms through the generations, conclusive evidence the sisters were carbon copies of each other. Although to be fair, Belinda had aged more kindly than Doreen had, but Lorne put that down to Belinda's more affluent lifestyle.

Unfortunately, there was no disguising it. From the woman's build, Lorne was one hundred per cent certain they had just identified the mystery body lying in the mortuary. She groaned inside. How the hell was she going to find the right words to tell this frail old lady her sister had been brutally murdered beyond recognition?

Doreen was still leafing through the album, offering a little anecdote to every page she turned. "And this one was taken on the dodgems at Battersea funfair, nearly thirty years ago."

Doreen's concentration seemed to slip momentarily. "This is going to sound strange, but I'm going to tell you, anyway. The day we realised Belinda was missing, I had a weird feeling inside."

"In what way, Doreen?"

"I don't know if you're aware, but some identical twins can be linked psychically to the other—symbiosis, I think it's called. For instance, when I was in labour with my daughter Colleen, Belinda felt every contraction I had, at precisely the same moment."

"How often does this kind of thing happen?" Pete asked, in an 'I don't believe a word of it' tone.

"It happens pretty regularly—usually Belinda is the one who feels my pain, but on the odd occasion, it's reversed. She had a tooth pulled out when she was sixteen, which had crumbled. Anyway, I was the one who ended up taking the painkillers for the day, instead of her."

An unexplained sadness swept over Lorne.

Doreen was quick to spot the change in her. "What's wrong, dear? You look as if you've just discovered you have a flat tyre or something."

"I was just thinking how magical that must be, to be so close to a twin like that," Lorne said, totally at ease with the woman, briefly forgetting Pete was in the room.

He cleared his throat reminding, her why they were there.

The astute woman asked, sensitively, "I take it you're an only child, my dear?"

"No, I have a sister, but our brother died when he was four days old. He was my sister's twin. My parents found the experience very traumatic. They refused to try for another child, after that." Lorne's eyes filled with tears.

"A great loss for both you and your parents, I would imagine," Doreen said quietly, echoing her grief.

Reality pulled Lorne back in line. She took a deep breath and pushed the family secret back to where it belonged, locked in the vault of her memory bank. "It was a long time ago."

Doreen straightened and asked, "Is there a particular reason you've come here, today?"

"That'll be your psychic powers kicking in, then, Doreen." Pete laughed at his own stupid insensitive joke. Lorne glared at him.

He shrugged a silent apology, and Lorne cleared her clogged throat. She gathered the woman's right hand in her own. It was cold to the touch.

"After studying the photos you've shown us, Doreen, I'm afraid I have to tell you we may have found your sister after all."

Doreen stood up and began firing questions as she paced up and down her living room, momentarily forgetting about her aching hip.

"Oh, my God, where? Why didn't you tell me sooner? Is she all right? When can I see her?"

Lorne felt the bile rising in her throat. She glanced at Pete for support. He gave her a 'You're the boss' look. She was on her own—as usual, when that type of situation cropped up.

"Doreen, I need you to sit down, love." The woman sat. "Like I said, we were unsure until you showed us the photos. Now… Well, now we think that the body found last night in Chelling Forest is that of your sister, Belinda."

"I don't understand. 'Body', you said 'body'. Is she *dead*? Why wouldn't you have made the connection as soon as I opened the door? She couldn't have changed that much in a month. Everyone can tell within seconds we're identical twins. Why couldn't you?"

Lorne didn't think telling Doreen her sister had been decapitated was a good idea. "I understand how upsetting this must be, Doreen, and I regrettably have to inform you that we believe your sister was murdered."

"What?" The old woman gasped for air as the two detectives looked helplessly at each other.

"My tab…lets. Over there…" The woman's blood had drained from her face. She anxiously pointed to the small bottle of pills sitting on the mantelpiece.

Pete was the first to react. Grabbing the bottle, he asked Doreen how many tablets she needed.

"One," she replied, breathlessly.

The bottle had a child safety cap on it. Pete's large hands fumbled over it without success. Lorne snatched the bottle from him and quickly tipped a handful of the tiny pills into her palm.

Doreen's hand shook as she grabbed one of the pills and tucked it under her tongue.

The change was dramatic. Seconds later, the woman became calmer. Lorne ordered Pete to fetch a glass of water from the kitchen.

He returned with the glass to find his boss rocking the woman back and forth in her arms as if she were a child.

"I have angina. The shock must have brought on an attack."

Once she'd recovered, Doreen insisted they tell her about her sister's death, but the detectives refused to divulge the horrifying injuries her sister had sustained, fearing the shock would bring on another attack. Lorne did, however, ask the woman if it would be possible to take a DNA sample from her, so they could use it to formally identify the victim. Doreen agreed.

Pete telephoned Arnaud, who dispatched a colleague immediately to the woman's address.

In the meantime, Lorne telephoned Doreen's daughter, explaining briefly what had happened and arranged for her to come over to be with her mother.

Ten minutes later, a blonde dishevelled-looking woman let herself into the bungalow. Instead of makeup, there were smudges of chocolate and flour on her face. Her eyes were swollen and red.

"Mum, are you all right?" Dropping to one knee, Colleen picked up her mother's hand and tenderly kissed it.

Doreen weakly introduced the two detectives as she lovingly wiped away the chocolate from the younger woman's cheek with the corner of her apron. "Oh, Colleen, whatever am I going to do? She's dead. Your aunt is dead," she babbled as tears rolled down her wrinkled cheeks.

"I know, Mum. We'll get through this. I promise we will."

Colleen showed the two detectives to the door.

"Your mother had a slight turn. We had to give her one of her tablets." Lorne gave the woman one of her cards. "When someone arrives from pathology, they'll take a buccal swab, instead of a blood sample. Ring me if I can be of any help."

"That's a sample from the mouth, isn't it? When will the results of the DNA come through?" The young woman's voice shook with emotion.

"That's right. It's less invasive, and it's supposed to yield a higher amount of DNA. Results should be back in the morning. We'll let you know as soon as we have them. Will you be staying here with your mother?"

"Yes. My husband is going to look after the children. A neighbour's sitting with them at the moment. I'll stay here for as long as Mum needs me. Oh my God, what about Oliver, my cousin? Who'll tell him?"

"If you'd rather we did, that's fine. I'll sort it out. Let's leave things as they are for now. As soon as the results are back, I'll contact you first, then give him a call. We have his number at the office."

They shook hands, and the detectives left the grief-filled bungalow. As they walked down the path, the blood red roses edging it bowed a graceful farewell in the breeze. In the distance, a dog barked at its elderly owner, who was teasing it with a gushing hosepipe. It was a relief to hear the hum of normal healthy lives being led.

"How come you never told me you had a kid brother who died?" Pete asked as they got in the car.

"It was no concern of yours, Pete. It still isn't." Lorne promptly changed the subject. "We'll drop by the doc's office on the way back, see if the report's ready."

One thing her father had taught her long ago was never to mix work with your personal life.

Pete threw her a thunderous look, but thankfully he thought twice about challenging her.

Chapter Ten

They picked up the report and returned to the station. When they arrived, the incident room was a hive of activity. Even Molly was busy tapping away on her computer.

Lorne said, "Give me five minutes to go over this report, and I'll summarise it for you. Then, before we call it a day, we'll recap what we have or haven't achieved today, okay?"

The team shouted, "Yes, ma'am," in unison. Work had been non-stop lately for all of them, and their spirits rose at the thought of knocking off early.

The report did little to raise Lorne's spirits. In fact, it proved to be a total disappointment, full of conjecture and uncertainties. It emphasised the need and urgency to recover the missing limbs before the cause of death could be ascertained.

Doctor Arnaud suggested there was a distinct possibility the body might have been placed in a freezer for a week or two before they'd discovered it. He also stated that, although the torso had suffered many blows with a blunt instrument, none of the sustained injuries would have been fatal.

The skin around the neck was jagged in some areas and torn in others, a sign that it had been removed impatiently by the perpetrator with some kind of saw. It appeared that the decapitation had been carried out around the time of death, as the extent of blood loss incurred had been maximum, from what he could gather. The fingertips of the left hand appeared to have been removed in the same way.

The victim had suffered four broken ribs, and during the assault, the sternum had also sustained several fractures.

Lorne read on and was horrified to find that a piece of wood five inches long and three inches in diameter had been discovered wedged deep inside the victim's vagina. That find suggested that the crime had been a sexually motivated one, although no semen had been found in, on, or near the corpse.

The doctor had finalised his report by saying: "If—and it's a big if—the victim had lived, the internal injuries she suffered would have meant she would have had to endure months of recuperation and numerous corrective operations. Putting it bluntly, the victim's death proved to be a blessing in disguise."

Stunned and disgusted, Lorne slammed the report shut. If the victim was verified to be Belinda Greenaway, what kind of sick animal were they dealing with? The woman was sixty-five years old, for Christ's sake. No one in their right mind would subject a woman of that age—or any age—to such a horrendous ordeal, would they?

She had to concur with Arnaud's view, that death had been the better option for the poor defenceless woman.

A sudden urge to call home and hear a friendly voice overtook her. She dialled.

"Hello?" the young voice of her daughter answered.

"Hello, darling. Did you enjoy your sleepover?"

"It was all right. Susie had another fight with her mum, and…"

"And?"

"And I love you, Mum."

Her eyes misted up instantly, and her throat felt restricted. She cleared it with a slight cough. "Oh, Charlie. I love you too. Did you have a good day at school?"

"Not especially. One of the teachers was off sick, and the deputy head stepped in for Maths. A bummer, really."

"Charlie, you mind your language," Lorne chastised, holding back a laugh. "Is your father there?"

"Yeah, where else would he be?"

Where, indeed, but for how much longer?

Tom picked up the phone and said light-heartedly, "I hear Charlie just gave you a sample of the latest word she's picked up at school."

"God knows where she's getting it from. Anyway, I'm just about to wind things up here. Fingers crossed I should be home within the hour. Shall I pop by the off-licence on the way?"

"Nope. I took care of that earlier. Just hurry home. I've made lasagne."

Lorne didn't have the heart to tell him she'd eaten pasta for lunch. He'd obviously made an effort; any fears she had of her marriage coming to an abrupt end diminished rapidly during the call. He'd spent time preparing her favourite meal. Perhaps he'd had time to think about their circumstances and decided to forgive her for not being around much lately. *Or is that purely wishful thinking?*

She quickly tidied her desk. Then, with the report tucked under her arm, she stepped back into the incident room. The team listened without interruption as she read out the report, every gruesome detail.

Despite their best efforts, the group had come up with nothing further at the end of the day. Without a positive identification of the body, it was impossible for them to identify any kind of motive for the crime. Lorne was sure now that they were on the way to making a formal ID, things would start falling into place soon. "Okay, we might as well call it a day. John, can you do one final job for me before you head off?"

"Sure. What's that, boss?" he asked, delighted to be singled out for the task.

"Organise a press conference for the morning: TV, newspapers, and radio. We should have an ID on the body by mid-morning, so around eleven would be ideal."

"What about an incident van at the scene?" Tracy said, poised with phone in hand, ready for action.

"Good idea. I'll leave that with you, Tracy."

The young officer nodded, already dialling a number.

Lorne dismissed the team and made her way out to her car with Pete tagging along beside her.

"It's been a helluva day, boss."

"That it has, Pete. Hopefully, things will look a little clearer, tomorrow."

"Ah... Hum... You don't think you're getting a bit too involved in this one, do you?"

She stopped abruptly and frowned at him. "What gives you that idea?"

They had reached the outside of the building. There was still a lot of activity around the station, with fewer officers clocking on than coming off shift.

Pete leaned forwards and said, voice hushed, "It's just that, well, when you were giving us the low-down on the PM report...um...you seemed a tad emotional. I was there today, remember—you know, when you told Doreen about your little brother…"

"You're reading things into it, Pete. I'd say I was seething about the case rather than upset. Every case touches us in some way. You know that. Be honest. Hasn't this one affected you?"

"Not really, boss."

Flabbergasted by his admission, she asked, "Is that because the victim is a woman and not a man?"

"I can't believe you said that, boss. You know damn well, I treat every victim the same, no matter what gender they are."

"I apologise. I was out of line. There's a lot going on around me at the moment, Pete, things I can't go into—but let me assure you, I'm *not* 'getting too involved', as you put it. This is the worst case we've had to deal with in a long time, even you have to admit that."

He nodded in agreement but didn't interrupt her.

"I have a feeling we haven't seen the last of this bastard. Call it women's intuition, if you like. That, my dear chap, is why maybe I'm a little bit more emotional about this case than I should be."

He held his hands up. "I was just making sure, boss. I guess I've never seen you like this before. It's bound to make me wonder what's going on."

"Wonder away, Pete, but remember: I didn't get to be an inspector without some professionalism under my belt. Now if you don't mind, I have a husband and daughter I'm eager to get home to."

"You and Tom have made peace then?" he asked, nodding at the plaster still sitting above her eye.

"I believe so. What have you got planned for tonight? Anything?"

"The usual—a few cans in front of the telly, a microwave meal I overheat at an extremely high temperature, in case of salmonella, that ends up going crusty round the edges."

She knew he was fishing for an invite to dinner. Her heart went out to him. Any other time, she would have felt sorry enough to invite him back for a meal with the family. But not that night. She really wasn't in the mood to socialise. Besides, she had a lot of making up to do with Tom, and she wouldn't be able to do that with Pete there.

Lorne bade him a guilty, "Have a good evening," and headed off home.

Chapter Eleven

It was dark when Lorne arrived home at seven. The night sky was clear, and the air had an autumn chill to it.

She crept into the house. It felt like stepping into a library. Then she heard the faint sound of voices coming from upstairs. She climbed the stairs and tiptoed along the hallway, avoiding the floorboards she knew creaked and stood outside her daughter's room. She could hear Tom and Charlie laughing and keys tapping on the computer keyboard as they played a game.

Eyes closed, Lorne leaned against the wall outside Charlie's room. She heard Charlie's door open and close, then felt his lips lightly touch hers. Her arms slithered around his neck as he seductively placed tiny kisses over her face and neck.

Sensations she feared had gone forever suddenly sprang to life. Tom brushed his groin against hers. She gasped at his firmness as he began grinding his hips urgently against hers. She moaned softly in his ear, giving him the encouragement he needed to continue.

He swung her slight frame into his arms with ease and headed for their bedroom. Charlie was caught up in a computer game, and they knew she would be occupied for hours. Tom dropped her gently on the bed, and she watched him eagerly tear off his T-shirt and jeans before he turned his attention to her again. Reaching behind her, he unfastened her skirt, giving it the merest of tugs as he eased it down over her round hips, and tossed it to the floor. Next he removed the matching blue blazer and threw it in the same direction. Then, one by one, he undid every button on her white blouse, placing a kiss on each bare patch of skin revealed. Finally, impatience getting the better of him, he ripped off her bra and panties. His boxer shorts completed the pile of eagerly discarded garments.

Tom hesitated; Lorne reached for him. His animal instincts took over, and he stalked her like a tiger and pounced as if she was his prey in the jungle. It had been a long time since they had touched each other like this and it took an immense effort to keep control.

Her hands stroked his back with feather-light touches, and he groaned. His lips found her taut nipples and sucked at them. She writhed with desire as her hands travelled down to grasp his buttocks. She moulded them with her hands, roughly digging her nails into his flesh, his groans intensifying with every touch.

His impatience reached its summit. Tom guided himself into her wet crevice, and they both cried out with joy as he thrust deeper—he was back where he belonged. They clawed, bit, and sucked at each other as he plunged into her again and again. He flipped her over, positioning her on top. Together, they erupted, and she crumpled in a heap on top of him.

He settled her down beside him, and the sound of their irregular breathing filled the room, words seemingly inadequate at such a euphoric moment. Their erratic breathing finally slowed, and they both drifted blissfully off to sleep.

They awoke in the same position the next morning.

"Are you ready for an encore?" Tom snuggled closer, then got on top of her.

"Sounds tempting," Lorne purred.

He began kissing her but stopped abruptly. "I hear the patter of tiny feet. Quick—pretend you're asleep."

They both managed to shut their eyes before Charlie pushed open the door.

"Get up, you two. It's half-past seven," she shouted, before exiting their room and banging the door shut behind her.

Tom chuckled, seeing the pile of discarded clothes littering the floor on his side of the bed. He bent over and kissed Lorne hard on the lips. She responded enthusiastically, but he pushed her gently away from him. "We'll have to continue this at a more convenient time, sweetheart. I have a starving daughter to feed, and you've got a job to go to."

"Life just isn't fair, is it?" She threw back the duvet, revealing her naked body, letting him know clearly what he was turning down. She seductively opened and closed her legs and immediately noticed the bulge developing beneath his robe.

He threw her bathrobe at her in mock disgust and ran around the bed to pull on his boxer shorts, no doubt hoping that their bagginess would disguise his growing manhood before he went downstairs. "You can be positively evil at times, Mrs. Simpkins."

"Don't you know it, baby." She quickly reached over, tugged one leg of his boxers down, then ran from the bedroom, along the hall, and into the bathroom.

Chapter Twelve

Lorne arrived at work sporting a wide grin.

Pete noticed the change in her demeanour immediately. "You look like the cat that got the canary."

"Anything new to report?" Blushing, she ignored his wisecrack.

"Nope."

The phone in her office rang. *Perfect timing.* Lorne answered it on the fifth ring.

"Finally. I was just about to hang up," admonished a grumpy voice she recognised.

"Doctor Arnaud. I take it you have the results of the DNA?"

"Indeed. The body in the mortuary is a perfect match to the DNA we took from Mrs. Nicholls. Will you inform the relatives?"

"I'll do it straight away. Thanks for the call, Doc." Her heart sank with the news they'd been expecting. *So much for starting the day off in a good mood.*

She took a few deep breaths before making the calls she needed to make. The first was to Doreen, although it was Colleen who took the call, as her mother was still in bed after having a sleepless night. She relayed the information they'd all been dreading. Understandably, Colleen broke down. Lorne informed her that a press conference had been called for later that morning.

The second call she made was to Colleen's cousin. She introduced herself to Belinda's son, gave him her condolences and told him of their findings. She also let him know that a conference was taking place that morning.

"Thank you for calling, Inspector. I'd like to attend the conference, if that's okay?"

"I think that'd make a lot of sense, Mr. Greenaway. The conference has been arranged for eleven o'clock. Can you make it up here by then?" Lorne remembered that Pete had told her he lived almost two hundred miles away.

"No problem. I'll fly up in the company helicopter. Perhaps I can see Mum before the conference?"

The question floored Lorne. "Do you think that's a good idea? I've just explained the extent of her injuries."

"It would help me put into perspective what the bastard did to her."

The more Lorne tried to deter him, the more insistent he became. She decided to leave it to Arnaud and his staff to talk Oliver out of it.

Pete popped his head round the door after she'd finished her final call. "Coffee?"

"I'd love one, thanks."

When he returned with a cup of steaming liquid that only he could describe as coffee, he asked, "What's up?"

"The DNA's back. It confirms that the body is that of Belinda Greenaway. Her son's on his way. He wants to be involved in the press conference, *and* he's requested to see his mother's body."

"You're kidding! You told him the injuries she sustained?" Pete shook his head in disbelief.

"Does this face look as if I'm joking? I'm hoping the doc can put him off the idea."

"Beats me why anyone would want to put themselves through that. Leave it to the doc; he'll get Greenaway to change his mind. Did you have a good evening?"

Her face flushed deeper than a ripe cherry. "Lovely, thanks. What about you?"

"Same old thing, nothing to write home to granny about," he said, staring into his murky- coloured coffee.

"Sorry I didn't invite you back for dinner. Umm...Tom and I had a lot of sorting out to do." She busied herself with some paperwork, letting Pete know that if he valued their friendship, the questions needed to stop there.

"I understand, boss." Pete tapped his nose with his forefinger. "By the size of the grin you were wearing when you came in this morning, I'd say you were pretty successful in your mission."

She groaned inwardly. Was she really that easy to read? Or had Tom secretly placed a sticker on her head that read '*Had the shag of my life last night*'? Drastic evasive action was called for. "What time is the conference today?"

"Eleven o'clock on the dot," Pete replied with a smirk.

"Thanks for the coffee, Pete. I'll be another thirty minutes here, then we'll bounce some ideas around with the rest of the team, see what we can come up with."

"I'll take that as my cue to leave, then."

She ignored him and set about reducing the pile of paperwork on her desk.

The team was ready and waiting for her thirty minutes—and the beginning of a headache—later. "Right, now we know who the victim is, we can finally get down to solving this crime."

"So it was Belinda Greenaway?" Mitch asked.

"That's right. Mitch. Start delving into the background of Belinda and her husband, Jack, will you?"

"Am I looking for anything in particular, boss?"

"Anything that can be perceived as dodgy in Jack's business. The oil business must be full of people bearing grudges from lost contracts, things like that."

"Didn't her husband die in a helicopter crash?" Pete chimed in.

"You're right. See if there was anything suspicious about the accident, Mitch. Molly, I want you to poke around in the son's background. See if he's involved in anything untoward."

"He lives two hundred miles away," Molly groaned.

"Your point being what, exactly?" Lorne bit back.

"Any likely associates he has down there would hardly come all this way to bump off his old mum, would they?"

"I don't know, Molly. Why don't you do what I suggested and try to find out?" she told the sour-faced DS, who was stretching Lorne's patience to the limit. She was sick to the back teeth of Molly continually challenging her authority. Lorne wondered briefly if then would be a good time to get the woman transferred out of her team, while the chief was still around to support her.

The rest of the team watched but remained silent as the two women glowered at each other. Molly broke eye contact first.

Lorne resumed delegating tasks. "Tracy, I want you to question the neighbours, see if the Greenaways ever had any public arguments—that sort of thing. Find out what Belinda got up to while Jack was away on the rigs?"

"Sure, boss. By the way, the incident van will be on-site by ten this morning, as instructed." The new recruit looked pleased with herself.

Lorne smiled and wondered why the other woman on the team couldn't respond to her in the same respectful manner. Tracy had been like a breath of fresh air since she'd joined the team three months before—volunteering to do any job, however menial, just to show everyone how eager she was to learn and progress. Twenty and blonde, with the looks and figure all the men in the team appreciated, Tracy was refreshingly different from the sullen thirty-year-old Molly, who dug her heels in when asked to carry out the simplest of tasks.

"John, see what you can find out about their finances. Try to access both personal and business accounts. Anything inappropriate, I want to know about it."

"Okay, boss. What about the son?" John, another exceptional member of her team, was a renowned workaholic and one of Pete's best mates.

"Go for it. Pete, I want you to get access to the Greenaway's house. We'll go over there this afternoon, once the conference is out of the way," Lorne said.

"Okay, what time is the son due?"

"He's flying up from Cornwall—should be here about ten. I'll take him to the mortuary. If the traffic's bad and he knows we're on a tight schedule, he might think twice about wanting to see his mum—fingers crossed, anyway. He's aware of what time the conference is."

The phone rang on Pete's desk. While he answered it, Lorne brought the meeting to a close.

"Hold on a minute," Pete said.

Lorne raised an eyebrow.

Pete put the caller on hold as Lorne crossed the short distance to his desk. "The river police have just picked up a black bag in the Coll River. It contained a right arm."

"Shit. Tell them to get the bag over to Arnaud's office right away."

"There's something else." He looked perturbed.

"What?"

"The desk sergeant says a girl was reported missing last night in the vicinity of Chelling Forest."

"It could be a coincidence, Pete. Get the details, and we'll follow it up later."

As Pete continued his conversation with the desk sergeant, Lorne headed for her office. Like Pete, she feared the day had suddenly spun off in an ominous direction. *Is it a coincidence, or do we have yet another murder on our hands? Could we be dealing with a serial killer?*

She hunted in her drawer for the packet of Nurofen she hoped would ease the throbbing pain in her head. If she did something about it immediately, she'd be able to handle the strain of the conference far better.

Oliver Greenaway arrived at ten on the dot. Considering he'd just lost his mother, he appeared to be holding it together remarkably well. They left for the mortuary immediately.

Thankfully, Arnaud insisted he couldn't let Oliver view his mother's body; it wouldn't have been proper.

Oliver's resolve crumbled. Collapsing into a chair, he cradled his head in his cupped hands and cried, repeating the same words over and over. "Why Mum? Tell me why someone would do this to her? She was the kindest, most caring person who ever lived. I'll get the bastard if it's the last thing I do—I'll get him. I'll make sure he suffers the way he made her suffer."

Lorne stepped forwards to comfort Oliver, but Arnaud caught her arm. Lorne suspected he was accustomed to such reactions and knew Oliver's response was an important part of the grieving process some distraught family members had to go through.

It brought home to her how much she cherished her own parents and made a mental note to give them a ring as soon as she could. She felt even guiltier when she realised that because of her recent heavy work schedule, it had been a month since she last contacted them.

Lorne took Oliver to the canteen for a much-needed cup of coffee.

Pete caught up with them ten minutes later. "Boss, the conference is due to start."

"Are you sure you're up to this, Oliver?" Lorne asked.

"Would you be, if that was your mother lying in the mortuary?" He'd barely uttered a word since breaking down.

"I think it would be good if you came along, but it isn't obligatory. The choice is yours."

"I'll be fine. I want that bastard to see how he's destroyed me and what's left of my family," Oliver said, his fighting spirit quickly returning.

The Chief Inspector opened the conference then handed over to Lorne. She went over the suspected times, dates, and places of the crime and called for any witnesses to come forward to help with their enquiries. She purposely neglected to inform the media of any of the injuries Belinda had incurred.

Then it was Oliver's turn. For a moment he hesitated, searching for the right words; but as he became more comfortable in front of the camera his tone grew more aggressive. "Help the police find the bastard who did this. Who knows—your mother, sister, or wife could be this maniac's next victim!"

It was a cry from the heart, which Lorne knew was sure to strike a chord with the viewers. His sincerity also strengthened Lorne's belief that Oliver had nothing to do with the murders.

After the conference, Oliver accompanied the two detectives to his mother's home. The house was more like a mansion, situated on an exclusive estate on the outskirts of the village of Bournley. The tree-lined drive was an indication of the grandeur they were about to encounter. Landscaped gardens surrounded the immaculate *White House.*

"My dad was fascinated by the American presidential home," Oliver enlightened the two detectives.

"You don't say!" Pete said, picking his chin up off the path.

"Why on earth did your mother continue living here after your father died?" Lorne was awestruck by the sheer size and elegance of the property.

"She insisted that Dad was still around her and refused to leave the security she felt in the home. That seems a bit ironic now, after what's happened to her…"

"Did your mother employ staff?"

"They've been with my mother and father for years. Surely you don't suspect them?"

"Give Pete their names and addresses. They'll have to be checked out."

They searched every room, drawer, and cupboard in the house. Lorne felt like an intruder as she rifled through the dead woman's belongings. The more they hunted, the more their frustrations grew. They found nothing. No signs of a break-in or of Belinda being killed there. Again their investigation had hit a brick wall.

Was this a random killing, after all?

Two frustrating hours later, they left the grieving Oliver to his memories and returned to the station.

En route, Pete asked, "What do you make of the son?"

"In what respect?" Lorne shot him a puzzled glance.

"Can we regard him as a suspect?"

"Jesus, Pete, I think you've been watching too many cop shows on that damn telly of yours." She laughed, but then realisation came crashing down on her. "Oh, I get it. You think he killed her for the inheritance money, is that it?"

"Stranger things have happened." He shrugged his broad shoulders.

"You haven't quite grasped it yet, have you, Pete?"

"What's that?" It was his turn to look puzzled.

"You haven't quite mastered the knack of gauging people's reactions."

"You mean we're back to women's bloody intuition again? Well, I'm sorry to have to inform you, boss, but I ain't no woman with no magic powers. I have to go about things my way, which happens to be the force's way. So, if I've got suspicions about someone, I have to follow up on those suspicions."

"That's why we're such good partners—because I can share my God-given ability with you. Read my lips: There is no way Oliver

Greenaway killed his mother. It is definitely not an avenue I'm willing to pursue, got it?"

"Don't blame me if you're wrong. There's always that saying, 'Look at the in-laws before looking for the outlaws.'"

"Another wonderful analogy from one of those American cop shows you love so much. What else have we got?"

"Hey don't knock it, honey," he said in the lousiest American accent he could muster. In his normal cockney voice, he said, "Absolutely sweet FA, which is why we should check him out. Unless the doc comes up with a match to the mud found on the body, we might as well wrap this case up now."

"What about the staff?"

"I'll get someone to do some digging when we get back."

"Chase up any leads we have regarding the girl who was reported missing last night, as well. The evening news will be airing the conference soon, we should get a flurry of calls from that."

The rest of the team had also had a very disappointing day. The helicopter accident had proven to be just that, an accident. The bank accounts showed nothing dubious, except that Belinda Greenaway had been a very wealthy woman. It didn't take a genius to work that one out. The neighbours said that the Greenaways had been a wonderful couple and never any bother. Finally, much to Pete's annoyance, Oliver came up smelling of roses—Mr. Squeaky, Squeaky Clean, in fact.

"And the missing girl?" Lorne asked her partner over a cup of coffee and a jam doughnut in her office.

"She's sixteen. Kim Charlton. Left her friend's house at about eleven. She called for a taxi. When it failed to show up, she got impatient and decided to walk. Her house is about two miles from her friend's." Pete reeled off the facts he'd gathered from one of the team and took a huge messy bite of his doughnut.

"Does she make a habit of going missing?"

"Generally, she's a hundred per cent reliable. But according to her parents, she's recently started going out with a boy they don't fully approve of," he spluttered through a large mouthful of cake.

"Did the parents call him?"

"Yeah, he was on the other side of town with his mates. Hasn't seen her since the weekend."

"Get someone round there to question him. He might be telling the parents what they want to hear."

"Anything else, boss?"

"Get Mitch to check out the staff—previous employers, reliability. You know the kind of thing."

Chapter Thirteen

Every news channel ran the footage of the conference that evening, and the local newspaper carried the headline: "CORPSE FOUND IN COPSE". Somehow they had tracked down Doreen for an interview, and she was pictured holding a photo of her taken with her sister. The woman looked ghastly, and Lorne was livid at the paper's intrusion into her grief. She made a mental note to call round to see the old lady the following day.

* * *

"I don't believe it," his sister cried in disbelief as she stared at the front page of the local evening paper.

"What's that?" he asked.

"That woman."

"What bloody woman?" he demanded, tired of the guessing game.

"The woman you killed… You made a mistake."

He snatched the paper from her trembling hand. His gaze darted across the main storyline, and his pulse raced as the anger mounted. He shot his companion a venomous look.

"What do you mean, *I* made a fucking mistake? You're the one who gave me the information, you dozy cow." He threw the paper across the room, and it drifted to the floor, the front cover landing face up, taunting him further.

"I…I thought it was her, when I saw her in the paper giving that award. I put two and two together and…"

"Came up with five. What have I told you about getting your facts right?" He jumped up from his seat and towered over her. His companion reacted quickly, putting her hands up to cover her face. Noticing her trembling, he took pity on her and knelt beside her, taking her in his arms he gently rocked her back and forth. He started singing a lullaby that had soothed her in their childhood. She hummed along to the tune and sighed contentedly in his strong arms.

His thoughts returned to his childhood; the beatings he and his sibling endured from their over-dominant parents; the sexual favours he had to perform on his mother and father and the many friends they invited into their shabby home.

"But, Dad, please. I don't want to do that," he had pleaded from the age of six, but his begging had been shamefully ignored. And when he refused to accommodate one of his father's friends, he was beaten to within an inch of his life and thrown in the cellar for days.

He became a recluse at school, but no one bothered to analyse him. He was just another pupil they had to deal with. Years passed, and when his sister was nine and tiny breasts developed, their father turned his attention to her.

The boy struck his father on more than one occasion, trying to defend his sister, and his mother clobbered him with a bar from behind. He was locked in the cellar while his sister was forced to carry out unspeakable sexual acts on groups of five or more men. The boy heard his sister's screams. He felt ashamed and riddled with guilt that he was unable to help her. To protect her.

After that terrible ordeal, he decided to ask for help at school. But the school stupidly told his parents what he'd confided. The children's lives were a darn sight worse after that. Pain and anger had gnawed away at him for months before finally he gained enough courage to end their ordeal.

Chapter Fourteen

After a good night's sleep—and before Tom woke—Lorne set off early for the station. The dewy autumn morning caused her to shiver slightly. She switched on the car heater to combat the chill lingering in the car. It pleased her to hear the radio station still running the conference and the number for the information line. That usually generated a good number of leads, so she prepared herself for a long day ahead.

Call after call flooded in. They had to draft in extra personnel to man the phones. Lorne and Pete personally chased up a few of the calls, but they proved to be hoaxes, stupid ignoramuses in search of their fifteen minutes of fame.

Lunchtime came and went. They sent out for sandwiches while continuing to man the phones. Lorne delved into her bag and pulled out her mobile phone, ringing her sister as she ate her ham sandwich. "Hi, Jade, how's things?"

"Huh, so much for calling me back the next day." Her sister admonished her in a mock hurt tone.

"God, did I really say that? Sorry, hon. It's been a tad chaotic around here."

"Yeah, I heard how chaotic it's been from Tom, especially in your bedroom."

"You're kidding, Tom told you abou…?" *Is nothing sacred in my private life?*

"Every last detail. Especially the bit about—"

"That's enough. You wait till I see that bloody husband of mine."

"Aw, come on, Sis. Don't drop me in it. Tom will never trust me again."

"That's what I'm hoping." The phone on her desk rang. "Hang on a minute, hon. I've got a call coming in." Lorne reached for her work phone as her sister protested about being interrupted.

"Boss, I have Doreen Nicholls on the line for you?" Tracy told her.

"Shit, I forgot to ring her. Give me thirty seconds, then put her through, will you?"

"Will do, ma'am."

"Hi, Jade. Sorry, but…I've got to go—there's a really important call waiting for me."

"It's only important if it's to do with work, isn't it, Lorne? Well, family is just as important, you know."

Lorne said a quiet goodbye and picked up her office phone. "Doreen, hello. How are you?"

"Bearing up, dear. Any news for me?" The older woman sounded weary.

"The response from the appeal has been phenomenal, but it will take us a few days to plough through all the leads. Is Colleen still with you?"

"She's just popped out for some groceries. I don't keep much in the larder nowadays, you see. Can't afford to. Oliver came to see us last night."

"The conference and trip to the mortuary was a daunting experience for him. How's he holding up?" Lorne heard the woman's front doorbell chime in the background.

"Just a minute, dear. That'll be Colleen. She must have forgotten her key."

The phone clattered onto the table, and Lorne heard Doreen shuffle away from the phone. Muffled voices filled the earpiece, and Lorne busied herself with some papers.

The woman's piercing scream sent a chill rushing through her.

"Doreen? Doreen are you there?" Lorne shouted down the phone.

She heard a man yelling, then several thuds as if something or someone was being struck, and Doreen's pitiful cries for help, followed by three more heart-wrenching screams.

"Pete, get in here, now," Lorne screeched, cupping her hand over the phone.

Seconds later, Pete rushed into the office. "What's up?"

"Get the nearest Panda car over to Doreen's immediately—she's being attacked. Go! Do it, now!" *Please God, keep her safe until we get there.*

Chapter Fifteen

Lorne felt sick to her stomach. There was silence on the other end of the line. No more begging. No more tormented screams. Nothing.

Realisation hit home—she'd heard Doreen's last pitiful moments on this earth.

"They're on their way, ETA five minutes, they reckon," Pete said, as he returned to her office.

Lorne dropped the phone and threw herself into her chair, shaking her head slowly she whispered, "It's too late, Pete. I'm sure she's dead."

"Shit, and you heard the whole damn thing?"

"Every last fucking torturous detail."

"Are you okay?"

"I'll be all right. We better get over there."

Obviously, despite Pete's warning, Lorne had broken all the ground rules and become emotionally involved with Doreen Nicholls. It was something she had never experienced before. She would have to dig deep into her resolve, and quickly. They had a killer to catch. *Come on, girl. Pull yourself together, quick smart.*

"We'll go over there all right, but I'll drive, and we go in my car."

"Yeah, whatever. I'm in no mood to argue with you. As long as we get there in one piece, I really couldn't give a shit who drives."

"I'll bring the car round. See you outside."

Lorne took three deep calming breaths and pronounced herself ready for action. "Let's get this over with," she said, shaking her arms out in front of her. She headed for the entrance and jumped into the 'Sherman tank' a few minutes later.

"What the fuck happened? What did you hear?" her partner shouted above the noisy engine.

"Doreen was asking me—"

"You'll have to speak up, boss. You're mumbling."

"I am not. It's this pathetic heap of yours. Are you sure you didn't get it out of a war museum? I'm sure I've seen it in an old *Pathé News* clip."

"Ha bloody ha. You were saying?"

"I was saying that Doreen was asking me how the investigation was going, when her doorbell rang."

"But her place is as secure as the Tower of London. How on earth did the bastard manage to get past three bolts and a security chain?"

"She thought Colleen might have forgotten her key—she'd just popped out to do some shopping. I suppose Doreen forgot to put the chain back on after she left. I heard the front door burst open. It banged against the wall—the force probably knocked her off balance."

"I better put my foot down. We don't want Colleen finding her mother like that." Pete managed to reach sixty on the speedometer before the car started to shudder violently.

Far from amused, Lorne clung to the passenger seat as if her life depended on it. "Jesus, Pete, this piece of shit belongs in a scrapyard. Slow down, will you? Unless you're planning to beat Doreen to the mortuary."

He eased the car back to forty, and they continued the rest of the journey in silence.

They walked up the path of the dead woman's house. Two uniformed police stood guard outside the front door.

"You stay here for a few minutes. I want to see Doreen by myself," Lorne said.

"I don't think that's a good idea, boss."

"It wasn't a request, Pete."

"Make sure you don't disturb anything, boss," he called after her.

"Pete," she warned.

The entrance hall was like a scene from a macabre low budget film set, only it was no movie. Doreen lay in a pool of blood, one hand over her chest, the other above her head. Her neck looked broken. Her face was unrecognisable; her left cheekbone protruded through her skin. Blood spattered the walls, the floor, the furniture—even the ceiling.

Lorne walked gingerly past Doreen's battered body, avoiding the bloodstains on the carpet, taking a new pair of latex gloves from her handbag. Pulling on the gloves, she walked over to the hall table and put the phone back in its cradle, putting an end to the high-pitch tone hindering her concentration. At the back of the phone, she noticed a few unpaid bills, a business card for a taxi firm—obviously used by Doreen, as she didn't have a car—and the woman's post office savings book. Surely, if the suspect's intention had been to rob, wouldn't he have taken her savings book with him?

Returning to the body, she systematically ran her eyes over the lifeless frame. She swallowed back the lump that had formed in her throat and noticed the old woman's knickers had been pulled down to her ankles. Bending down, she raised the hem of the woman's woollen A-line skirt and was sickened by what she saw.

Jesus Christ. What kind of sick piece of shit are we dealing with?

There, between the woman's legs, was a hand broom, the handle of which had been impaled in her vagina.

A woman's scream halted any further assessment.

Shit, Colleen.

Rushing from the house, she found Pete trying his best to restrain the sobbing woman, whose numerous shopping bags lay scattered at their feet.

Pete stood back as Lorne grabbed Colleen by the shoulders. "I'm so sorry, Colleen. We got here as soon as we could, but it was too late to save her."

"You mean… She's *dead*?"

Lorne nodded slowly, and the woman fell to her knees, taking Lorne with her. Colleen screamed, shouted, and finally sobbed as Lorne held her tight, fighting to control her own tears.

One of Doreen's neighbours came over and offered to make Colleen a cup of tea, and once Lorne had settled Colleen at her mum's neighbour's house, she rang the devastated woman's husband at work.

The forensic team arrived a few minutes later. Arnaud was with them.

"I see that protecting the sister wasn't high up on your list of priorities, Detective Inspector Simpkins," Arnaud said, when she arrived back at the crime scene.

Lorne found his observation offensive, and it was hard to resist the temptation to swipe the smug grin off his face. *Forget it, Lorne. He's not worth it.* "For your information, Doctor, it's not the force's policy to protect the family members of a homicide victim. If we did, we wouldn't have enough officers to catch the bastards who carry out crimes like this, would we?"

He grunted a response and proceeded with his examination, while Lorne stepped outside to find Pete. "Did the guys see anything when they arrived?"

"When they got here, the door was wide open, and Doreen was already dead."

"They didn't go in the house, did they?"

"No, they said it was obvious she was dead and thought it best not to tamper with anything, unlike someone I could mention."

"All right, Pete. You've made your point. Her neck was broken, and he knocked seven bells of shit out of her. Look, Colleen's husband is on the way. In the meantime, I suggest we knock on a few doors—see if anyone heard or saw anything."

"They're retirement bungalows, so we might be lucky. I'll take the houses on this side of the road, if you like."

Five minutes later, a car screeched to a halt outside Doreen's house. A man in a suit slammed the driver's door shut and headed up the path, but the two officers stood their ground and refused him entry.

Lorne guessed who the visitor was. "Mr. Shaw?"

The man looked disoriented as he turned. "That's right. Where's my wife?" His hair stood on end as though he had been running his hands through it, and his pink striped tie hung low around his neck.

"I'll take you to her."

"What the hell happened?" he demanded, as he followed Lorne to the neighbour's bungalow.

"We're not sure. We'll know more after the post-mortem."

"Why? Why did this happen? Why wasn't she protected after what happened to Belinda?"

"We had no reason to suspect she was in danger. As far as we were concerned, Belinda's murder was a one-off, a random killing."

"I'm not trying to tell you your job, Inspector, but I think that assumption can be put to bed now, don't you?"

"I'll need to ask you and Colleen some questions. When do you think you'll both be up to it?"

"How long does grief usually take to get over, Inspector—a year, maybe two?"

"I know this isn't easy, Mr. Shaw, but please don't make our job any harder than it has to be. The sooner we talk, the quicker we can catch the one who did this."

"It would be better if we left the interrogation until tomorrow—providing, of course, that Colleen is up to it then," he snapped.

"I'll give you a call in the morning."

"You do that, Inspector."

Lorne walked back to Pete's car, a feeling of helplessness draped around her aching shoulders. Should she have protected Doreen more? In the last half hour, two people had told her she should have. Guilt replaced the helplessness as she mentally pictured the fear Doreen must have experienced during the attack.

"I take it the husband didn't take the news too well, then?" Pete asked as he returned to the car and stood alongside her.

"He blames me."

"For what?"

"He has a point. I should have asked a uniform to check on the area every half hour. It would have served as a deterrent."

"You're being hard on yourself. Can we start looking in Oliver's direction now?"

"Why are you so damn suspicious of him, Pete?"

"You know what they say: Before looking at the outlaws, you have to look at the in-laws."

"Do you take pleasure in repeating yourself?"

"No, but you have to admit it makes sense, boss. At least seventy per cent of homicides are committed by friends or relatives of a victim."

He had a point, although he would have to come up with an astonishing motive before she suspected Oliver of not only murdering his own mother, but his aunt too.

"Do me a favour, Pete. Ask the Doc when the PM is likely to be. I don't think I could face any more of his odious comments at the moment."

By the time he returned, Lorne had belted herself into his tank. "He reckons he's gonna be another three or four hours here. Says he's found quite a lot of trace evidence already. Looks like another late night down at the mortuary."

"Let's get back to base, see what progress the team has made."

"Did the neighbours come up with anything?" Pete asked.

"The old man at number seven saw a man approaching Doreen's door, but he didn't get a good look at him. He'd heard her nephew was in town and presumed he was paying her a visit."

"Perhaps it was. How come he didn't mention it to the boys in blue?" Pete replied.

"Because he couldn't give any details; didn't even notice what colour his hair was."

"Great. He eyeballs a fucking murderer and can't give us jackshit. What hope have we got of finding the creep?"

"It's called old age."

"Promise me one thing, boss?"

"What's that, Pete?"

"That you'll shoot me if I ever lose my marbles like that."

She nodded her agreement.

The chief was waiting for them when they entered the incident room. The phones were quieter than when they'd left.

"Lorne, Pete, where are we up to?" the chief asked, perching on the edge of Pete's desk.

"We think Doreen was killed by the same person. Looks like the same *modus operandi.*"

"Any witnesses?"

"Nothing worth chasing. Doctor Arnaud says his team have found quite a lot of trace evidence at the scene, which looks promising."

"Do you have any suspects?" the chief asked.

"I reckon we should start digging deep into the son's background," Pete piped up before Lorne had a chance to reply.

"Why's that, Pete?"

"There's something about him that don't quite ring true, Chief."

"Are you of the same opinion, Lorne?"

"No, I'm afraid Pete's on his own with that one."

"If suspects are thin on the ground, I'm afraid I'm with Pete: You should start looking at the son. What about her will? Do we know whom she left her money to? If the son was the sole beneficiary, it could be a motive. I'll leave it with you; keep me informed." He left the room looking worried, his shoulders slumped as if he had a colossal weight on them.

Lorne watched him go with an odd ache in her heart. Then she slowly turned back to Pete and gave him a thunderous look. "Don't think you just got the better of me, Pete Childs. I'm neither in the mood nor the right frame of mind to argue with you at the moment. Get in touch with Belinda's solicitor. Delve into Oliver's personal and working life."

While Pete began his mission, Lorne set out on one of her own. Beginning with Tracy, she made her way round her team, gathering any snippets of information they had collected while she'd been out.

"Can I have a quick word, ma'am?" Tracy asked.

"Sure, what's up?" she smiled reassuringly at the young woman she regarded as her protégée.

"I received a letter from Head Office this morning."

"You did, did you? Well, tell me more." Lorne pulled up a chair and positioned it next to Tracy's desk.

"They're encouraging new recruits to enrol in a forensic course they're introducing."

"Sounds intriguing. What's involved?"

"It would mean losing me from the office for one day a week, a total of eight weeks." Tracy winced and waited, as though expecting Lorne to explode.

"I don't see a problem with that. Perhaps you could make notes and fill the rest of us in when you get back. Forensics is a vital part of the investigation process, nowadays—it's hard to keep up with all the new procedures. Will you be attending a post-mortem?"

"Unfortunately not."

"So what will the course entail?"

"Each week a different specialist will be giving a talk. We'll be looking at ballistics, scene analysis, fingerprinting, toxicology, things like that."

Lorne could see the enthusiasm in Tracy's eyes and would've found it hard to deny her the opportunity, even if she hadn't already given her the go-ahead to attend the course.

"You could give me a few pointers on the poison front. It might come in handy, for a few members of the staff," she whispered straight-faced, but when the younger woman's mouth flew open and her eyes nearly burst free of their sockets, Lorne laughed. "It was a joke, Tracy. Guess you haven't been privy to my wicked sense of humour yet. Mind you, if you listen to Pete, he'll tell you I had a humour transplant years ago."

The pair laughed, and the rest of the team looked their way.

"Keep them guessing," Lorne whispered behind her hand as she went on to the next member of her team.

A short time later, Lorne had jotted down all the relevant information they had gathered and transferred it to the notice board. Ten different vehicles, three men that no one could put a name to—clues were agonisingly thin on the ground.

Maybe Pete has a point about Oliver, after all?

Chapter Sixteen

The man burst through his front door and shut out the crazy world behind him. His clothes were spattered with blood, and his neck covered in scratches. Leaning against the front door, he panted breathlessly as he waited for his heart rate to return to normal.

Banging noises and cries for help echoed through the house. He raised his eyes to the ceiling when he realised the soundproofing in the cellar would need his attention, sooner rather than later.

"Well, how did it go?" The woman rushed towards him.

"I got her, this time. She won't be hurting anyone else again."

"I've had a hell of a time with that one down there."

"I'll get rid of her after I've had some dinner, I promise." The man smiled down at the woman, hugged her lovingly then kissed her on the forehead.

"I've made your favourite, roast lamb—it'll be ready in ten minutes. Why don't you get cleaned up, and we'll open a bottle of wine to celebrate?" the woman replied.

They sat down to eat. Incessant crying spoilt their meal.

"Damn it. I've had *enough* of her!" he said.

While the woman took their dirty dishes to the kitchen, he tore back the rug and angrily ripped open the trap door. The girl stopped crying instantly. He climbed down the rickety ladder and watched her tremble as he approached.

"Please, please not again. I promise to be quiet. Please don't hurt me. I didn't mean to laugh at you."

"Ah, but you did, didn't you? You'll be free soon," he assured her.

The girl wrapped her arms around her knees, hiding her nakedness from his intimidating gaze.

She sobbed again, and he towered over her like a vulture ready to swoop. He bent down beside her, stroked her hair as if she was his pet dog, then his hand began its journey. Starting on her cheek, his fingers outlined her lips, down past her throat, lingering on her arm before finally caressing her shapely thigh. "Shh. There, there. It's all right."

As he reached to undo his belt, she screamed.

Chapter Seventeen

Doreen Nicholls' post-mortem drew to a close at one in the morning.

"Therefore, I conclude that the cause of death was due to a fatal blow to the head," Arnaud finished, before turning off his recorder.

"Poor Doreen." Lorne watched Bones stitch up the Y-section to the woman's lifeless body. It was hard to find a reason why someone would despise Doreen so much as to want her dead. As post-mortems went, this had been her toughest yet. But Lorne had insisted that she needed to be involved, feeling she owed the dead woman that much.

"Poor Doreen, indeed. Even though she had a bad heart and was still very weak from her recent operation, she still managed to summon up enough strength to put up a fight for her life. The defence wounds across her hands and arms tell us that."

"She had an angina attack when I told her about her sister's death."

"I'm not surprised. She had arteriosclerosis."

Lorne frowned, confused.

Arnaud explained, "Which basically means the flow of blood through the coronary arteries is restricted. The result is a shortage of oxygen travelling to the heart muscle. In my opinion, it was at an advanced stage. Her life would have been shortened considerably by the condition."

The doctor sounded surprisingly emotional. *Is this his way of showing me he has compassion?*

"It'll be of little consolation to her family. But it may ease their pain a little, knowing she didn't have long to live, anyway. When will the forensic results be back, Doctor?"

"Twenty-four, maybe forty-eight, hours, as it's the weekend—for some of us, at least. I will let you know. We found several hairs and fibres on the body; a piece of dirt, possibly from the offender's shoe; skin under her fingernails; and a few fingerprints on the broom. The killer was very sloppy this time. He even managed to leave a bloody shoe print on the doorstep. Perhaps distant sirens scared him off. It's a shame your colleagues weren't a little nearer when you called for their assistance."

"She lives on the outskirts of town, in a small village. The closest squad car was on another call at the time," she said, sharply, sticking up for her colleagues.

"Never mind. The deed is done now. I'll wait to hear from you."

Lorne left the mortuary alone. The frosty night air caught her off guard, and she pulled her jacket tight around her already chilled body. Pete had insisted he would accompany her to the post-mortem, but she had ordered him to go home and get some rest. She suspected the days ahead of them would be long and laborious. It would've been pointless for both of them to be dead on their feet.

Chapter Eighteen

That Sunday, Lorne and Pete were the only ones in the office. She went over the findings of the post-mortem with him and asked how far he'd got with his quest to nail Oliver as their prime suspect.

"Bearing in mind that it was Saturday yesterday, I reckon I did well. I tracked down Belinda's solicitor at about five o'clock. He was on the golf course at High Wycombe—not too happy about being disturbed, I can tell you." He paused to take a sip of coffee. "Anyway, after his initial unwillingness to co-operate, and with a little friendly persuasion from yours truly, he finally came up trumps."

"In what way?" Lorne knew how much Pete liked to make a mountain out of the tiniest molehill.

A cocky tone slipped into his voice as he said, "Well, guess who the main beneficiary of Belinda Greenaway's will is?"

"Stop building your part up, Pete. Just give me the damn facts."

"Touchy this morning, ain't we? Anyway, Mr. Franklyn-Lewis, Belinda's solicitor, told me that ninety per cent of her money was heading in Doreen's direction."

"Really, and what do you glean from this snippet of information?" she said, raising an expectant eyebrow.

"Actually, *I glean* quite a lot from what he said. Especially as he went on to tell me she changed her will a few months ago because she'd fallen out with her son." He finished reading from his notebook and triumphantly threw it on the desk between them.

"Did he say why?" Lorne sat forwards in her chair as the implications behind these new findings sank in.

"Nope. All she would tell him was that it was a personal matter, one she didn't wish to discuss."

"It nearly chokes me to admit this, but I think you might have stumbled onto something significant."

"I told you, boss. He's shifty, and I don't need any goddamn women's intuition to tell me that, either."

"Hang on a minute, before you get too smug. If Belinda's money was on its way to Doreen, what happens now?"

"I'm not with you?"

"Well, wouldn't Doreen's money go to her own daughter, Colleen?"

"I guess so." He shrugged.

"So why in God's name would Oliver kill his aunt?"

"Because he's not as clever as he looks. Maybe his next victim is going to be his cousin." Pete's eyes beamed.

"Nope, sorry, Pete, I don't buy it. He seems a pretty shrewd individual to me. There's another matter we should be considering here, too."

"What's that?" His brow crinkled.

"The sexual aspect of the case. Would he subject family members to that kind of sick behaviour?"

"I beg to differ with you on that one. There are some sick folks out there. Anyway, I ain't finished yet. I also got in touch with his firm, Callick Oil, and they told me things haven't been going too well for him over the last two or three years."

"Meaning?"

"Apparently, he's lost the company millions. He promised to bring in more business if and when he got promotion, but instead he *lost* them a few lucrative contracts."

"I thought Oliver came up squeaky clean when we did the initial checks on him?" Lorne searched through the case file.

"Depends who's asking the questions," he said, tapping the side of his nose. "Let's just say my charm works wonders, on occasion."

"You're a good cop, Pete, if a bit highly strung and lacking in foresight, at times. But basically, I wouldn't be without you." Her smile broadened as she noticed the colour rising in his chubby cheeks.

"Aw, give it a rest, boss. As you're always telling me, we make a good team."

"I'll drink to that," she said. They raised their coffee cups and clinked them together.

"Don't you find it strange, though?" Pete asked as he settled back in his chair.

"What are you talking about now?"

"If your aunt had just been murdered right after your mother, wouldn't you be down to the cop shop straight away, demanding to know what the hell was going on?"

"I'd be there before the ink had time to dry in the attending officer's notebook. Do we know where he's staying?"

"I'll have to check, but I think it's the Deerfellow Hotel in town?"

"You check while I tidy up here. I think it's time we paid Oliver Greenaway a little visit."

"Yes, ma'am." Pete hurried out the door like a man on a mission.

Chapter Nineteen

The receptionist at the swanky four-star Deerfellow Hotel informed them Mr. Greenaway had checked out at ten that morning.

With their suspicions heightened that their prime suspect had left town, Lorne and Pete decided to pay Colleen a visit. Maybe she'd be able to shed some light on what they had discovered about Belinda's will.

"How could you *think* such a thing? Oliver loved his mother, and he always visited my mum whenever he was in town." Colleen nervously twisted a tissue in a figure eight around her fingers.

"Some details have come to our attention that makes us suspect all's not well with your cousin. Has anything strange happened over the last few months, anything at all?" Lorne asked.

"I'm trying to think. At the back of my mind, there is something I found strange. Give me a few moments, and I'm sure it'll come to me. My mind's all jumbled up because of what happened to Mum. I've got to go to the mortuary today. Don's coming with me." She smiled at her husband as he entered the room, carrying a tray holding four mugs of coffee.

Don handed round the drinks, then sat on the sofa next to his wife. He placed an arm around her shoulder and asked, "What's up, Col?"

"About a month ago—it might've been two—something happened with Aunt Belinda. I can't remember what it was, can you?" Her frown deepened as her frustration to think clearly mounted.

"That's right, Belinda and your mother came to Sunday lunch, and we were shocked by what she had to say."

"Was it something to do with changing her will?" Lorne asked.

Don ran his fingers through his hair and looked pensive. "No, she definitely didn't tell us about that. She did tell us she was angry with Oliver about something, though. What the hell was it?"

"I know!" Colleen seemed pleased with herself. "Bel—that's what we used to call her; she hated being called 'Aunt Belinda'—she was livid with Oliver for losing one of the firm's biggest contracts.

Jack—her husband—had treated that customer with kid gloves, bowed and scraped to their every need, because of how valuable they were. But Oliver was rebelling for some reason, he said he was fed up with having to kiss arse all the time."

"How did Belinda find out?" Lorne asked.

"The chairman of the board rang her. He was Jack's best friend. He'd stayed close friends with Bel after his death. He promoted Oliver to director. I think he felt obligated—guilt played a huge part in his decision. After all, Oliver's father did die on board one of the firm's helicopters."

"Did you see Oliver after he fell out with his mother?"

"No, he kept his distance. I rang him because he hadn't replied to our christening invitation. He apologised and said he wouldn't be able to make it. I was furious and put the phone down on him." Sadness filled her features. Colleen gazed over at the christening photo of her daughter nestled in her mother's arms.

"What was his excuse for not attending?"

"He said work commitments meant he was working seven days a week and couldn't afford to take the time off."

"When you met up after his mother's death, how did he seem to you?" Lorne probed carefully.

"That's really hard to answer, because he's a difficult man to figure out. He was an only child, spoilt rotten—always carried a rather large chip on his shoulder when he was growing up."

"Was he upset, do you think?" Pete pressed, eager to pick up Oliver.

Colleen looked flustered by Pete's insistence. "I suppose so. I did find it strange that he wanted to see Bel's body, especially when—you know, the way it had been...mutilated. I'm glad you managed to talk him out of it, Inspector." She wiped away the tears that had started to roll down her face.

Lorne noticed Don's expression pleading with the detectives to give Colleen a break. She took the hint, and they left soon after, leaving the couple to their grief.

On the car ride back to the station, Pete said, "I have to agree with her, actually. We both thought it strange when he demanded to see his ma's body like that."

"Hmm," Lorne said, contemplating their next move.

"Will the boss sanction a visit to Cornwall? I know funds are low, but I think we should pay Oliver a visit ASAP, don't you?"

"I'm sure the chief will want us to go down there. Leave him to me."

"Any chance we can call it a day soon?" Pete glanced at his watch.

"Some big game on the telly you want to watch?"

"The boys are meeting their biggest rivals today. I just thought if we couldn't do much down at the station, it being Sunday and all, I could make it home for the kick-off."

Pete was a lifelong Gooner, just like Tom. Both besotted with Arsenal, they could talk together for hours about the team, especially about the fabulous youngsters Arsene Wenger was developing. Their favourite saying at the moment was 'Who needs Patrick Vieira when you have a talent like eighteen-year-old Cesc Fabregas?'

Lorne had managed to get them tickets to last season's cup final, when the team had beaten Man Utd in a penalty shoot-out. Vieira had moved to Juventus straight after that match. Lorne always made out that she couldn't give a damn about football, but secretly she enjoyed it just as much as they did. God forbid if Pete ever found out the truth; her life wouldn't be worth living. Their crime solving statistics would drop overnight if her partner climbed on his soapbox every day, especially if the words Abramovich or Chelsea happened to be mentioned.

"I have an idea. Why don't you come over and see the match at our house? We'll pick up a few beers on the way, and I'll knock up some food before the game starts?"

"That'd be outstanding, boss! You sure Tom won't mind?"

"He'll be chuffed to bits to have someone else in the house who knows the offside rule as well as he does." She laughed as she crunched into gear and headed for the off-licence on Drake Street.

The Gunners lost, unfortunately. Arsene Wenger said the team were going through a transitional period. The team just looked disjointed to Lorne.

After drowning his sorrows a little too deeply, Pete ended up spending an uncomfortable night on Lorne's sofa.

Chapter Twenty

As Lorne came down the stairs at seven the next morning, she heard Pete shout, "Get off me, mutt."

Henry must've woken him up. She bounded into his makeshift, bedroom, fully clothed and ready for work. "Morning, Pete. Sleep well?" she asked loudly, with a devilish glint in her eye. She had little sympathy for anyone suffering from a hangover.

"Can you keep the decibels down this morning, boss? And to answer your question, I can't remember if I slept well or not." He steadied himself by gripping the back of the sofa as he rose.

Henry jumped up at him.

"Oh, no… The room's starting to sway." Pete dropped back down onto the sofa. "Just give me a minute or two to wake up properly, will you? There's a good boy."

Henry barked his agreement.

Lorne suppressed a chuckle. "You've got five minutes. Come through to the kitchen when you're able to stand up. Breakfast won't be long."

"Black strong coffee will do, and plenty of it." That time, he stood up successfully, and he staggered his way up to the bathroom.

The tempting smell of bacon wafted through the house, and when he appeared in the kitchen, Lorne thrust a full English breakfast on the counter in front of him.

"Guess coffee looks different in my house," he said. "Don't order me to eat this, boss."

"Get it down your neck. It'll do you good. Christ, it's like having another kid around the place when you stay over."

"Remind me not to stay over next time, if this is how you treat your guests. Force feeding ain't very hospitable, now is it?"

"Two minutes and counting, Pete," Lorne folded her arms and glanced up at the clock on the wall.

She backed down when she saw how much he was enjoying his breakfast. Ten minutes later, they were on their way to Cornwall.

It took them almost four hours to get to Callick Oil. Pete slept most of the journey, giving Lorne the opportunity to mull over Oliver's motives. She was still having trouble convincing herself that Oliver was the killer. But until they had another suspect in mind, it was a necessary avenue they had to explore.

They reached the top floor by the glass lift that rose on the outside of the building. The view over the rolling hills was breath-taking. But the speed of the lift had a detrimental effect on Pete's stomach. Against the odds, he somehow managed to hang on to his breakfast.

Oliver's secretary was a smartly dressed, well-spoken, middle-aged woman, who was surprised by their unannounced visit. "I'm afraid you've wasted your time. Mr. Greenaway *never* sees anyone without an appointment," she said, guarding his office as if it contained the crown jewels.

Pete grabbed the woman by the shoulders and guided her back to her desk. "He'll see us, darlin'. We're old friends."

While Pete distracted the secretary, Lorne took the opportunity to step into Oliver's office.

He appeared stunned by the intrusion. "Detective Inspector, what can I do for you?"

"We were in the area," Pete blurted out, barging into the office behind her.

"I tried to stop them, but he manhandled me," the secretary whined over Pete's broad shoulders.

"It's okay, Trisha. Hold all my calls for the time being, will you?" Oliver stepped around the desk to shoo the woman out the door.

"She's a bit of a Rottweiler. Thought you executive types went for curvy dumb blondes for secretaries," Pete said.

"She's usually capable of keeping the wolves from the door," Oliver bit back, obviously disliking Pete's tone.

Lorne interjected, "We need to ask you a few questions about your mother, if you don't mind, Mr. Greenaway?"

"I thought I'd answered all your questions already." He returned to his chair and motioned for them to sit down opposite him.

"What about the will?" Pete blurted out. Lorne shot him one of her *back off* looks, and he shuffled his feet sheepishly.

"What about it?"

"Were you aware that your mother changed it a short time ago?" Lorne asked.

"Totally aware, thank you."

"Can we ask why your mother would cut you out of her will?"

"She didn't. If you had bothered to do your research properly, you would know she left me ten per cent of her savings—which amounts to a very tidy sum—plus the house."

"Up until two months ago, you were the sole beneficiary, were you not?" Lorne asked, studying the man's reactions carefully.

"That's correct."

"I repeat, why would your mother change her will like that?"

"Actually, it was my suggestion," he admitted, surprising the two detectives.

"Oh?"

"You look shocked, Inspector. Yes, my mother was a very wealthy woman, but then, I'm a very wealthy man."

"Correct me if I'm wrong, Mr. Greenaway. You gave up your mother's millions because you already have millions of your own?"

"Half correct. I gave up the capital but kept the house that's worth around three million pounds. Forgive me, Inspector, but have I broken a law somewhere that I'm unaware of?"

"Why?" Lorne asked for the third time.

"Aunt Doreen needed the money more than I did. You saw the way she was living. I thought my mother should've helped her out more." He picked up his gold fountain pen and passed it through his fingers.

"Why didn't your mother help her out when she was alive? She could've arranged private medical care for Doreen to help with her hip replacement." Emotion crept into Lorne's voice.

"They were both stubborn. Mum was too stubborn to offer, and Doreen was far too stubborn to ask for any sort of handout. Pride and stubbornness, they're family traits.

"So, when Mum started going on about what I'd inherit one day, I told her I didn't want it. I felt Doreen needed it more. Mum was livid—she said I was being ungrateful. It took me ages to get back in her good books."

"Why didn't you just accept your mother's wishes and make provisions for your aunt?" Lorne asked as it dawned on her that her initial feelings about this man were correct. She was certain he had nothing to do with either death.

"I knew I could talk my Mum round, but not Doreen."

"Okay, that makes sense, but why did you leave town so soon after your aunt's death?"

"Yeah, that's what I want to know," Pete piped up, eyeing his chief suspect with growing scepticism.

"I'm in the process of negotiating a rather large contract. I checked with Colleen if she could cope, and she assured me she could. I plan on returning in a few days once the bodies have been released, to sort out a joint funeral." His eyes misted up, and he cleared his throat before continuing, "Right. I've taken the time and trouble to answer your questions, Inspector. Now you can answer one for me."

"What might that be, Mr. Greenaway?"

"Am I a suspect in my mother's and aunt's murders?"

"We're just covering all the bases. No one is accusing you of anything sinister, I assure you. Thank you for your help. We'll keep you informed of any progress we make." Lorne rose from her chair and offered her hand. Pete stood up too but planted his hand deep in his pocket.

Oliver Greenaway shook her hand and held her gaze for the briefest of moments, then he uttered quietly, "I'm a victim in this crime, Inspector, not the perpetrator."

"I know, Oliver. We'll get the person who did this, I promise." She meant every word of it.

"I'll leave it in your capable hands. My 'Rottweiler' will show you out," he said, smiling.

"You fell for it, didn't you?" Pete asked in disbelief when they entered the lift.

"If you're asking if I believe him, then yes, I do. We'll have to start looking in another direction, Pete, because as I said right from the beginning, I'm ninety-nine-point-nine per cent certain Oliver Greenaway did not kill his mother. Or his aunt, for that matter."

They stepped out of the building into the warm lunchtime sun, with Pete vigorously shaking his head in disapproval and Lorne vigorously nodding hers in contradiction.

After filling up with petrol and grabbing a quick sandwich at a motorway service station, they headed back up to London. The traffic was worse than anticipated because of road works on the M4, and they arrived back in the office at just before six.

Lorne sensed something was wrong the second they stepped into the incident room. She saw the chief's outline through the frosted glass window to her office.

"What's up?" she whispered to Tracy, as she swept past her desk.

"They've found the missing girl."

"That's good, isn't it?" Lorne asked, hopeful.

"She turned up at an allotment, two miles from Chelling Forest. She's dead, ma'am."

Shit. When is this bloody nightmare going to end?

Chapter Twenty-One

October 4, 2007.

Dusk was descending as they arrived at the allotment. Large drops of rain had started to fall, making the ground muddy underfoot.

Since leaving the station, Lorne had been in a foul mood. Her meeting with the chief hadn't gone well, and her call home had gone even worse. Her constant sighing in the car warned Pete his usual wisecracks wouldn't be welcome.

The forensic team were already on site. Cameras clicked, and people shouted "Be careful where you're stepping!"

The victim, Kim Charlton, lay face down on the wooden floor of a shed situated on the edge of the allotment. Arnaud had a scalpel in his hand and was gently taking samples of blood and soil from the victim's back.

"Why are you bothering to do that here, Doctor?" Lorne asked as she watched him put the samples into Perspex tubes.

"Ah, Inspector Simpkins, we really must stop meeting like this."

"I can assure you, Doctor, it's unintentional on my part," she snapped and immediately regretted her tone. "I'm sorry. It's been a long day."

Arnaud nodded his acceptance and continued with his work. "I'm taking the samples here because the body is transported to the mortuary facing upwards. Any trace evidence found on the victim's back would become smudged or possibly wiped off, when the body is placed in the body bag."

His willingness to hold a proper conversation with her for a change intrigued her. "I see. Why can't they transport the body the way they found it?"

"Because of lividity."

"Lividity?"

"More commonly known as *livor mortis.* It's when the heart stops pumping the blood. The red blood cells settle according to gravity, and this produces a maroon hue to the skin. We call this the colour of death.

"Funeral directors try to prevent lividity wherever possible. They say it causes loved ones unnecessary grief. Since the high-profile case of O.J. Simpson in the States, a directive has been issued that if the body has to be turned over, then samples must be taken from all exposed areas at the scene."

"You mean when they failed to take samples of the traces of blood found on Nicole Simpson's back? Yes, I remember it well. The police came in for a lot of stick on that one."

"Rightly so! And so did the forensic team. Some of them were morons. They traipsed through the blood of the victims with no protective shoe coverings. Was it intentional? I don't know. But that night, basic forensic and police protocol were ignored, proving to be detrimental to the prosecutor's case. I do my utmost to prevent that kind of mishap from happening in this country," he said as he walked over and stood beside her.

She suddenly felt awkward as his six-foot-four frame towered above her.

"Was there something else, Inspector?" His voice was soft, and he gave her a devastating smile.

She'd never seen this side of him before and was unsure how to react. Lorne's sudden discomfort baffled her. *Jesus, get a grip, woman.* She cleared her throat before saying, "I know it's early, but do you think we could be looking at the same killer?"

"You know how much I dislike conjecture, Inspector. However, yes, I believe there is a connection."

"Oh, fuck," Pete cursed, peering at the girl's naked body over Lorne's shoulder.

She turned and pushed Pete back outside the shed. "What did the owner of the shed have to say?" Lorne felt relieved to be outside and didn't have a clue why that was.

"The paramedics are giving him the once-over. He's in shock. Keeps saying that's his favourite fork sticking out of her vagina. Poor sod."

"Was the shed locked?"

"Yeah. He said he found the broken lock on the floor outside."

"Did he touch anything?" Lorne surveyed their surroundings for possible access and getaway routes. From where she stood, she could only see one.

"No, he saw the body and rushed out, shouting for help. One of his gardening buddies came over, saw the girl's body, and called 999 straight away. Our boys and the ambulance arrived within minutes."

"What's his name?"

"The guy who owns the shed is Jim Wilkinson, and his mate is Frank Gee."

Wilkinson was sitting on the steps of the ambulance, shaking uncontrollably despite the paramedics wrapping a fleece blanket around his shoulders. Gee was leaning against the vehicle's door. Both men looked stricken with shock, and the colour had drained from their ageing faces.

"Mr. Wilkinson, I'm Detective Inspector Simpkins. I understand what a shock this must've been for you, but are you up to answering a few questions?"

The poor man's hand shook as he placed the oxygen mask that had been lying in his lap over his nose. His gaze nervously darted in every direction. Finally, he nodded and looked up at his friend for reassurance.

"It'll be all right, Jim. Just tell the Inspector what you know." Gee patted his shaking friend on the shoulder.

"What time did you arrive?" Lorne asked as Pete took out his notebook.

Removing the mask, Wilkinson said, "Sometime around four, I suppose. I came down to pick some veggies for my dinner."

"When did you last come down here?"

"That'd be yesterday afternoon."

"What time?"

He took another long pull on the oxygen before answering, "I suppose it was earlier than usual because I wanted to see the match. Must've been about three—a few of us left at the same time. We watched the match together down the pub, same as usual."

"And you didn't return at all yesterday?"

"No, it would've been too dark after the match. I never come down here in the dark, miss."

"Did you see anyone hanging around when you left?"

"No one who shouldn't be down here, no. A few of the guys who weren't interested in the game stayed here. I'll give you their names, if you like."

"Thanks, that'd be helpful. Is there someone in charge around here?"

"No, there's usually no need. Nothing untoward *usually* happens around here. Zac McKinlay and Walter Moore are the guys we left down here. They come down in the afternoons, more or less every day, but I'm afraid I don't know where they live."

"That's okay. We'll find them. What about you, Mr. Gee? What time did you arrive today?"

"It was probably about two o'clock. I was the first one down here."

"What about yesterday?"

"Nope, family commitments. I rarely come here on a Sunday."

"You say no one is actually in charge? Does that mean the gates are always open, that anyone can get in here if they wanted to?"

Frank Gee took over the explanations as his friend sucked in more oxygen from the mask. "That's right. We're pretty much left to our own devices. Every now and then, a man from the council comes round—you know, to see if we have any problems."

"How many people have plots down here?" Pete asked.

"Fifteen, at the last count. I suppose you'll be needing all their names and numbers?"

"That would help us out considerably. Here's my card. Are you feeling any better, Mr. Wilkinson?"

"A little, they want to take me off to hospital, but I'm not sure about that." The old man pulled the blanket tighter around his sloping shoulders.

"It wouldn't hurt to get checked out. I'm afraid your shed will be out of bounds for a few days," Lorne apologised, her gaze scouring the area.

"That's okay. I don't intend going in there for a while anyway. Jim said that if I need to, I can borrow his tools. I can't believe this has happened to me again."

"Again? What do you mean 'again'? Have you been broken into before?" Pete exchanged glances with Lorne.

"Yeah. Two, maybe three weeks ago."

Pete asked, "Was anything taken?"

"No, but something was left behind."

"Oh? What was that?" Lorne asked.

"I was away for two weeks. Went to Benidorm with the wife. I came down here on the Sunday after we got back and found the lock lying on the floor, just like this time, and there was a patch of blood on the floor of the shed."

"Did you report it to the police?"

"Yeah, they came down, showed no interest whatsoever, said they would log it as a break-in. When I asked them about the blood, they said the burglar must have cut himself and that I should clean it up."

"You're kidding. What station was this?" Pete asked, incensed.

"I don't know. The young copper was only here five minutes." Wilkinson gulped down more oxygen.

They thanked the two men and wandered round the plots.

"Look into that when we get back, Pete. That's shoddy policing."

"Righto, boss. You know, one more murder, and he'll be a serial killer, according to the experts."

"Thanks, Pete. That's just what I needed to hear. Always looking on the bright side of things, aren't you? With any luck, we'll catch the bastard before he kills someone else. I can't seem to get my head round this one. What the hell are we missing? What's the bloody connection? Apart from the victims all being women, that is." She wildly kicked at a lump of earth lying in her path.

"If it's the same killer, the crimes are getting worse, and he's getting braver."

"We don't know how the girl died yet, so how can you possibly know he's getting worse?"

"Where has she been holed up for the last few days? You can't tell me the killer didn't have some fun with her before he finished her off."

"Shh, keep your voice down. Let's get back to the station, see what we can come up with. We'll have to oversee another midnight post-mortem later. I spend more bloody evenings at that damn place than with my own family at the moment."

"Talking of which, what's with you and the doc?" Pete nudged her arm with his and gave her a knowing wink.

"What the hell are you on about?" Lorne's foul mood quickly returned.

"You seemed pretty pally in there when I came in. Usually you do everything you can to keep a safe distance from him, but there you were, side by side, all nice and cosy."

"We were in a damn five-foot garden shed. I'm afraid it's your warped mind playing tricks on you again, Pete."

"Whatever you say, boss. Whatever you say. By the way, are you gonna tell me what the chief said?"

"He gave me a bollocking for not getting anywhere with the case, and he was furious when he heard about the latest murder on his patch. He told me to start pulling suspects in. He's given us another ten days to get the case solved." Lorne immediately regretted letting her tongue slip.

"How come?"

She had to come up with a plausible excuse. "Er, budget. We went way over on our last case. He wants this one wrapped up within two weeks."

"Shit. Does he think we're supercops or something?"

Lorne shrugged innocently.

Chapter Twenty-Two

"Gather around, ladies and gents," Pete shouted when Lorne and Pete walked into the incident room.

Chairs scraped and the noise of rustling notebooks filled the room as the team gathered.

Lorne took up her position beside the whiteboard, and Pete sat on the edge of the desk nearest to her.

"I know that you're all doing your best, but we have to dig deeper, think harder. Look outside the box. Feel free to throw any ideas at me as we recap," Lorne said.

"Victim number one: Belinda Greenaway, a sixty-five-year-old widow. By all accounts, she had no known enemies. Victim number two: Doreen Nicholls, sister of Belinda Greenaway."

"Twin sister of victim one," piped up Molly, in her usual bored tone.

"Meaning?"

"And not just twins, but *identical* twins. We could be looking at a case of mistaken identity," Molly told the group matter-of-factly.

"It's a possibility, but Doreen Nicholls was a very inoffensive old dear. Can't see what the motive would be there," Pete pointed out.

"Okay, it's a start. What else have we got?"

"There is one thing, boss," Mitch told her, hesitantly. "While you were out a courier brought over a package, it's in your office. Um… It's from Arnaud's office."

"Get it for me, Pete, will you? I should've been told about this straight away."

Pete returned with the large brown envelope in his chubby hand and gave it to her.

Lorne quickly scanned the post-mortem report on Doreen Nicholls and jotted down snippets of information on the board beneath the woman's name. Three hairs found on the body that hadn't belonged to the victim. Minute green fibres found in the clasp of her watch had been sent for further analysis. The skin under her fingernails belonged to someone other than the victim and traces of blood also found under her nails, came up as O Positive. *Great, that accounts for at least thirty-seven per cent of the population of the UK.*

Forensics managed to find two decent fingerprints, experts were searching through the database for a match. The soil samples from the shoeprint were similar to those found on the body of Belinda; further analysis was being carried out on both samples. All results were due back at the end of the week.

"What about the sexual aspect to the crimes?" Tracy asked quietly.

"Good thinking. Mitch, check the Sex Offenders Register, see if it highlights any offenders living in that area? You might as well check the paedophile list while you're at it, because Kim Charlton, the third victim, is only sixteen."

"That brings me nicely onto Kim Charlton, victim number three. According to her friend, she rang for a taxi the night she went missing, but it didn't show. Does anybody know what firm she used?"

"I'll get on to it straight away, ma'am," John said.

"Tracy, I'd like you to chase up a crime number for me. The allotment shed where Kim's body was found had been broken into a couple of weeks back. I'd like a word with the idiot who attended the scene, ASAP."

"Yes, ma'am. By the way, the incident van has been withdrawn from the forest. Their leads didn't amount to much, I'm afraid."

"Okay, Tracy. I might want them to set up shop at the allotment. I've got to think about that one. I'll get back to you on that."

After the meeting, Lorne grabbed a coffee from the vending machine en route to taking refuge in her office.

"Make mine a coffee, milk, two sugars," Pete said, creeping up behind her.

"Sugar is bad for the waistline, Pete. I'm cutting you back to one sugar, no arguments." Placing the coins in the slot, she hit the white coffee button, bent down to retrieve the steaming cup and handed it to her disgruntled partner.

He followed her to her office. "Sorry, boss. I'm having trouble workin' somethin' out."

"What's that, chunky?"

"How is cutting my sugar intake down gonna benefit my waistline, when you've already thrust a full-English down my neck this morning?"

"That was purely medicinal. It's a well-known fact a greasy fry-up is the best cure for a hangover," she said, smirking.

"One rule for one, and one for another. I ain't ever gonna win an argument with you, am I?"

"Nope. I've only got your best interests at heart."

After their drink, Pete helped Lorne with some paperwork. An hour later, a knock on the door disturbed them.

Tracy poked her head in. "I've got the constable outside who you wanted to see, ma'am."

"What's his name?" Lorne mouthed to the younger woman.

"P.C. Bulmer, ma'am," Tracy whispered back.

"Show him in, Tracy, and good work by the way." Lorne smiled as Tracy thrust the door open wide and stood back to let the young constable past her.

"Ma'am. You wanted to see me?" The constable, in his early twenties, looked worried.

"Indeed I did. I'd invite you to sit down, but I'm afraid my partner here's got the only available seat."

"That's okay, ma'am, I prefer to stand."

"P.C. Bulmer, how long have you been with the force?"

The young officer proudly thrust his shoulders back and chest out. "I'm just beginning my second year, ma'am."

"Are you enjoying your role as a police constable?"

"Why yes, ma'am, most definitely, ma'am." He appeared more relaxed.

"I have a few hypothetical scenarios to put to you, if you don't mind. It'll give me an insight into the type of training you've been getting."

"Fire away, ma'am."

"You're on the beat, in the middle of town, at one o'clock in the morning. Suddenly you see a rowdy group of youngsters attacking innocent bystanders, what would you do?"

"I'd call for backup via the walkie-talkie, ma'am. Arrange for a paddy wagon to come and aid me at the scene. If I was by myself, I wouldn't approach the crowd until backup arrived. But if I was with a colleague, then I would try and calm things down the best I could." He brimmed with confidence.

"Excellent, excellent, Bulmer. Okay, what would you do if you saw a young lady being sexually assaulted and her attacker took off as soon as he spotted you?"

"Ah, now that's a bit more difficult. Obviously the girl would need urgent attention and shouldn't be left alone. On the other hand, if her attacker is close by, should I leave her and chase after him?"

He pondered for a moment before Lorne urged him for an answer. "So?"

"Right, I'd call for immediate backup, giving them details of where to find the girl, ask the girl if she was okay and run after the assailant straight away. Once I caught him, I'd return to the scene and wait for assistance."

Lorne and Pete glanced at each other but showed no emotion. Then Pete said, "So the girl's lying there, bleeding, feeling ashamed and demoralised, and you, first of all, leave her alone, vulnerable to another attack. Then, once you've caught the suspect, you bring him back—presumably cuffed, you forgot to mention that part—and hold him there in the same vicinity as his victim until you receive backup. Which could take anything up to twenty minutes to arrive."

"Oh, I see what you mean. Maybe I would just stay with the victim and call for backup, wait for them to arrive before giving chase." Bulmer nodded, approving his revised answer.

"So, when does the ambulance arrive at the scene to aid the girl?" Lorne asked mischievously.

"I suppose I forgot that part." Bulmer coloured up with embarrassment.

"The trouble with policing, Bulmer, is that what we do at the scene is crucial. We don't get second chances. Last scenario, a burglary has been committed, the window is broken, and there is a pool of blood on the floor. What would be your initial course of action?"

"I'd ensure nothing was moved, question the proprietor about what they thought had been taken. Let the station know what was going on, and possibly call in the forensic team."

"Good. Why do we call forensics in? What can they do that we can't?"

"Well, they can analyse the blood for DNA and dust everywhere for fingerprints to help ascertain who the burglar might have been. If he or she has a previous record, their fingerprints would be on the register." Bulmer smiled again.

"Supposing there is blood at the scene but no proof that a window has been broken, what then?"

"I don't understand, ma'am."

"No shit, Sherlock. Does the scenario sound familiar at all to you, Bulmer?" Pete piped up, bored.

"Should it?" Bulmer forgot the protocol when speaking to a superior officer.

"'Should it, *sir*,' to you, sonny!" Pete corrected the bemused constable.

"Sorry. Should it, sir?"

"Let's cast our minds back to Saturday, 16th September, shall we?" Lorne watched the constable frown as he searched his mind. "Mr. Wilkinson placed a 999 call to say that his allotment shed had been broken into."

"Yes, ma'am. I remember the case."

"There was blood at the scene. Had a window been broken?"

The penny finally dropped. "No, ma'am. As far as I can remember, the window wasn't broken."

"So where the *hell* did the blood come from? I presume you asked Mr. Wilkinson if it belonged to him?"

The constable's hand nervously swept over his face and then ran through his hair. "I neglected to ask, ma'am."

"No, you simply logged it as a regular burglary and told the old man to clean it up. It takes professionals like DS Childs and myself to come along and solve your crimes for you. I'm reporting you to your superior officer, and I'll be recommending you recap your basic training before being let loose on the general public again."

"I'm truly sorry, ma'am."

"That may be, but for your information, Bulmer, we suspect the allotment shed was used to store the body that was discovered in the forest a few days ago. Now get out of my bloody sight."

"Yes, ma'am... Thank you, ma'am. Once again, I'm very sorry, ma'am."

"Get this cretin out of here, Pete."

"Come on, son. Let's go." He led the dejected constable out of the room.

Lorne picked up a file lying in front of her and smashed it back down on her desk, venting her anger. Incompetence on the job pissed her off. She couldn't believe Bulmer had been let out unsupervised on the streets. What the hell was going on? She made a note on her pad to bring it to the chief's attention—she didn't have time to chase up crap like that.

Her dad would have a field day when she told him of Bulmer's incompetence. As an ex-copper, it infuriated him when he heard about police cock-ups through the media. The unfortunate Soham murders were a prime example. He knew as soon as Ian Huntley spoke to ITV news that he was the murderer. He even rang a few of his old colleagues who were still on the force to tell them, but no one cared enough to chase it up. In the old days, her father had told her, a lot of crimes were solved by a copper's nose. True coppers could smell out a criminal at a hundred yards. What had changed since her father's time on the force? *Why are coppers nowadays so incompetent?* Was too much emphasis being put on employing university graduates with little or no common sense, or was it a case of the criminals getting smarter?

It was nearing nine when she rang Arnaud to see if Kim Charlton's body was ready for post-mortem.

"I was about to ring you, Inspector. Will you come alone?"

His question momentarily floored her. She cleared her throat. "No, my partner will be attending the post-mortem with me."

She had intended to send Pete home early, but Arnaud's question changed her mind. She shuddered at the thought of being alone with Arnaud in his creepy workplace.

"I'll have his seat waiting for him, nearest the door as usual," he said and laughed.

Feeling uncomfortable, Lorne ended the conversation promptly, telling him they'd be with him in half an hour.

She tidied her desk, picked up her car keys, and dismissed the team for the night. Pete pushed through the swing doors at the top of the stairs and walked towards her.

"Fancy going on a little trip?"

"Not if it means spending time with a stiff," Pete groaned as his stomach rumbled.

"We'll pick up some chips on the way."

"You're joking, right? There's no way I could handle a post-mortem after stuffing my face. I'd rather starve."

"So be it. Don't blame me if you pass out in there. The doc would love that."

"You're always on about my weight anyway. Maybe I'll be a few pounds lighter in the morning."

"Whatever," Lorne shouted back over her shoulder as they took the stairs down to the car.

Chapter Twenty-Three

They arrived at the mortuary suited and booted.

"Ah, Inspector. Come. Stand beside me." He pointed to the floor, barely a foot away from him.

Pete remained by the door in his usual place. Lorne suspected he'd forgotten his hunger the minute he'd laid eyes on the dead body lying on the table.

Lorne relaxed as the post-mortem got underway and Arnaud focused on cutting up Kim Charlton's body.

Before he made the Y-incision, the pathologist pointed out all visible injuries the girl had suffered: At least ten bite marks were visible on her neck, thighs, and breasts. The right nipple was missing and had not been recovered at the scene. Had the killer kept it as a trophy? Her face was bruised and bloody after receiving ten to twelve blows from a blunt object. Her jaw was broken, and her right cheekbone was smashed to pieces.

As Arnaud removed the garden fork from the victim's vagina, he described her appalling wounds into the recorder alongside him: "The deceased's vaginal vault shows signs of penetration caused by a round-ended cylindrical object—the garden fork handle—and was inserted with a moderate degree of force. The lack of visible bruising in relation to the injury suggests that it happened after death."

The doctor shook his head in disbelief, then continued, "There is a second vaginal injury, consisting of a red abrasion on the vaginal vault. This injury was caused by the insertion of a different hard object. The latter injury looks as though it occurred during forceful intercourse."

He raised his gaze to Lorne before saying, "The bruising on both arms and hands are typical defence wounds. Here, there is a three-inch wound to the chest. I will know more about this once the torso is opened up."

Arnaud took swabs from every orifice before making the first cut of the Y-shaped incision. The cuts began behind both ears and descended at a forty-five-degree angle along the neck. The two cuts met at the top of the chest and ran vertically as one down to the pelvis. He turned on the recorder again and said, "I am pulling back the skin over the skull and it is here that I notice bruising to the left occipital area. The brain is swollen where it has been hit with a blunt object."

The plastic door slapped shut. They both looked round. Pete had exited the room.

"It never ceases to amaze me, Inspector, why you bring him with you. He has yet to complete a full post-mortem, whereas you—well, what can I say?" he said, eyeing her with admiration.

Lorne blushed. *Is he flirting with me? Or is it my weary imagination working overtime?* "Let's just say I have a stomach for the gruesome things in life, and, well... Pete just has a stomach." She chortled, but she glanced back at the door, praying for Pete to return.

"Ah, so you do possess a sense of humour, after all. I was beginning to wonder."

"It's extremely difficult to remain buoyant all the time in my job—as with yours, I should imagine. Anyway, as long as my hubby appreciates my sense of humour, surely that's all that matters." She hoped casually dropping her husband into the conversation would make Arnaud think twice about coming on to her.

Appearing to receive her warning, Arnaud resumed with the examination. Further investigations to the chest wound showed that a sharp object, probably a knife, had entered the pericardium at the front of the heart, and he suspected this injury had proven to be fatal.

Lorne and the doctor left Bones sewing up the body. Pete was seated in the corridor, his head buried between his oversized thighs. The pair walked past him and into the changing room.

"We found out today that the shed where Kim Charlton was found had been broken into a couple of weeks ago. The owner found a patch of blood inside and called the police. Unfortunately, a very junior officer attended the crime and didn't think to call in forensics. Is there any chance you can take another look at the shed for me?"

"Has the blood been wiped up?"

"Afraid so. Can you do anything?"

"Leave it with me, Inspector. I'll go down there tomorrow and see if the Luminol shows up anything. Even if there's no blood to see with the naked eye, we will find it. I trust you dealt with your incompetent colleague?" Arnaud asked as they stepped out into the hallway.

"He won't make the same mistake twice, I can assure you."

"I'm glad to hear it. Now, if you will excuse me, I have a cup of cocoa waiting for me at home. I'll be in touch, Inspector, and I hope you feel better soon, Sergeant." He chuckled, opened the door to his office, and disappeared inside.

"He can be such a smarmy shit." Pete didn't bother to hide how much he disliked the doctor.

"Come on. Let's get home and get some sleep. Do you want to crash at my place? Otherwise, I'll have to drive all the way back to the station to pick up your car."

"Two nights on the trot sleeping at your gaff? People will talk." Pete laughed and winked at her.

"Only if you tell them. Yes or no, Pete?"

"Why not? Any chance of a bite to eat when we get there?"

"Will an omelette do?"

"Sounds good to me. I can honestly say you spoil me rotten at times, boss."

"Hmm… You don't deserve it after wimping out on me in there."

"Afraid to be left alone with the doc, were ya?"

"Don't be so ridiculous. That's not what I meant at all, and you know it. Besides, Bones was there, remember? Get in the car, chunky."

Pete's eyes rose heavenwards as she called him the nickname she'd recently bestowed upon him—not because of his weight. No, she'd chosen the nickname because he'd suddenly acquired a penchant for Kit Kats, the chunky variety.

* * *

The next morning, the pair left Lorne's house in differing moods. Pete was grumpy and moving around as though he had aches in places he never knew existed after spending the last two nights on her uncomfortable sofa. And Lorne was in one of her 'tread carefully around me' moods. She and Tom had been arguing till three AM about her taking him for granted.

The atmosphere at breakfast had been colder than a freezer. Lorne and Tom had exchanged hateful glances across the breakfast bar.

The weather did nothing to brighten their moods. A torrential downpour had followed them all the way to work.

Pete eyed the darkening sky. "You got an umbrella in the boot?"

"Yeah, but I doubt you'll appreciate the colour."

"It's girly pink, is it?"

"Yup. Actually, it's polka dot pink, a present from Charlie at Christmas. Apparently it's the 'in' thing. I'll drop you as close to the station as I can, okay?"

Disgruntled about her decision, he mumbled something incoherent under his breath. Whenever he stayed over, she always insisted—to prevent unnecessary rumours flying around the station—they should never arrive at work in the same car first thing in the morning.

"Jump out at the next set of lights."

"You're kidding! Shit, that's miles away from the station."

"It's a few hundred yards. The jog will do you good. Now, shoo," she said, as the lights changed to red.

Lorne drove past him a few seconds later and blasted the horn as he battled against the gale-force wind and rain. She glanced in her rear-view mirror and smiled when he gave her a V-sign. He already looked as if he'd swum twenty lengths at the local baths in his overcoat. She braced herself for a tongue-lashing when he arrived at work.

She bought two cups of coffee from the machine and checked through her post while she waited for him to arrive.

A few minutes later, she cringed when she saw her drenched partner zigzag his way between the desks.

"Forget to take your car home last night, Pete?" Mitch teased.

"No!"

"Did you spend the night with a nice bird, Pete?"

"No! What gives you *that* idea?"

"You're wearing the same clothes you had on yesterday—and, come to think of it, the day before that—plus your car was parked in the car park all night." Mitch tapped the side of his nose.

Pete grunted and cast a few looks around as he wrestled his way out of his soaking wet trench coat.

Lorne suppressed a smile when he entered her office. His hair— what was left of it—was plastered to his face and he left a trail of water on the carpet behind him.

"Morning, Pete—"

"Don't you dare make any quips about it being a lovely day," he warned her, sitting in the chair opposite.

"Wouldn't dream of it. What've you got there?" she asked, referring to the package in his hand.

"The desk sergeant said it was left outside for you this morning." He placed the twelve-inch square box in front of her on the desk.

"I got you a coffee."

He sat down again and wiped his face with a handkerchief.

Lorne stood up, picked up the letter opener, and tore the tape around the edge of the box. "This will probably be the new stationary I ordered last month."

"Where do you want me to start today?"

She flipped the lid up and reached inside to pull out a large packet wrapped in bubble-wrap. Throwing the box on the floor, she sliced through the wrap as she carried on their conversation. "We'll see what the team came up with after we left last night, then—"

A maggot fell out of the package and landed on her desk. Lorne jumped back in horror.

Then the smell hit them.

"Shittin' hell," Pete cried almost tipping back in his chair.

Lorne opened her drawer, pulled out a pair of latex gloves and a few of masks. She threw one of the masks to Pete, and he hurriedly placed it over his nose.

"Here, let me do it, boss." He volunteered, but she pushed his hands away.

"I'll do it. Here goes."

After ripping away the rest of the tape at the top of the bubble-wrap, she peered inside.

Lorne just made it to the bin before her breakfast came up.

Pete moved towards the package, but she put her hand up to stop him. "Pete, don't! I think it's Belinda Greenaway's head."

Chapter Twenty-Four

October 5, 2007

Doctor Arnaud arrived half an hour after Pete rang him.

Lorne discovered a note inside the box she'd thrown on the floor. It read:

HERE LIES THE MISSING PART TO YOUR FIRST PUZZLE.

She was studying it when Arnaud entered her office. "Are you okay, Inspector?"

"I'm fine. Well, as fine as I can be, when confronted with something as macabre as this first thing in the morning. What do you make of it?" She handed him the note.

He pulled on his latex gloves before accepting it.

"Curious, is it not? It looks to me as if the typeface belongs to an old printing set."

"You mean a John Bull type printing kit? I had one when I was a kid." Her voice shook.

"Look, why don't you take a break? Splash some cold water on your face or something. I'll be here for a while."

"That sounds like a good idea to me," Pete said from the doorway.

"Okay, okay. Back off, the pair of you. I know when I'm outnumbered. I'll be back in ten minutes."

"As you wish, Inspector. It is your office, after all." Arnaud placed his bag on the floor and moved towards the package on her desk.

* * *

"Jesus, we're definitely not dealing with your run-of-the-mill type of killer here," Pete said over a strong cup of coffee in the canteen.

"Can you remember if the address was handwritten?" Lorne asked, sipping from the chipped mug. Her mind was racing. Puzzle, the killer had mentioned "the missing part to your first puzzle". So far, the whole frigging case had been a puzzle. *Does that mean this is the first of many pieces? What does this guy have in mind?*

"Yeah, it was in black ink, no address. It just read 'Detective Inspector Lorne Simpkins', and in the corner in capital letters, it said 'personal'."

"After we've had this, go see the desk sergeant. See where it was found and at what time?"

"I'll check the CCTV footage."

"Good idea. You okay, Pete? You've hardly had the best start to the day, have you?"

"Me? Yeah, I'm fine. How about you?"

"What's that old adage? It never rains but it pours. That's pretty succinct in this instance, wouldn't you say?"

"Yup. See you in a while." He gulped down the remains of his coffee and left.

Lorne walked through the incident room, stopping only to tell her team what had happened. She left them discussing the event and returned to her office. Arnaud was bent over, still examining the head. She crept up behind him and peered over his shoulder.

He turned his head slowly to face her. Lorne immediately jumped back.

"My, aren't we jumpy?"

She ignored his comment and quickly regained her composure, looking beyond him at the head displayed upright on her desk. "Found anything, apart from the obvious, Doc?"

"I fear it is the head of our first victim. At least now we can lay her to rest in one piece. I'm certain of the COD now."

She raised a quizzical eyebrow.

"COD—Cause of death—and I wish you would call me Jacques. Especially as we seem to be spending a lot of time together lately." His eyes sparkled, and she couldn't help but notice the attractive little laughter lines that appeared at the corner of them.

"I would prefer to keep things on a professional basis, Doctor."

"I can take a hint, Inspector." His face grew serious, and he explained, "She was hit several times with a blunt object and sustained the same kind of injuries as Kim Charlton."

"Have you had a chance to take another look at the allotment shed yet?"

"I was en route when your partner rang me. Of course, I came straight here. I will send someone down there later to do the necessary tests. Right now, I'd like to get this back to my lab ASAP. I'm sure you can't wait to get rid of it or the smell. I might suggest you use a different office for the next few hours?"

"Thanks for the advice. Can I help you out with that?"

"*Merci*. Can you take my bag out to the car, while I carry the box?"

They walked through the stark grey corridor and out to the car park in silence. Reaching his car, Lorne asked, "When will all the results be available? I hate to rush you, but my boss wants this case wrapped up in a few weeks."

He handed her the keys, she pressed the button, and the central locking system unlocked the boot. Jacques placed the box and his bag inside. Lorne followed him round to the driver's door.

"Does your boss usually make such unrealistic demands?"

She stepped back as he opened the door and got in. "Not usually, but there are extenuating circumstances in this instance. He has his reasons for wanting the case wrapped up quickly."

"Would you like to share those reasons with me?"

Lorne shuffled her feet and shrugged. "I've been sworn to secrecy, I'm afraid. Pete doesn't even know."

"Would you like me to have a word? I could impress upon him what sort of time scales we are looking at for each procedure and test." Arnaud smiled up at her as he started the engine.

"There's no need for you to do that. I'm sorry; I think I might've given you the wrong impression. He's not an ogre—far from it, in fact. I'm just going to see him now. I'll reassure him that everyone is doing their utmost to bring this case to a swift conclusion. I'll see you soon, Doctor." She closed the door to his sleek black BMW sports car, and he roared off.

As she watched him leave, an unfamiliar churning stirred deep inside of her. *Don't be so ridiculous, Lorne. You're a happily married woman—well, a married one, at least.*

"I've got the CCTV tape. Do you want to go through it in the conference room?" Pete asked when she rejoined the team.

"Can you make a start, Pete? I better bring the chief up to date."

"Will do. Tracy, you want to sit in on this one?"

"I'll meet you in there. I'll grab a few coffees," Tracy answered, heading for the machine.

"Atta girl. Mine's white with two sugars."

Lorne and Tracy watched Pete make a hasty getaway.

"He means he's trying to cut back, and one sugar will do. Thanks, Tracy."

They both chuckled as they went their separate ways.

Chapter Twenty-Five

"Lorne, come in. I was just about to come see you. What was all that commotion about earlier on?" the chief asked.

She filled him in on the package and its gruesome contents.

"That's awful. Here, take this." He handed her a tumbler half-filled with Scotch.

"I can't drink this, sir. I'm on duty."

"You've had a shock. Get it down your neck—that's an order."

"I wanted to advise you on the state of play, sir. With the second and third victims, we found trace evidence at the scene. But the results won't be available until the end of the week." Lorne knocked back a large mouthful of the amber liquid and immediately coughed and spluttered.

"Is there any chance of hurrying things along?" The chief's brow furrowed.

She couldn't help but notice how tired he looked; his skin was grey and lifeless. His weight had suddenly dropped, too, but she'd been too busy to notice before. His once tight-fitting collar hung loosely around his neck.

"Sorry, sir, but no. I had a word with the pathologist, and he assures me they're rushing the tests through, but it's bound to slow things down a bit, with three victims and a mountain of evidence to try to match."

"Keep on top of it, Lorne. By the way, they've appointed my replacement," he said, quietly.

Stunned, she shook her head. "They have, already? Who is it, sir?"

"They're keeping it under their hats for the moment. Whoever it is will be taking over on Monday."

"What do they hope to achieve by keeping it a secret?" Lorne swallowed the last drop of Scotch, her need for the amber liquid suddenly increasing.

"There's too much of this 'I know something you don't know' going on in the force. Actually, I'm quite relieved I'm leaving, even if it is through ill health. We'll have to wait and see who walks through the door on Monday. The rumour mill has been surprisingly quiet about this one. Usually, you get a list of ten possible applicants, but not this time."

"One thing's for certain: I won't have the same relationship with the new chief as I have with the outgoing one." Lorne's eyes misted up.

"I'll keep in touch when I leave, Lorne. You know I regard you as a daughter. You'll be fine. I'm positive your strong will and determination will pull you through. It always has in the past. I seem to remember we haven't always seen eye to eye. Take that case where the social worker killed his wife—Len Craven, wasn't it?"

She nodded.

"I was convinced it was an accident and warned you to back off. Thankfully, you were too stubborn to listen; you put him under a twenty-four-hour surveillance. He was into drugs in a big way as I recall, accumulating huge debts and came up with the hare-brained scheme of killing his wife for the life insurance. When you solved that case, I was forced to eat my words, wasn't I?" He smiled as he reminisced.

"Yes. But no matter how fraught our relationship has been in the past, neither of us bore a grudge, did we, sir? On the whole, you generally let me go with my instincts. Others might perceive that as me being bloody-minded. For instance, the case we're working at the moment. Pete was adamant that Oliver Greenaway killed his mother and aunt. I was absolutely certain he hadn't. Pete's always decrying the fact that I rely on my woman's intuition too much, but it hasn't let me down yet."

"I completely understand your concerns. What about when I appointed Pete as your partner? You screamed and cursed like a woman possessed. Now you think he's the greatest thing under the sun."

"Point taken. I just know it's not going to be easy obeying the rules of a new kid on the block. Que sera, sera. Anyway, I've come to the conclusion that there's no use worrying about things beyond my control."

The chief proved how well he knew her and asked, "Are you and Tom having problems?" He reached across the desk and placed a hand over hers.

Tears of frustration sprang to her eyes. Without looking up she replied, "Sorry, sir. Slip of the tongue. Ignore me. That package probably affected me more than I realised."

He gripped her hand tightly. "Look at me, Lorne." She obeyed him. "If you want to talk any time, you know where I am."

Easing her hand from under his, she said, "I'll remember that, the next time we have an argument and I'm contemplating my life's journey at three o'clock in the morning."

"Ah, don't think the wife would be too keen on that idea, do you?"

They both smiled, and Lorne stood up to leave the room.

"I meant what I said, Lorne. Don't ever forget it."

She nodded and left his office. As she headed down the corridor towards the conference room, she took a few deep breaths to help push down her bubbling emotions.

Chapter Twenty-Six

"What have we got?" Lorne asked, walking into the incident room.

"At 4:32 AM, a suspect delivered the package. Take a look." Pete nodded at Tracy, and she started the video.

A shudder ran up Lorne's spine as she watched a man, dressed from head to toe in black, deposit the box on the top step of the station. He arrogantly stopped to wave at the camera, obviously knowing his every movement was being taped. His hooded sweatshirt obscured his face; it was impossible to make out his features as he mocked the camera.

"Is there any way we can find out how tall he is? It would be a start."

"I'll line a few of the guys up—varying heights, of course. See what we can come up with. I'll get on it straightaway," Pete said.

Lorne and Tracy checked the video, frame by frame, for clues. Nothing—no rings, no glimpses of tattoos. Nothing.

Mitch burst into the room and threw himself into one of the vacant chairs. He placed a list on the table and slid it across to Lorne. "Fifteen perverts in and around the Chelling Forest area."

"By 'perverts', I take it you mean registered sex offenders, Mitch?" she asked, studying the list.

"Actually, what I meant to say was, there are fifteen names on the list—thirteen sex offenders and two registered paedophiles."

"Good work, Mitch. I want you and Tracy to pay everyone on the list a visit. Bring in anyone looking shifty." Mitch opened his mouth to speak, and she raised her hand to stop him. "Yes, I know this type always look shifty, but you know what I mean. If we start bringing in some of these bastards, word will soon get around. It might make our killer think we're closing in on him."

"Only if he's connected to this group, ma'am. What if he's not?" Tracy pointed out.

"Then we're back where we started, up shit creek. Paddleless."

"Molly has made an interesting discovery, too." Mitch tucked his chair back under the long table and stood behind it.

"What's that?"

"Shall I send her in to see you, ma'am?"

"Can't you tell me, Mitch?" Lorne asked, desperately trying to avoid yet another confrontation with her least favourite member of staff.

"There're a lot of details involved. It would be better coming from her."

"Okay." Lorne sighed. "Send her in."

Tracy cleared her throat. "Umm... Can I speak freely, ma'am?"

"Of course, Tracy."

"It's about Molly, ma'am." The young sergeant hesitated, her gaze focusing on the worn oak table between them.

"What about Molly? I know she can be out of order at times, but if she's upset you in any way, I want to know." Lorne's blood started to boil. *If that bloody woman has done anything to upset my star pupil, I'll string her up by the nipples.*

"She had a word with me the other day. I don't really know how to say this, ma'am, except to come right out with it. She feels that you pick on her."

"She *what?*"

"She admits she has an argumentative nature, but she says she tries hard to control it. She's desperate to sort things out with you, ma'am. She doesn't appreciate having a final warning hanging over her head."

"So, she asked you to mend some fences for her, is that it?"

"No, ma'am. I knew I shouldn't have said anything. Me and my big mouth. She's trying to find the right time to have a word with you, but things are so manic around here at the moment, it's difficult for her."

Lorne could see how upset Tracy was. The poor girl was stuck in the middle, trying to help both sides concerned. "I'll see you later. Be careful out there." As the younger woman reached the door, Lorne called after her, "And Tracy, thanks for speaking up for Molly."

Maybe she was wrong about Molly. Perhaps it was *her* fault that Molly acted the way she did towards her. A possible clash of personalities? Why didn't Pete have a problem with Molly?

Lorne didn't have time to dwell on the problem any longer, because Molly entered the room. She welcomed the woman with a forced smile, hoping it would break the ice between them. "Hi, Molly. Mitch tells me you've got something interesting to tell me about the case."

Molly stood at the front of the desk, and Lorne pulled out the seat next to her and gestured for her to sit.

"You asked me to check out the Greenaway's staff. There's a housekeeper and a butler/chauffeur/odd-job man. They're a married couple—Mr. and Mrs. Ron Hall. Employed by an agency, they've been with the Greenaways for over ten years. The agency insisted the couple were model employees. When I asked the owner of the agency to look back over their employment record, she told me that they'd left their previous post under a cloud."

"Was it a storm cloud?" Lorne smiled.

Molly, visibly relaxed now, said, "I suspect it was, although there was no actual complaint filed against them. They were ordered to vacate their employer's home immediately. The woman became cagey the more questions I asked. I think it would be worth a follow-up call. To me it sounded as though she was covering something up."

"Do you fancy going over to see her?"

"Me? But I never leave the office."

"Here's your chance, then. How would you feel about following up on your own lead, Molly? What do you say? Shall we call a truce?"

"I'd like that very much, ma'am. I know my fuse is a tad short at times, and I apologise for that."

Lorne raised her hand. "Enough said. Welcome aboard, Molly." She held out her hand, and her colleague accepted it with gusto.

"Thank you, ma'am, glad to be back. Shall I take John with me to question the woman at the agency?"

"Why not? Pete and I will reverse roles with the pair of you. It should be fun." She prepared herself for an ear-bashing from Pete. "Let me know how you get on."

Lorne sat back in her chair and exhaled a huge sigh of relief. It felt good to sort out at least one relationship that had gone sour, especially with the new chief arriving in a few days.

* * *

"The guy was approximately five foot nine, according to the scientific tests I've just carried out," Pete proudly announced, when he re-entered the room.

"Great. Now all we have to do is find a suspect that height, and the case will be solved. Easy, this police work, ain't it?" Lorne retorted sarcastically.

"Who's rubbed you up the wrong way?" Pete asked, his enthusiasm crushed.

"Sorry, Pete, you didn't deserve that. I've sent the others out for the day. That leaves you and me answering the phones and going through this list I've prepared."

"Suits me. I'll just grab us a couple of sandwiches from the canteen first, shall I?"

"Always thinking of your stomach. What am I going to do with you? Make mine a tuna and mayo."

He ignored her comment and set off.

Lorne sat at Tracy's desk, still adding to her list when the phone rang. "DI Simpkins speaking, can I help you?"

Initially she was greeted by silence, then she heard a man's muffled voice in the background. "Say it. Tell her."

"Hello, who is this?" Lorne asked. She heard a slap, and a woman's pitiful whimper.

The phone went dead.

"Hello? Hello?" Lorne sat holding the receiver, with the sickening realisation that the caller had been the killer. From the sound of it, he'd captured his fourth victim. *Shit!* How long did they have before she ended up like the others?

Chapter Twenty-Seven

Lorne sprang into action, picked up the phone, and ordered twenty-four-hour surveillance at the allotment, the only place connecting at least two of the victims. Then she ordered a trace to be set up on all incoming phone lines in the incident room. Had the killer known that she would be at the station when he'd made the call? Was he watching her? She ran to the window. To the left was a concrete tower block and to the right nothing but waste ground. *You're being paranoid, Lorne.*

Pete barged into the room, making her jump. "One tuna and mayo as requested. What's up, boss?"

"He's just made contact. He's got another hostage."

"Shit. What did he say?" Pete tossed the two sandwiches onto his desk.

"That's just it. He didn't *say* anything. Not to me, anyway. He was threatening a woman, to force her to talk, but she was too scared to speak. He slapped her and put the phone down."

"How did he know you were here?"

"I don't know. Get the team back in here. I've ordered traces on all lines and surveillance at the allotment. If he can't go there to get rid of the body, it might delay the woman's death a bit longer, if that's where he kills them."

"We don't know that yet, do we? I'm gonna ring Arnaud and see if he can rush the results of the fingerprints through," Pete said.

"Okay, you do that while I haul the team back in." Lorne's heart pounded.

The four sergeants promptly arrived back. Lorne noticed Molly wearing a scowl. She thought she owed the woman an apology for dragging her back to the station.

Appreciating Lorne's explanation, Molly asked, "What can I do?"

"You can help the technical bods when they arrive. Tracy, Mitch, I want a twenty-four-hour surveillance set up at the allotment. Uniforms are on their way over there now. Do you fancy doing the nightshift?"

"Sure, okay by me," Mitch said. "What about you, Tracy?"

"I'll have to call home first, but sounds fine to me."

"Right that's one less thing to worry about. While you're in the office, go over the sex offenders list, see if anything recent pops up, and pull the fingerprint files on them all. Pete's just rung Arnaud to hurry along the prints found at the scenes. As soon as they're in, we can match them with what you come up with; and we'll be on our way, hopefully. John, look into Doreen's background. She was a head teacher. Find out where."

Lorne's stomach was complaining about it being way past lunchtime. "Pete, come on. We'll grab a bite to eat."

He didn't need telling twice. He grinned, picking up the two packets of sandwiches he'd bought earlier, and followed her along the hall into the conference room. "What a bloody morning."

"Trouble is, we've got too many leads to follow up at the moment. That call has put a spanner in the works." Lorne massaged her temples.

"Headache?"

"No thanks, Pete. I've already got one," she replied and smirked.

"Nice to see you ain't lost your sense of humour."

"God knows how. I don't mind telling you, I was more freaked out about the call than unwrapping the head this morning."

"That's because you feel helpless. You know somethin' is gonna happen, and you can do fuck all about it. But it's not just the case that's bugging you, is it?" He downed a bite of his sandwich.

"You can be extremely perceptive at times, partner." Lorne gave him a weary smile.

"I'd like to agree with you, but I'd be lying. I heard you and Tom arguing till the small hours."

"I'm sorry if we kept you awake. I don't know what's going on with him at the moment. He seems to pick a fight over the slightest thing."

"Now, don't go off the handle at me." Pete eyed her warily. "Do you think he might be having an affair?"

"We're talking about Tom here, Pete." She laughed, but her smile faded as his words sank in. "Has he said something to you?"

"Why the hell would he tell me?"

"What made you say it, then?"

"You said he'd changed." He shrugged. "All the women's magazines tell you that's what happens when a bloke's got something to hide."

"Since when did you start reading women's magazines? I think you're wrong. He has changed a little over the last few months, but I put it down to Charlie pissing him off. She's just coming up to her teens and starting to show a rebellious streak. Sometimes I'm glad overtime keeps me away from home. Oops, shouldn't have said that."

"Why do ya think I've never settled down and had kids? Have you tried talking to him?"

"Yeah, every chance I get. He refuses to open up. We'll get through it; we always do. That's not the only thing that's bugging me though. There's something else I've got to tell you, but you need to promise me you won't say anything to the others. I can't keep it a secret any longer."

"When's it due?"

"I'm not pregnant, you idiot." She scoffed at the thought. "The chief told me last week he's leaving."

"When?"

"When I went to see him about our gruesome package this morning, he told me the new chief will be starting next Monday." Lorne walked over to the water tank in the corner. She thought a drink would help shift the sudden lump that had appeared in her throat.

"Did he say who his replacement is gonna be?"

Lorne sensed her partner wasn't overly concerned by the news. As far as he was concerned, Lorne was his next in command. Any flack coming from the new chief would be aimed at her first. "He couldn't give me a name. Looks like it'll be an outsider."

"So you're worried, is that it?"

"I wouldn't say I'm worried, exactly—concerned, maybe. The chief and I have a good rapport. I doubt I'll get that with anyone else. It's like me telling you that I'm getting a new partner. How would you feel?"

"Pleased. Delighted. I'd be dancing around, jumping for joy."

Lorne felt hurt.

Pete chuckled and hastily reassured her, "I'm kiddin'. I understand completely, but it's no good getting yourself in a tizzy about it. Wait till Monday. See who turns up, eh? Then start panicking."

"You're right, of course. Enough of this doom and gloom. We'll finish our lunch and then see what we can get out of this taxi firm."

"Do you mind if I chalk that one up? It's not often you admit I'm right about somethin'."

She poked her tongue out at him, and they both tucked into their sandwiches.

Chapter Twenty-Eight

"You should've spoken to the nice detective when I told you to. Now I'll have to punish you." The man's menacing black eyes penetrated the woman's core.

"I'm sorry. I was so scared. Call her back. I promise I'll talk to her this time. I'll say anything you want me to say, do anything you want me to do. Please don't hurt me. I'm begging you." The woman cowered away from him. She shivered from the cold of the cell and her mounting fear. Her legs and arms throbbed with pain from the beatings he'd given her. She'd been stripped naked, but thankfully he hadn't raped her—yet. Maybe her constant prayers had saved her from that.

"She's no use to us. Kill her," his accomplice said, emerging from the shadows.

The naked woman cried and wrapped her arms tightly around her legs. She sat on the cold floor of the cell and rocked back and forth. "Please don't kill me. Why are you doing this? Tell me who you are, please?"

"Ah, she doesn't remember us. Just like the other one. *Make* her remember. *Punish* her till she can beg no more." The woman lunged forwards and kicked the prisoner in the leg, adding to her bruises.

The man grabbed his demented accomplice, picked her up, and swung her around. "Leave us for a minute. Go calm down. I need this one to do some work before I'm finished with her."

The man waited while his accomplice trudged up the ladder, which creaked under her weight, before he attacked the prisoner with his belt.

* * *

Lorne and Pete were just passing through the incident room when the call came in.

"Just a minute." Mitch clicked his fingers to gain the team's attention. The room fell silent, and Lorne grabbed the nearest phone. Mitch transferred the call to her extension, and the trace began.

"This is DI Simpkins. Who is this?"

Again, Lorne heard a woman whimpering. Another pitiful yelp followed, then the woman said softly, "He—he wants to know—if you received the package?"

"I did. Has he hurt you?"

The woman's voice trembled when she spoke. "I'm okay. They're treating me well."

They. Did she just say they? The sound of a slap on flesh came through the phone and made Lorne wince. Her heart went out to the woman. "What do they want?"

"She says, 'What do you want?'"

Silence.

Then the woman said, "He wants—retribution."

Colin, tracing the call, held up two fingers.

Two more minutes, and we'll have the bastard. "Retribution for what?"

"She wants to know for what?" The terrified woman's voice shook as she was forced to act as a go-between for the police and her kidnappers.

"For those they've failed and keep failing," came the reply, before the line went dead.

"Don't go! Tell us where you are?" Lorne shouted into the mouthpiece, her gaze seeking out the colleague tracing the call. Colin shook his head in regret.

"Thirty bloody seconds. Why couldn't I keep her talking for thirty seconds more?" Lorne asked Pete, thumping her clenched fist on the desk.

"He's not stupid. He must've realised we'd be tracing the call. Don't go blaming yourself, boss. At least we know the woman's still alive."

"Yeah, but for how long? She said *they* were treating her well. We're looking for more than one suspect here."

Chapter Twenty-Nine

As they drove through the town centre, Lorne found it hard not to glance down every alleyway, every turning they passed.

"I'd like to get to Toni's Taxis in one piece, if that's all right with you, boss." Pete sounded frustrated.

"You will. We've got to keep our eyes open."

"Correct me if I'm wrong, but I thought there was two of us in this car. One who's driving—that'd be you—and the other who's constantly on the lookout—well, that'd be me. If you want to swap roles, be my guest, but don't feel as though you have to carry out both jobs on my account, please."

Lorne nearly ran a cyclist off the road.

Pete grabbed the steering wheel. "Shit, that was close. What's it to be, boss? You want to concentrate on the driving, or do ya wanna swap?"

"I *am* concentrating. The idiot shouldn't be on the road anyway. It's about time the council introduced bus and cycle lanes around here."

"Take the next turning on the right, and the taxi office is halfway down on the left." Pete shook his head.

The taxi firm was located in the worst part of town, known to the locals as 'Squatterland', with prostitution and drugs part of daily life.

They entered the office, finding the vile stench of urine and vomit difficult to ignore.

"Ain't got nothin' for at least half an hour." The overweight controller dunked her chocolate chip biscuit into a cup of dark liquid that was either well-stewed tea or very strong coffee.

Lorne glanced around and cringed. How the hell someone could work an eight-hour shift in that godforsaken place was beyond her.

"We don't want a taxi. Is the manager around?"

"Don't be worrying about the mess. You kinda get used to it. She's out on a job."

"Is she likely to be long?" Pete asked, in the obnoxious tone he tended to use when he didn't fancy staying in a place for long.

"I can give her a shout if you like. Who wants her?"

The pair flashed their warrant cards. Lorne couldn't tell if the woman was squinting because she needed glasses or scowling at them for being cops.

"Toni, are ya gonna be long?" the woman called through the mic in front of her.

A woman's angry voice came back over the airwaves. "I'll be as long as I need to be. Why?"

"There's a couple of cops, er...police officers, here to see you."

"I'll be back in five."

"This place been open long?" Pete asked, showing his disgust at his surroundings.

"About four years." The woman appeared to let out a sigh of relief when the phone rang. "Toni's Taxis... Yeah... It'll be about half an hour.... Please yourself." She slammed down the phone and scribbled through what she'd already written on the docket. "He couldn't wait, wanted it yesterday."

The three of them remained silent until Toni returned.

Lorne wasn't expecting the stunning redhead who walked through the door. It was hard to imagine the aggressive voice they'd heard earlier coming from the slight, almost fragile-looking woman.

Toni wore white skin-tight jeans and a low cut blue top that accentuated her curves. "What's the urgency?"

Lorne introduced Pete and herself. "We're investigating a murder. Four days ago, Kim Charlton—who I believe was a regular punter of yours—arranged for a taxi to pick her up from a friend's house. For some reason, your driver overlooked her. After waiting thirty minutes, she decided to walk home. The problem is, she didn't make it. We'd like to talk to the driver who should've picked her up, if that's possible?"

"Is he a suspect?"

"We'd just like to have a word with him. Do you know who the driver was?"

"Pull out the dockets for last Thursday, will you, Mary?"

The fat controller grunted her disapproval of having to move from her comfortable chair. She reached up to the top shelf of the unit on the back wall and pulled down a box-file marked September. She waddled back to her desk and fell into her chair, looking and sounding exhausted. She rifled through the dockets and handed the relevant one to her boss.

"Get Wacko on the radio, Mary. Call him in for a break."

The controller had already put across the airwaves that the police were around, so if the guy had nothing to hide, he'd come in. If, however, he chose to do a runner, they'd know straight off he was guilty of something.

"How many drivers were working that shift?" Pete walked over and studied the planner on the wall.

"It was a busy evening, I think eight of the ten drivers worked that night. The other two covered the day shift."

"Got a list of names and addresses of all your drivers, just in case?"

"In case what? I'm not sure I'm with you, sergeant?"

"Just in case we need to ask 'em all some questions. You know, to help us with our enquiries."

"I'll supply it, but don't go hassling my guys just for the sake of it. I don't want them getting twitchy."

"Oh, and why might they get twitchy? You employ a lot of ex-cons or somethin'?" Pete said, eyeing Toni suspiciously.

She shrugged. "Drivers are hard to find nowadays."

"So you turn to ex-cons to help you out?" Mystified, Lorne glanced around the office and caught the controller watching her. Something unnerved her about the way the woman studied her. Her stare was intense and went beyond the normal inquisitive eye you give someone you've just met.

"They've done their time, Inspector. They're entitled to a second chance in life, aren't they?"

"Depends what kind of crimes they've committed. I don't suppose you know that kind of information, do you?"

"Might do. It's confidential. The council insists the drivers inform us on their application forms. It's up to the council and the Criminal Records Bureau to say if they get the licence or not. So if you have any gripes, you should take it up with them, not me."

"You're acting as though you know one of your drivers is guilty of something. We told you we're simply making enquiries."

"None of my drivers are murderers, I can assure you of *that.*" Toni poured boiling water in a cup.

"Are you with these guys 24-7?" Pete asked, with a note of sarcasm.

"Of course not, but I know my staff."

"You wouldn't know a killer if he came at you with an axe. They don't wear stickers on their foreheads advertising the fact, you know."

"That's enough, Pete." Lorne noticed the way Toni was scowling at him. "I apologise. We're anxious to get the killer off the streets before he kills anyone else."

"You mean you're looking at more than one murder? Hey, wait a minute... Weren't you the one on the TV the other day? I remember now—you were after information about the body found in the forest."

"Yes, that's right. At the moment, we have no way of knowing if the two murders are connected, hence our enquiries. Now, are you willing to let us have a copy of the drivers' application forms, or do I have to come back here with a search warrant?"

Toni sighed and moved towards the battered filing cabinet.

The door from the street swung open, and in stepped a six-foot man in his mid to late thirties who was in desperate need of both a haircut and a shave.

"Wacko, this is DI Simpkins and DS Childs. They'd like to have a word with you," Toni said, as he threw himself into one of the vacant chairs.

"Have I done something wrong?"

Lorne pinched her nose, the putrid smell of the office filling her nostrils. "Not that we know of. Last Thursday, you were supposed to pick up a Miss Charlton at eleven PM from her friend's house on Hill Bank Rd. Why didn't you turn up?"

"You expect me to remember every job I have? I've probably picked up about five hundred punters between then and now. Let me think for a minute."

Toni gave the driver the dockets. He flicked through them, frowning as he tried to recall what happened that night. "That's right. I had a drunken bum in the car that I couldn't get rid of. I was about to pull him out when he puked. Had to clean up the bloody mess before another punter got in."

"Did you tell anyone what was going on?" Lorne scrutinized the controller, who seemed to be pretending to be busy while listening to their conversation.

"Yeah, I radioed in, but the other drivers were too busy to cover the job."

"Where did you clean up your car?" Pete had his notebook and pen at the ready.

"There's a garage in Rossyard Street. I got there at around ten fifty-five PM. I cleaned the inside up and dropped by the girl's friend's house at about eleven thirty PM. Her friend said my pickup got tired of waiting and decided to walk. I was annoyed at the time, but I suppose I would've done the same thing, if I was in her shoes," Wacko told them, placing his ankle across his other knee.

Lorne cast a critical eye over him and decided he appeared harmless enough. He hadn't seemed anxious or nervous at all during their questions. "Did you look for her?"

"Should I have?"

"You bothered to turn up for the job even though you were over half an hour late. You could've kept an eye open for her on your way back," Lorne challenged.

"As it happens, I did look out for her in the roads near her mate's house, but I soon gave up. I figured she would've made it home by the time I turned up. It's only a few miles to her house. So I radioed in a no-show, and they gave me another job."

"Who was on control that night?"

"It was you, wasn't it, Mary?" Wacko called over to the controller.

Mary blushed before answering, "It was me, what?" as if she hadn't heard.

Lorne knew differently, and she studied the woman through fresh eyes.

"You were on control last Thursday evening." Wacko blew out a frustrated breath.

"Yeah, I was on duty. What's it to you?"

Lorne sensed an underlying hatred between the two of them. "Did you send another cab to pick up the girl?"

"He just told you all the other drivers were busy. I didn't have anyone else to send." Mary fiddled with a pile of paper clips on the desk.

So, she had been listening to their conversation, after all.

"That can't be good for business, to leave a regular punter waiting around like that," Pete commented, frowning.

"It ain't my fault if she orders a taxi at kicking out time. We're always busy when the pubs shut. All firms are."

"How long does the average trip take?" Lorne asked Wacko.

"How long's a piece of string? Generally, they're shorter trips around that time of night. The maximum trip would be about twenty minutes."

Toni handed Lorne the copies of the application forms, and Lorne decided to leave the questions there. "Thanks. We'll return these as soon as possible."

"Hang on a minute," Wacko called after them as they headed for the door. "I don't get what all this has been about."

"Sorry, my mistake. The girl you should have picked up on Thursday was found dead yesterday. She never arrived home that night. Even if her house was only 'a few miles' away."

"Jesus, she was a nice kid. I've picked her up a few times before. Told me she wanted to be a model. We used to have a laugh. She used to pose in the back of my car. She always sat in the middle. Wanted to make sure that she was the centre of attention in my rear view mirror. She used to pout and pose. I laughed but never thought anything of it. She was just a kid, after all."

Lorne and Pete left. When they reached the car, Pete asked, "What are you thinking?"

"I don't know, really. There's something not quite right about that controller. What did you make of her?"

"Apart from her being the size of a rhinoceros, you mean? I got the impression she doesn't get along too well with Wacko. That aside, she seemed okay."

"Let's get back and go over these applications, see what we can dig up."

Chapter Thirty

"This guy's been in and out of prison for years. I reckon he knows the system inside out, because he commits minor crimes that carry minimal custodial sentences," Pete said as they went through the application forms Toni had given them.

"It's either a cry for help, or he prefers prison food to his own culinary skills."

"That's no excuse. He could get a take-away every night like I do."

"Perhaps his desire to remain slim is greater than yours. Tell me, Pete, does a vegetable ever make it past your lips?"

"You heard of saag aloo?"

In mock concern, she gasped, "Is it contagious?"

"Have you heard of it?"

"No, I can't say I have." Lorne's left eyebrow tilted upwards.

"It's spinach and potatoes. They're veggies, ain't they? I have a side order of that every time I have a chicken korma."

"I meant wholesome vegetables, not ones that have the goodness fried out of them and end up floating in fat."

"Veggies are veggies, no matter how you prepare them."

"Whatever. I think we'll agree to disagree on that one. Toni employs ten drivers. A quick gander at these forms tells us eight of them are ex-cons. Not a ratio I'd be happy with, if I was an employer."

"Yeah, we got all sorts here, ranging from burglary to sex offenders. Anything over three to ten years, and they're clear. I know I wouldn't want a sex offender driving my kid around, no matter when they committed the crime. How do you want to play this?"

"What is it now? Five thirty. I bet most of these guys will be on duty, so there's no point calling on them now. We'll leave it until morning."

"What about the missing woman?" Pete closed the file and placed it on the desk.

"I really don't know what more we can do, this evening. I've got Tracy and Mitch covering the allotment overnight. We don't know where else he's likely to take her, do we?"

A knock on the door interrupted them, and Tracy popped her head round it. "Sorry to interrupt, ma'am."

"Come in, Tracy. Take a seat."

"I hope you don't mind. I took the liberty of taking the tape of your call from the killer down to a friend of mine. He analyses background noises and can tell a lot from voice recognition."

"How?" Pete asked.

"It's all done by computer. He can pick up the slightest sound—if someone dropped a pin in a room, he'd recognise it. Anyway, he played the tape as it was, with the voices, then cut the voices out and came up with some interesting data. There was some sort of echo, as though the conversation was taking place in an uncarpeted room. He compared the data with other tapes he had and believes the walls to the room were bare, no wallpaper or plasterboard on them."

Pete's mouth dropped open. "Jesus, how the hell can he tell that?"

Tracy grinned, obviously in her element as she continued, "If the walls are bare, the noise rebounds off them; but if there is paper or some kind of covering on the walls, then the sound would be dulled by the covering. He believed the walls contained a certain amount of moisture, too."

It was Lorne's turn to be astounded by what Tracy was telling them. "He can tell that just by listening to a tape?"

"My friend is a bit of a geek. He compared our tape to hundreds he has access to. He believes the call came from a cellar. That's not all—something else cropped up on the tape, too. In the background, he heard a train, the rumble of it travelling on a track; and a few items in the cellar sounded like they rattled with the vibration, so the track must be relatively close to the house."

"Get me a map of the area, Tracy, will you?"

Moments later, Tracy returned with the map and spread it out on the desk.

"The forest is here. There's no hint of a railway line near there," Lorne said.

"And the allotment is over here. A track runs alongside that, but they can't be there, because uniform are down there at the moment, and forensics have been in and out of there all day," said Pete, pointing at the map.

"Get the others in here, will you, Tracy?"

Seconds later, six of them gathered around the table leaning over the map. "Does anyone know of any houses with cellars around this area?" Lorne asked.

"My mum has one. She lives on the outskirts of town." Molly pointed out a road on the right-hand side of the map.

"No good. The railway isn't in the vicinity. Anybody else?"

"A friend of mine lives here. The house has a small cellar, but they keep it blocked up. Not sure what size it actually is." John pointed at a different road, one where the track ran directly along the back of the houses.

"Bingo!" shouted Pete.

"Not so fast," Lorne said. "We need to study the map in detail, carefully. We can't bank on that being the right road. We'll leave it tonight. First thing, I want Molly and John to visit the council and see how many houses there are in the area that fit the bill? Some of them might have been renovated recently."

"We'll go there first and then shoot over to the agency, see what we can dig up about the Halls," Molly said.

Lorne nodded and turned her attention to Tracy and Mitch. "Are you sure you two will be okay on the stakeout tonight? Keep the car tucked away out of sight. Anything at all suspicious, you call for backup immediately, right?"

"Yes, ma'am. What time shall we report in tomorrow?" Mitch asked.

"I'll be here from about seven. As soon as it gets light, report back here and fill me in before you go home to get some sleep."

The group dispersed, leaving Lorne and Pete surveying the map.

"With all the leads we've got now, boss, don't you think we should get some extra staff in on the investigation?"

"Cutbacks, Pete. They won't let us have any. We'll just have to do the best we can. Why don't you get off home? You look done in.

A night in your own bed will do you the world of good. I know what kind of state I'd be in, if I'd spent two consecutive nights on my couch."

Pete arched his back and stretched, as if he'd just remembered how much he'd suffered the last few nights. "I'll take you up on that one. Are you calling it a day, too?"

"I'm going to make a few calls and then head off home."

After Pete left, Lorne called home. "Hi, Tom. It's me."

"Don't tell me you'll be working late tonight!"

"Tom, please don't be like that. Is Charlie there?"

"No."

"Oh. Where is she?"

"Her grandmother came to pick her up for the night, so we could have some time together. Guess she needn't have bothered."

"I'm sorry, darling. There's no way I can leave now. I've far too much work to do."

"Delegate."

She could just imagine him shouting that through clenched teeth, and rather than admit she'd dismissed her staff for the evening, she said, "The team's busy chasing up leads. I'll be home as soon as I can, I promise."

"Don't bother on my account. I'll go out with the lads. Expect me when you see me." He hung up.

She replaced the phone and sat for a few minutes with her head in her hands. Her marriage was a mess, and she didn't have a clue how to rectify that.

The phone startled her, and she almost jumped out of her seat. "Hello, DI Simpkins. How can I help you?"

"Inspector, *comment ça va?*"

The French accent was unmistakable and sent shivers dancing along her spine. "Doctor Arnaud. What can I do for you?"

"Jacques," he reminded her. "I have a print from the letter. It matches that found at Doreen Nicholls' house. Unfortunately, I cannot identify the person for you."

"Is it possible for me to pop by and see you?"

"Now?"

"If that's okay?"

"Why not? I have nothing better to do. Have you eaten?"

"There's no way I want to eat in the mortuary. I'll grab something afterwards."

"Whatever you like, Inspector. I'll see you soon."

After ending the call, Lorne found the file of sex offenders and paedophiles. She wedged the file in her handbag and headed off to the mortuary.

When she pulled into the car park, Jacques Arnaud was waiting at the entrance.

Lorne felt uneasy as his gaze took in her every move. When she was a few feet from him, his gaze settled on her face. She tried to hold his stare, but her nerve abandoned her. She laughed self-consciously. "I wasn't expecting a welcoming committee."

"I wanted some fresh air. Besides, the doors are locked at six, so I would have had to come down and open up for you. You look tired, Inspector." He relieved her of the files and briefcase. The unexpected gallant gesture took her by surprise.

"It's been a hell of a day. My second wind's due to arrive at any moment."

"I am unfamiliar with that saying. Would you care to tell me what you mean?"

"I'm sorry. It means: After a short rest, I'll summon up enough strength to see me through the rest of the day. At least, I'm hoping that'll be the case." They reached Arnaud's office.

He pointed to a soft leather chair he'd placed alongside his own. "Please, make yourself comfortable."

They were inches apart, and the churning she'd felt earlier that day, when she watched him drive away from her, had returned with a vengeance. Lorne picked up the file, and her shaking hand annoyed her. She dropped the file again before Jacques noticed.

She kept her gaze fixed on the file. "You said you found a print on the note. I've brought a file of suspects with me. Perhaps we can go through them together to see if any of them match."

Jacques smiled. "Why are you scared of me, Inspector?"

The colour rose in her cheeks, and for a moment, words failed her. She stood and walked to the window. She could feel his eyes boring into her. Feeling like a teenager, she struggled to find the right words. Her head was pounding, and she wanted to run. But to where, and why did she feel the need to?

Lorne sucked in a few deep breaths and slowly turned to face him. Focusing on the shelves behind him, she asked, "Why should I be scared of you, Doctor?"

"Ah, that is a typical response by a detective, to answer a question with a question. I asked my question first." His grin never wavered.

"I'm not scared of you, just the surroundings." She returned to her seat.

"I find that hard to believe, Inspector. You are usually strong and at ease in the mortuary, unlike your partner."

"Perhaps I'm feeling a bit jumpy at the moment. I've already told you it's been a day from hell for me."

His smile faded, and his tone became understanding. "It must've been awful to have been confronted with first the head this morning and then the call from the killer this afternoon."

"Actually, I've had two calls this afternoon. On both occasions I spoke to a woman whose life is in jeopardy, and there's not a damn thing I can do about it."

"I see. I was only aware of one call. What did the woman say?" He placed his elbows on the desk and watched her.

"Her abductor was telling her what to say. When I asked what all this was about, he said—via the woman—that he wanted retribution. For what, I have no idea. The woman let it slip that there were other people behind her abduction, for which she received a slap."

"Why have you taken this case to heart, Inspector?"

"I don't know. I feel I owe Doreen Nicholls something. She touched my heart; we built an instant bond. She was a very perceptive woman, and I can't help feeling I've somehow let her down. Does that sound strange?" She made full eye contact with him for the first time since arriving.

"Not at all. As a pathologist, I am supposed to distance myself from the people who lie on the table before me. But once I cut them open, I feel responsible for them. I owe them the right to be heard in death. We call them the 'silent witnesses', and it is true. I believe a higher council has blessed me with a skill to look beyond what others see. To fight hard to bring justice to the silent witness, and sometimes—though not very often—I fail and feel as you do now. But I reprimand myself and force myself to continue fighting even harder for the victims."

"This case seems so beyond me at the moment," Lorne admitted, surprising herself.

"By all accounts, you are usually a very efficient policewoman. Ask yourself this question—what is so different about this case that you find yourself struggling to deal with it?"

"That's just it. I can't put my finger on it. Normally, I can say this is wrong or that is wrong, but right now I'm unable to do that." She slumped back in the chair then sat forwards and bashed her forehead twice with the heel of her hand before Jacques grabbed her wrist, preventing her from doing it a third time.

"Please don't punish yourself in such a way. There are other ways of dealing with things, I promise you."

"I think I prefer you as Mr. Hyde. At least then, I knew where I stood. You're confusing me with your kindness."

"It can be arranged. I can change just like that," he said, clicking his fingers. "Inspector, forgive me for asking, but do you have problems at home?" His concern seemed genuine.

It didn't feel like he was intruding into her personal life, so she was truthful with him. "Things could be better, I admit. Everyone has problems in their personal lives, but that shouldn't detract from their ability to carry out their job properly."

"I agree, but it obviously is. Your husband, what is his job?"

"He's a house husband."

"Ah, this is a species of male that is alien to the French. How many children do you have?"

"Just the one. Charlie's twelve."

"Could your husband be rebelling against being tied to his apron strings? That is how you say it, is it not?"

She chuckled. "Sort of...but I get what you mean."

"It is not uncommon for men to change their minds—it is not only a woman's prerogative, you know." His smile returned, and though their conversation had started out as a serious one, it was now in danger of becoming a light-hearted look at the gender's roles around the house. "So he irons, dusts, vacuums, and cooks, I assume?"

"He does, and I'm the one who works twelve, fourteen, sometimes sixteen hours a day."

"No wonder things aren't good between you. There is no time for *amour.*"

The way his tongue lingered on the word *amour* sent her pulse racing, which sent her into a panic again. Why the hell was she divulging such intimate information to a stranger—a very handsome stranger, at that?

"I didn't say there was no love in our marriage—"

"Ah, there may be love, but is there the passionate variety?"

"Do you mind if we talk about something else? I'm feeling a tad uncomfortable with this subject."

"That is where the French and the British are so different. You British treat love as if it should be hidden, confined to the bedroom. Whereas the French, we enjoy showing the world how passionate we are." He made a dramatic sweeping gesture with his arm but was interrupted from continuing his dramatic performance by a buzzer sounding at the end of the corridor. "Excuse me one moment, Inspector."

"The name is Lorne."

He returned to the room with a brown paper bag accompanied by an unmistakable smell. "I hope you like Chinese food, Lorne?" he asked, trying out her name for the first time. It sounded good with a French accent.

"You shouldn't have. I would've grabbed something on my way back to the station." She felt relaxed for the first time that day, despite the tense conversation they'd just had.

"Knife and fork or chopsticks?" Jacques opened a drawer in his desk.

"Knife and fork. I wouldn't know where to start with chopsticks."

"It would be fun to teach you."

He removed the lids of the three containers, and one by one, the aroma of each sumptuous dish filled the air. *Sweet and sour pork, chicken chop suey and king prawns with noodles.* All her favourite dishes. She was in gourmet heaven.

"Please, as you British say, 'tuck in'."

"You have the cutlery but no plates. How bizarre."

"It is more intimate this way. Here."

She looked up to find a king prawn, squeezed between chopsticks, inches away from her mouth. "I couldn't possibly fit all that in my mouth," she objected, laughing.

"There is an answer to that, and if I weren't such a gentleman, I would give you it!"

"Is there a Madame Arnaud?" she blurted out between mouthfuls before she had a chance to stop herself.

"No. I am one of those people who believe commitment belongs in a mental institute. I have had many lovers, though. Ah, I see that I have embarrassed you again."

"Not at all. I find it quite refreshing to have such a frank conversation, even if it is with a stranger from a different culture. Do you mind if I ask you a personal question?" She played with her food.

Jacques smiled and raised an eyebrow. "Another one? Go ahead. I can always refuse to answer if I don't like it."

"Is there a significant difference between French and British women?"

"You assume that I have taken British women to my bed."

"Haven't you?" Lorne challenged.

"I have lived and worked here for twelve years, it would be foolish of me to deny it. We all need satisfying from time to time. I've had two British lovers, but they were very different. It would be impossible for me to compare them to French women. Have you ever had a foreign lover, Lorne?"

"Never." She swallowed hard. "Let's just say the opportunity has never presented itself."

"That is a shame, because according to what I hear of British men, the average lovemaking session is approximately five minutes. I find this to be an incredible statistic." He chuckled and shook his head.

By then she was intrigued, and she had to ask the obvious question. "And how long does it take you to satisfy a woman, Jacques?"

He smiled as he threw the empty cartons in the bin behind him, then swivelled back and looked her in the eye. "In my youth, lovemaking used to be marathon sessions, lasting for two to three hours." Lorne gasped, which made him laugh. "I did say in my youth. Now, a session would consist of at least an hour of foreplay, followed by thirty minutes of intense lovemaking."

Her gasp was louder that time. "You're winding me up?"

"Why would I do that? If you weren't married, I would say that I would take pleasure in proving it to you."

"It's a good thing I'm married, then. Six minutes is a marathon session in my house. God knows what condition I'd be in after half an hour. I probably wouldn't be able to walk properly for a week."

They both laughed, then Jacques said, "You have a beautiful smile, Lorne. You should show it more often."

"I'm hardly in a job that warrants me walking around like the Cheshire cat all day, am I?" She hesitated. "Well, I'd better get back to the station." Disappointment swept over her. Despite her earlier reservations, she'd enjoyed her time with him.

"You're not going home?"

"I have a lot of calls to make, and Tom is going out with friends tonight, making the most of Charlie being at her grandma's house. So there's no point me going home early."

"I'm not doing anything. Perhaps I can keep you company."

"That's kind, but there's no need." She picked up her briefcase and file and headed towards the door.

"Two heads are better than one. I can take a look at the case with a fresh pair of eyes. I really don't mind." He looked at her with lost-puppy-dog eyes, which she found hard to resist.

"Okay, okay. What about if you bring the post-mortem reports with you, and we'll go over them, too? And Jacques, thanks for listening, and thanks for a lovely dinner."

"It was my pleasure. Anytime you are at a loose end, feel free to drop by. And I promise, no more Mr. Hyde when we are called out to the same crime scene."

Chapter Thirty-One

"Lorne… *Chérie*… Wake up. It is six forty-five…" The voice sounded distant but vaguely recognisable.

She'd been in a wonderful dream in a faraway unfamiliar place. Lorne stretched her arms above her head and yelped. "Ouch! I think I've pulled a muscle in my neck."

"I'm not surprised. That will teach you not to fall asleep at your desk again." Jacques smiled at her.

"What time is it?" She glanced at her watch, but her vision was slow to adjust to waking up. Her hair stood on end, and creases covered her clothes. She felt—and no doubt looked—a mess.

"I repeat: It's six forty-five. I should be going."

"Yes, that's a good idea—before my team get in. God, I must look awful."

"Nonsense. You look stunning, as usual."

"I think your French lies are very admirable. How come you still look as handsome as ever?"

"It must be my superb French genes. I must go. I'll ring you this afternoon." To her surprise, he bent down and planted a kiss on her cheek, then left.

As Lorne watched him walk away from her for the second time in two days, she found it difficult to stop the tears springing to her eyes. A feeling of desertion filled her, body and soul. She feared her head was being slowly turned, and she felt powerless to stop it from happening.

Lorne and Jacques had accomplished a lot between them the previous evening. After observing and taking notes of Lorne's phone technique, Jacques had offered to help go through the list of allotment gardeners. When it reached eleven, Lorne felt it was too late to ring prospective witnesses at home, so they turned their attention to the post-mortem reports. They went over each one with the finest of toothcombs, questioning every detail, significant or otherwise. They'd painstakingly compared the fingerprints and drawn a blank.

During their time together, Lorne had grown more comfortable in his company, something that she couldn't have imagined only a few days before. They'd developed a friendship that went beyond that of working colleagues.

They had laughed, flirted, and even fallen asleep together, but they both knew the score. Lorne was married and determined to remain that way, but the temptation to wander was pulling at her. She saw her new friendship as the one positive thing to have come from hunting down the killers. She no longer doubted her abilities in the case—Jacques had pointed out that the clues were few and far between.

She searched through her desk for a clean top and the undies she kept tucked away for emergencies. She set off for the gym in the basement, where she grabbed a quick shower, changed into her clean clothes, and dried her hair under the hand dryer in the ladies'. Luckily, she wasn't the type of woman who relied on cosmetics to help her look good. A quick coat of gloss on her lips, and she was ready for yet another day in the line of duty.

Lorne heard voices as she approached the incident room. A final brush down of her suit, and no one would be the wiser about her night spent at the office.

"It was a total waste of time, boss," Mitch was telling Pete as she entered the room.

Lorne informed the small group, "I rang most of the gardeners last night. None of them have seen anyone suspicious hanging around down there lately."

"Is it worth putting an incident van down there, ma'am?" Tracy asked.

"Waste of time, I think. Why don't you two go home and get some sleep?"

"I'm fine, ma'am. I'd like to carry on, if you don't mind," Tracy said.

Mitch looked horrified at his colleague's eagerness.

"Everything all right, Mitch?" Lorne asked, amused at his reaction.

"Nothing a few zzzs wouldn't put right, ma'am, but I suppose that can wait." He shrugged his wide shoulders.

"Leave it till nine, then I want you to track down as many of these pervs as you can." She picked up the sex offender file and passed it to Mitch.

Pete followed her into her office, which had been cleaned early that morning. The putrid smell from the package had been replaced by pine disinfectant. Lorne opened the window to let in some fresh air.

"Did you sleep here last night?" Pete asked, studying her appearance.

Lorne sighed, "Nothing gets past you, Pete, does it? I made a few calls, had an argument with Tom, and crashed here the night."

"You've got to have a word with Tom, sort things out."

"I know. I will tonight. Shall we start by chasing up the taxi drivers?"

"Have you had breakfast?"

"Nope. have you?"

"Come on. I'll treat you to a fry up down at Kev's Café."

* * *

They arrived at the café, which only had a few spare tables left. Lorne picked a table close to a corner. "You can have the fry up; I'll settle for toast and marmalade."

Their breakfast arrived within a few minutes.

"Do you want to talk about it?" Pete took a mouthful of bacon and egg. Yolk seeped from the corner of his mouth, and Lorne averted her eyes.

"There's nothing to say. Tom's just going through one of his phases. It'll blow over soon enough." She nibbled at a triangle of lukewarm toast.

"So all this arguing is down to Tom, is it?"

"What the hell is that supposed to mean?"

"I don't know. You have to admit, you've been a little strange over the last week. Maybe it's the case, maybe it's the fact that the chief is leaving, and maybe it's something else I don't know about.

But *I've* noticed a change in you. All I'm saying is, have you considered taking a step back and looking at your relationship from Tom's point of view?"

"I haven't had time. I'm always bloody working." She shoved her plate away in annoyance, having lost her appetite.

"See, there you go again. You're full of anger. Why don't you ask for some time off?"

"Now you're just being ridiculous, I haven't got time for a holiday. What would the new chief think about that?"

"Okay, it was just a suggestion. You don't have to snap me head off. Forget I even suggested it."

"Have you finished?"

"Finished what—the lecture or the breakfast?"

Her chair scraped on the floor as she stood up. "*Both*," Lorne snapped, and she stomped out of the café.

Before closing the door, she noticed the other customers go quiet, then heard Pete's smart-arse retort, "She got angry when I asked her for money for the tip."

Pete followed her out. "Right. Where to first?"

Lorne's frostiness dissipated as they set off. "What have we got?"

"We've got three of the drivers on sexual assault charges. Four were had up for burglary, one ABH, and two with nothing at all to their names," Pete said, scanning the list. He'd matched the list Toni had given them with the files they had on record for each of the ex-cons.

"We'll go with the sexual assault charges first. Who's the first on the list and where does he live?"

"Josh Lampard. He's thirty-eight, got put away five years ago for touching someone up on the underground. He blamed the girl for leading him on."

"Sick shit." Lorne shook her head.

Pete gave her directions to Lampard's house, and they pulled up outside ten minutes later. The man's flat was a stone's throw from the taxi firm.

Pete rang the bell, then wiped his hand down his trousers in disgust.

A man in boxer shorts opened the door. They'd obviously disturbed his sleep. "Yeah, what d'ya want?"

Lorne produced her warrant card as Pete brushed the man aside and entered the flat.

"Hey, what the hell is this?"

"Get some clothes on. We've got some questions we want to ask you." Pete's nose wrinkled in apparent disgust as he surveyed their surroundings.

The man left the room and returned seconds later, buttoning up a shirt he'd put on. A half-dressed girl followed him into the room. No more than eighteen or nineteen, she was wearing a long T-shirt that stopped mid-thigh.

"What's going on, Josh? Who are these guys?"

Lorne ignored the girl and asked, "Last Thursday night, where were you at between eleven and eleven thirty?"

The guy scratched his head as he thought. He walked over to the table, picked up a packet of cigarettes, took one out, and lit it. "Working. Why?"

"What area?"

"How the hell should I know?"

"Look, we can either do this here or we can do it down the nick, it's entirely up to you, buddy," Pete said, annoyed at the man's tone.

"All right. Let me think. That was almost a week ago. Thursday... Busy night, that was. I was probably around the town centre about that time, but I can't be sure. Why?"

"One of your fellow drivers was supposed to pick up a girl from High Bank Road at eleven. He couldn't make it."

The driver thought for another few minutes as though piecing the information together in his mind. "Yeah, I remember. It was Wacko—he was in a panic, didn't want to let the girl down. I think he fancies her. Anyway, a drunk puked up in the back of his cab, and he wanted to clean it up before going to pick her up. As far as I can remember, he asked the girl to hang on, but she wouldn't, so Mary asked if anyone else could do the job. But everyone was busy. Wacko told me he swung by later, but she'd gone. He tried to track her down, but there was no sign of her. He was gutted."

The two detectives glanced at one another. Had they at last stumbled across something important in their case?

"Did he talk about her much?" Lorne asked.

"Not really, but he always made sure he was available when her call came in."

"Did he? Had she been a customer for long, do you know?" Pete asked.

"Couple of months, I suppose."

"Have you ever picked her up?"

"No, can't say I have. By all accounts, she's meant to be a stunner." The girl on the sofa coughed and Lampard corrected himself. "I mean, *Wacko* said she was really pretty."

Pete ignored the girl's presence. "So, given the opportunity, you would've liked to have met her?"

"What's that supposed to mean?"

"With your penchant for pretty young girls—you know in your past." He held up his file, and the man glared at him.

"That's just it—in the past. I ain't done anything like that for years."

The girl jumped up from the sofa. "What did you do?"

Lampard closed the gap between them and grabbed the top of her arms. "They're winding you up, sweetheart. Ignore them. It's just the police doing what they do best."

The girl looked at the two detectives, her eyes full of questions.

Pete shrugged. "It's up to him to tell you. Maybe it'd be better if you left us alone for a minute?"

She tore herself from the man's grip and ran from the room. They heard drawers banging, wardrobe doors slamming, and the girl cursing.

"Thanks a lot, pal. What the fuck have I done wrong?"

Lorne stepped in to calm things down. "Nothing. We're investigating a murder. The girl Wacko should have picked up that night was found dead a few days later."

"Shit. You're joking. But I don't see—what the fuck has it to do with me?"

"What my partner was trying to ask was, if you picked her up later? Or maybe you know if one of your colleagues picked her up?"

"Like I said, as far as I can remember, it was busy that night. Wacko got shirty with us because no one was willing to pick her up. Hey, there was no need to drag up my past in front of Jemma."

Lorne gave him a hard stare. She didn't like sex offenders, reformed or otherwise, but she tried to keep her distaste under wraps. "If you hear anything, give us a call."

Once outside, Pete said, "There's more to that relationship than meets the eye."

"What relationship are you on about?"

"Wacko and Kim Charlton, of course."

She flicked Pete a glance as they climbed into her Vectra. "Pete, you need to be a bit more careful about showing your feelings. You damn well made a difficult situation worse."

"I can't help it when it comes to sex offenders—and I know you feel the same way. Did you happen to clock how old the girl was in there?" He angrily jerked his thumb behind him.

"Yeah, I 'happened to clock' how old she was—well over the age of consent. There's no point pissing people off unnecessarily. Just leave the questioning to me next time. All you seem to do is get their backs up before we've gained their confidence. That's basic policing, Pete."

The air grew frosty again. That time, it was Pete's turn to be in a mood.

Lorne's mobile rang, breaking the silence. "Yes, Tracy?"

"Ma'am, a package arrived for you half an hour ago, and Mr. Greenaway is here to see you."

"Oliver Greenaway? What does he want?"

"That's right, ma'am. He wouldn't say."

"What about the package—does it look suspicious?"

"It's a Jiffy bag, ma'am, addressed to you. Hand delivered, again. The desk sergeant discovered it a little while ago."

"We're on our way. Show Oliver to the canteen, will you? We'll be about twenty minutes."

"Yes, ma'am."

"Wonder what *he* wants?" Pete said.

"I don't know, but remember: He's off the list of suspects. Treat him like a normal human being when we get back, okay?"

"Whatever. I'll let you deal with him. I'll see to the package."

"I'll do both, if you don't mind." Her mind raced. If the package turned out to be yet another of the killer's little party tricks, she'd need to get it over to Jacques straight away. Her heart rate spiked at the thought of seeing him again.

"Hey, take it easy on the accelerator, boss. What's the rush?"

She eased off, but the tension remained—she was desperate to know what was in the package.

Chapter Thirty-Two

The A5 Jiffy bag was addressed in thick black marker to DI Lorne Simpkins.

She snapped on a pair of latex gloves and opened it, tipping the contents carefully onto a piece of paper on her desk. Bubble wrap and a note fell out. The note read: *HERE IS THE SECOND PART OF THE PUZZLE INSPECTOR. IS IT COMING TOGETHER YET?* She tore open the bubble wrap. Inside was a blood-soaked tissue, and inside that was a severed nipple.

"What the hell is that?" Pete looked confused and disgusted.

She answered him in a whisper, "The only part of Kim Charlton that was missing... Her nipple."

"This guy gets frigging worse. What are you going to do with it?"

"As soon as I've seen Oliver, I'll take it over to Arnaud. He can analyse the note and the packaging. While I'm gone, see how the rest of the team got on this morning. I'll be back in a few hours."

She could tell by looking at him that her partner wasn't happy about staying at the station, but that was tough.

* * *

Lorne left the incident room and went down to meet Oliver Greenaway in the reception area. She shook his hand. "Sorry to keep you waiting, Oliver."

He smiled and seemed pleased to see her. "Inspector, nice to see you again. I didn't mean to turn up unannounced. I was in the area and wanted to see if you'd made any progress with the case?"

"I'm glad you're here, actually, I was going to contact you later. There's something important I need to tell you. It's not pleasant, I'm afraid."

"You're worrying me. Has something else happened to my family?"

"No, nothing like that. Yesterday, the killer made contact with me." Lorne paused, unsure how to continue.

"Go on."

"I received a large box. Inside the box was…" Her mouth dried up, and she called over to the girl serving in the canteen to fetch her a glass of water.

"Inspector, please go on."

The girl arrived, and Lorne took a large swig of water. "Inside the box was your mother's head."

He buried his head in his hands. "My God. What type of sick individual…?" Anger replaced his shock. "Was there a note, a postmark, anything that can be traced?"

"There was a note. You've got to promise me you won't tell anyone about this. We *have* to keep it out of the media. Otherwise, we'll receive hundreds of crank calls, and it'll slow down our progress."

"Of course I promise. What did it say?"

"It referred to a missing part of a puzzle."

"Have there been other murders, apart from my mother and my aunt?"

"Yes, a sixteen-year-old girl. I just received a second parcel with another note," Lorne confided. Even though she knew she shouldn't, she felt he had a right to know.

"You've received nothing from my aunt's murder, no parcel or note, I mean?"

"Nothing, but I'm not expecting anything. Don't forget, uniformed police disturbed the killer before he could take anything."

"Who's your main suspect, apart from me?"

"You're not a suspect, Oliver. I never thought you could do that to your own mother or aunt."

"Unlike your partner." He raised an eyebrow.

Lorne said nothing to that. She didn't want to criticise her partner in front of Greenaway.

"We haven't got any clear suspects at the moment, but the 'probable' list is growing daily. As soon as we have a suspect in custody, you'll be the first to know, I assure you."

"Thank you. Look, the reason I'm here is, we're having a double funeral at St Saviour's church tomorrow. I thought you might like to attend. It seems pretty ironic, to be burying them on the same day, after they came into the world together. Do you think Mum will be buried...um...intact? Whole?"

"I'm going over to the mortuary now. I'll make sure that happens, Oliver. Don't worry about that. What time is the service tomorrow?"

"Eleven. A wake is being held afterwards at the Thornton Hotel. You're welcome to come along."

"I can't promise I'll be able to attend the wake, but I'll definitely be there for the funeral. Thanks for letting me know."

"I'll see you tomorrow, then."

"I'll walk you to your car." Lorne smiled at him.

* * *

The slow-moving traffic infuriated Lorne as she made her way across town. Was she really that desperate to get to the mortuary? Who in their right mind would be in a hurry to get to such a depressing place? *Unless, of course, you had a rendezvous with someone interesting who worked there.*

It was three twenty when she arrived. Lorne watched Jacques through the porthole of the post-mortem suite for a few minutes before she knocked on the door.

He smiled and seemed surprised to see her, then mouthed that she should wait in his office. Holding up a gloved hand covered in blood, he signalled he'd be five to ten minutes.

Jacques walked into his office some minutes later. He'd replaced his surgeon gowns with smart black trousers and a caramel-coloured jumper that screamed, *I know what I'm doing, as far as fashion is concerned.*

Her heart flipped a somersault when he approached her and planted a tender kiss on both cheeks.

"I see my charms are irresistible to you, Lorne, that you can't stay away," he teased. His smile deepened when a flush of colour worked its way up her neck and settled in her cheeks.

"That's the trouble with arrogant French men—they think all women find them *irresistible*." She was happy to flirt with him, but her tone gave away that something was wrong.

He picked up on her mood in a flash. "Come. Sit down. Joking aside, I can tell when something is wrong." He removed her coat, and she tensed at his closeness.

"Oliver Greenaway came to see me. It's his mother and aunt's funeral tomorrow. I told him I'd make sure his mother was…umm…put back together again, if you like."

"Of course, I will ensure that happens. Is that all that is bothering you, because you could have told me that over the phone. Also, that is the general procedure, anyway."

She placed the Jiffy bag on the desk. "You might want to put your gloves on before you open it."

"Another package from the killer, I take it?"

"I suspect the contents belong to Kim Charlton, but I'd like you to verify it for me, if you would?"

Jacques looked inside. "Why do you think he might be taking parts of the bodies and sending them to you?"

"I thought about that on my way over here. Trophies?"

"*Peut-être*, maybe. But in my experience, when murderers take trophies from their victims, they usually keep the trophies tucked away in a drawer." He examined the nipple. "I'll get it tested; perhaps there will be some trace evidence on it that can help us build a case against this vile person. I'll be right back."

He took the package to a colleague. Tiredness swept over her. She rested her head on the desk and began to drift off. She almost jumped out of her seat when she felt a pair of hands on her shoulders.

"Relax. You are so very tense. Does your neck still hurt as bad as it did this morning?" His voice was as caressing as his hands.

"To be honest, I haven't had much time to think about it. Ouch! Yes, it does."

"Of course, a proper massage is much better when the person in need of it is naked."

His words tormented her, and his accent affected her in ways she found impossible to explain. She tried to break free from his grasp, but he was determined to finish what he'd started. It was useless to try to fight him—the moment she gave in to his powers of persuasion, she felt the knots untangling under his warm, experienced hands.

An unexpected moan of pleasure escaped her lips, startling her.

The spell was broken when the phone rang. He muttered something unintelligible and unrecognisable in his native tongue.

With the moment lost, Lorne hurtled back to reality with the speed of a spaceship re-entering Earth's atmosphere. While he was distracted with his call, she dashed to the coat stand to retrieve her coat. She glanced up. Feeling embarrassed, she ran from his office. She would ring him later to apologise. Confusion filled her every pore. She didn't want to run from him—it wasn't in her make-up to run scared. But then, neither was cheating on her husband.

She drove back to the station, trying not to replay the way she'd felt when his hands were on her.

The incident room fell silent when she walked in.

"The killer's been in touch again," Pete announced.

She shrugged out of her coat. "What did he say?"

"He wouldn't speak to anyone. Got annoyed when you weren't here."

"Did you tell him to call back?"

"I didn't get a chance. The woman was with him, though. The last call he made, he terrified her. She screamed, and then there was silence. I think he killed her, boss."

Lorne collapsed into a nearby chair. *Am I the reason he killed her? If she's dead, just because I wasn't around? The sick shit! Is this personal? Do I know him?*

Lorne coughed to clear her throat. "Are the uniforms still down at the allotment?"

"Yes, ma'am," Tracy responded.

"Call them off. You and Mitch get down there. Park your car a couple of roads away and position yourselves near the shed, just in case he decides to use it again."

"We'll get down there right away, ma'am," Tracy said.

"You okay, boss?" Pete perched a buttock on the desk beside her.

"To be honest, Pete, I feel as though someone's just kicked me in the guts. I should've been here. Maybe it would have prolonged her life. What time did the last call come in?"

"About twenty minutes ago. You can't go blaming yourself for this."

"*Can't I?*"

"No, you bloody can't. If the sick bastard is going to kill someone, it makes no odds if you're around to take his call or not." Pete walked over to the vending machine to get her a cup of coffee.

"Did anything come to light while I was out?" Lorne asked, trying to pull herself together.

"Molly called into the council. According to their records, there're two roads around the railway line where the houses have cellars large enough to stand up in." He pulled out the map and pointed out the two roads. "Clearmont Road, which is here, and Lehman Avenue, which is tucked away over here."

"Pass me the files of the taxi drivers, will you?"

Pete handed her the files and continued with his update. "Molly also dropped by the agency—you know, the one that employs Mr. and Mrs. Hall? She did well, getting the information out of the woman. Apparently, it turns out that before working for the Greenaways, they worked for a posh family in Harrow—the Mountbattens. The husband used to work away a lot—some kind of explorer, I think. Anyway, Mrs. Mountbatten became reliant on Mr. Hall, but one day he overstepped the mark and tried to kiss her. She threatened to call the police if they didn't resign and vacate their flat. They started at the Greenaways not long after."

Lorne's head stopped spinning, and her thoughts began to function properly. "Why did the agency keep them on their books?"

"The woman told Molly that because the Mountbattens hadn't filed a formal complaint or brought the police in, it would've been prejudiced *not* to offer the couple another position. They've behaved themselves ever since."

"Oliver told me the funeral of his mother and aunt are taking place tomorrow. I said we'd go. The Halls should be there; we can ask them a few questions then. But I think it'll prove to be a waste of time."

"I don't know. They had the opportunity to do away with Belinda. It's just a matter of motive."

"But what about her sister—and, of course, there's Kim Charlton to consider. It's obvious the crimes are linked because of the same MO. So how would Hall get to them?" Lorne frowned, and leafed through the files he'd given her.

"Well he must've known Doreen and where she lived, but like you say, what's the connection with Kim? How does she fit in?"

The phone rang. Lorne checked the technician was ready to trace the call before she answered.

"Hello. DI Simpkins. How can I help you?"

There was silence on the other end of the line.

"Hello, is anybody there?" Lorne listened carefully, trying to pick up on any background noise. She heard the shuffling of feet and heavy breathing.

"Hello?" she prompted again, then more softly, continued, "I can't help you if you won't talk to me."

A muffled voice replied, "You should've been there. You could've saved her."

Lorne closed her eyes. She wanted to shout and scream at the caller, but she needed to restrain herself. It was important to play things his way, to gain the killer's trust.

"I was on an errand. I can't be here all the time, waiting for your call."

"Didn't you spend enough time with him last night?"

Lorne's eyes flew open and found Pete's gaze. He raised an eyebrow, and she shrugged, pretending she didn't know what the killer was referring to.

"Ah, silence, a sign of guilt. I was watching you flirt. Is it his French accent that you admire, Inspector?"

"What have you done with the woman?" Lorne asked, a tremor to her voice. The bastard had been watching her. Thank God Jacques had spent the night with her. If she'd been alone, she might not be alive.

"Does his accent turn you on, Lorne?" the killer asked, determined to keep the conversation going the way he intended, not her.

Pete's eyes widened, and he shook his head. "Don't answer. Ask about the woman," he mouthed.

"Can I speak to the woman?"

The killer's breath came in short bursts as he became more annoyed with Lorne avoiding his questions.

"No, she's gone. I disposed of the body when you weren't there to take my call. You made me angry, Inspector. So very, very angry."

"I'm sorry. Tell me what you want, and I'll do my best to make things right."

The line went dead. Lorne looked across at the tracer, who shook his head. She hurried into her office and slammed the door, feeling both helpless and guilty.

There was a knock on the door, she hoped if she ignored it the person would give up and leave her in peace. No such luck—Pete entered as though on tiptoes and closed the door behind him. He said nothing, just sat down in the seat opposite. Lorne stared past him at the painting of the Lakes she adored that hung on the wall behind him.

"Boss, we need to talk about this."

"The bastard is watching me, Pete. Can you imagine how that feels? He knows my every move. Why? How?" Her hands shook as she raked them through her hair. She wanted to pull it out from the roots in frustration.

"I'm not gonna let you out of my sight, okay?"

"That's ridiculous, Pete. You can't be with me 24/7." She blew out a deep breath.

"Was Arnaud here with you last night?" His brow creased.

"Yes, but it was purely professional. We went over the case from every angle. He helped me make some calls. I shouldn't have to be explaining my actions to you, Pete. I haven't done anything wrong."

"You should make Tom aware of the situation. You know—that you're being watched, not..."

"I will later. What we should be doing now is looking for the body. Get uniform on to it, will you?"

As soon as Pete left the room Lorne reached for the phone. "It's me."

"Why did you run off like that? Am I that scary, *ma chérie?*"

"I'm sorry, Jacques. I've just received another call from the killer. He's killed the woman, but I have no idea where her body is." She was fighting to remain professional, but all she wanted to do was seek comfort in his arms.

"Did you manage to trace the call?"

"No, it was too short. He's not stupid. He knows you were here with me last night."

"How? *Merde*, he's watching you."

"We need to catch the bastard before I become one of his victims. Can you hurry the tests along for me?"

"It goes without saying. I'll get on to it immediately. Ring you later. Take care, *chérie.*"

"I will. Ring me as soon as you know anything."

Pete barged into her office as she hung up the phone. "There's a woman at reception demanding to see the person in charge of the case. The desk sergeant thinks she's a nutter, but he can't get rid of her. The woman's tried ringing me a couple of times, but…"

"She might have some information for us, Pete. At this stage, we can't discount anyone."

Pete set off to fetch the woman, mumbling under his breath.

The woman was dressed in black from head to toe. Silver rings jangled together as she swept her long black hair over her shoulder and sat in the chair opposite Lorne. The black on her lips and her eyes enhanced her weird beauty.

"My colleague said you've got some information about a case we're dealing with?"

"You mean *cases*, surely, Inspector. My name is Carol Lang; my stage name is Madame Xsarina. My talent was given to me by God to rid the world of evil."

Lorne raised her eyebrows. "I see… How?" Her interest was piqued. Out of the corner of her eye, she noticed Pete fold his arms.

She knew how he felt about outside influences on a case. He called it 'jiggery pokery' and was adamant there was no place for it on the force. In the past, he'd condemned other forces who had been open to using psychics and their 'special powers' to help solve cases. But Lorne felt differently about psychics, as her great-aunt had been one.

"I've had visions that up until now I couldn't explain. I believe three murders have been committed." When the two detectives neither confirmed nor denied her statement was correct, she continued. "I see the despicable deeds through the murderer's eyes. He is cold and calculated in his actions. I see a sheet of paper with three names on it. He's holding it in his hands and shares the information with another."

"What're the names on this piece of paper?" Pete asked, with his usual cynical tone.

"I can tell you're a non-believer, sir. If you can keep your scepticism in check for half an hour, I will prove that my visions are accurate."

"He will. Go on." Lorne shot Pete a warning glance.

"The names are unclear, they are blurred..."

"That figures," Pete muttered.

"I've read about the murders in the paper, but if I give you information that hasn't appeared in print, then will you believe me?" Miss Lang aimed her question at Pete, who shrugged his acceptance.

"If you want to leave, Pete, feel free. I'd like to hear what Miss Lang has to say."

"I'll stay. I promise to keep my opinions under wraps from now on."

"Two of the women were twins. Identical twins, I believe? One of the murders was a mistake."

"That's right, but that information has already appeared in the paper," Lorne said before Pete had a chance to jump in with another of his sarcastic comments.

"You're missing the point, Inspector. *One* was a mistake."

"There's no way of knowing if that's true at the moment, the investigation is still in its infancy."

"When you are putting the clues together, just bear it in mind. Kim, the sixteen-year-old, was not originally on the list either. She did something that angered the man, she was punished for that."

"Let's get this right." Pete chipped in. "One of the twins was a mistake, and now you're telling us that the last victim, Kim Charlton, was *also* a mistake. I guess that puts paid to your list of three names then, doesn't it?"

The woman ignored him and continued divulging what she'd seen in her visions. "The women are abducted and kept in a kind of cell."

Lorne was amazed by this revelation, a fact that had never been alluded to in the press. They had only discovered this particular piece of information yesterday, after Tracy's friend had listened to and analysed the tape. "Go on."

"The women are from his past. He's punishing them for something that happened years ago. I can't see what that is—perhaps it will come to me in the future. He beats them to death with a long, narrow object, with a hook on one end and some kind of spike on the other. I don't think you've found any semen at the scene either. I believe the man is impotent. He does, however, sexually assault them and leaves something like a calling card inside the victims."

"Jesus Christ, how the hell did you know that?" Pete's interest piqued, and he paced around the office.

"Do you believe me now, Sergeant? You have also been receiving body parts through the post."

Lorne couldn't believe what she was hearing. "When was the last time you had one of these visions?"

"A couple of days ago. The last few nights I've had trouble sleeping. Although I haven't seen it clearly, I think he may be holding someone else hostage. Is he?"

"I'm afraid I can't answer that."

"Inspector, I can help you get this man... Burning, I see burning."

Carol Lang's hand flew up to her forehead, and Lorne wondered if the woman was having another vision.

"Ah well, now. That's where you're wrong, because none of the victims have been burnt or found near a fire," Pete was quick to point out.

Lorne studied the woman as beads of sweat broke out on her forehead. Carol clutched at her throat and gasped for breath.

"I can't breathe. There's a thundering noise. Flames leaping up all around me. I'm in a tunnel—I can see the end of it. A river is a few feet away. If only I wasn't bound, I could dive in and put the fire out. Torture, this is torture! He's standing close by, laughing as the flames engulf me, goading me. Please. Please help me."

"Get the map, Pete." Lorne ordered. Pete left.

Carol Lang screamed. Pete rushed back into the room, map in hand. The woman had passed out in the chair. Lorne rushed past him to get a glass of water.

"What happened?" Pete asked breathlessly.

"She just passed out. Set the map out on the desk. We'll go over what she told us."

"If you believe what she just told you, you're as insane as she is."

"How can you say that? She's given us info that isn't common knowledge yet, like the body parts arriving in the post and the way he kills the victims. What else have we got to go on, Pete? Lighten up, for Christ's sake. Right, we're looking for water and a tunnel of sorts." Lorne checked the woman's pulse; it seemed normal. She kept a close eye on Carol as Pete and she studied the map.

Pete pointed at the map. "Here, the river runs along here—and shit, there's a bridge. Jesus, could that be classed as a tunnel?"

"Ring down to reception, get someone up here to look after her." Excitement churned up Lorne's stomach.

"Will do. What are we going to do?"

"Get down there straight away, of course." Lorne grabbed her keys and handbag.

"But it might not be that site. Who's to say she's right?"

"It's a chance I'm willing to take. Come on."

Chapter Thirty-Three

It was past six by the time Lorne and Pete arrived at the location; the light was fading fast. Something in the distance caught Lorne's eye. An orange glow beckoned them.

Pete bolted from the car, leaving the passenger door swinging in the breeze. Lorne contacted the station and called for backup. She also requested the fire brigade, an ambulance, and told the controller to place a call to Doctor Arnaud immediately.

Lorne searched the boot of her car. "Damn it!" All she found were a few carrier bags that had seen better days.

"Here. Get some water in these." She handed Pete the bags. He looked at them and shook his head in despair, then ran to the edge of the stone embankment and scooped his right arm into the murky river.

As he pulled the first carrier bag out, the handle stretched and broke under the weight of the water. "Shit!" He tried another bag, this time filling it with less water, and rushed over to the small fire burning by the bridge wall. The orange glow dimmed, only to flare up again when he threw the pitiful amount of water on it.

"It's no good; we need more water." Lorne said urgently as trepidation filled her. She placed the last two carrier bags one inside the other and handed them to her partner. "Take this. I'll see if I can find anything else." She hunted the area surrounding them and found an old metal bucket that had a large hole in the bottom, but the handle was good.

After Pete tipped another bagful of water on the flames, Lorne held the bucket out to him. "Put the bag inside to cover the hole. Hurry up; keep them coming. It's working; the fire's going out."

Lorne felt relieved when she heard the sirens in the distance. The fire engine pulled up as she threw another bucketful of water on the fire.

"Stand back, miss. We'll take it from here." The burly fireman gripped her by the elbows and guided her back towards her car.

"There's a body. We think she's dead. We just wanted to put the fire out. Be careful with her; try not to destroy any evidence."

"I understand. We'll do our best not to disturb any more than we have to."

Pete joined her, and they watched in silence for a while as the fireman put out the fire. Pete appeared to be just as traumatised as she was.

"This is my fault. If only I'd been around to take his call, maybe I could've prevented this. That poor, poor woman." When Lorne saw the charred remains, tears welled in her eyes, but she was determined not to let them spill.

"That's rubbish, Lorne. The sick bastard's got an agenda. He was set on seeing it through, whether you were around to take his call or not."

It was unusual for Pete to call her by her Christian name, and she felt strangely comforted by it.

A black BMW skidded to a halt in the gravel alongside them. Jacques walked towards them. He eyed her with concern. "Inspector?"

Lorne watched as sparks flew between the two men. "Pete, can you check what's happening, while I have a word with the doctor?"

"How did you know where to find the body?" Jacques stepped forwards as her partner walked away.

"Not long after I called you, a woman turned up at the station wanting to see me. She's a psychic, and she told me things about the victims that I've intentionally kept out of the media. She told us about a bridge—actually, she called it a tunnel. That it was by a river. She also told us she's been having visions and said she sees things through the killer's eyes. She also saw a list with three names on it. I know this is the fourth murder, but she thinks two have been mistakes. Maybe the other two women were in the wrong place at the wrong time. Who the hell knows? She even told me about the packages I've received.

"She made me think—the way he keeps ringing me and letting me know he's watching me, makes me wonder if he intends making me one of his victims. Perhaps mine is the third name on his list."

"Is that what you truly believe?"

"Why else would he be trying to make contact with me?"

"There could be a number of reasons. You're the lead investigator."

"Hmm…"

"It's plausible that he sees you as a friend rather than foe."

"If that's the case, why won't he confide in me *why* he's carrying out these murders? Why are his calls so brief?"

"Because he's not stupid. He knows you'll try your best to trap him, to trace his calls. Whatever happens, swear to me you will never agree to meet him, not alone."

"If it means I can save the lives of other women, that's exactly what I'll have to do."

"But that's ludicrous. You can't put your life at risk to save others."

"I joined the police force to protect and serve my fellow countrymen. If I turn away and run when things get tough, then I shouldn't be in the job, should I?"

He shrugged, defeated by her words. "I can see it would be useless to try and dissuade you."

Pete returned to them and shaking his head, he said, "I told you he was getting worse."

Jacques gave Lorne a puzzled look. She explained, "The crimes—Pete's got it into his head that each murder is worse than the previous one."

"It is not uncommon for a murderer to perfect his art. He becomes more confident and, I suppose, more adventurous in the way he kills."

"Tell us something we don't know," Pete muttered.

Jacques' eyes creased in annoyance at Pete's derogatory tone. "Far be it for me to tell you your job, DS Childs, but I think it would be better if you took DI Simpkins home. She's had a rough day, and she also spent an uncomfortable night at the station."

"Yeah, you'd know all about *that,* of course."

"Pack it in, you two, for God's sake. Thanks for your concern, Jacques, but I have a post-mortem to attend in case you've forgotten. There's no way I can call it a day, even if I wanted to. Which I don't."

After a moment's pause, Jacques said, "Is that the only reason you have to stay at work?"

"I suppose so," she replied, perplexed.

"Then I will postpone the post-mortem until tomorrow." When Lorne stared at him in open-mouthed disbelief, he added, "It is my prerogative, as leading pathologist on the case. No, seriously. Being practical, I would have to wait for the body to cool down before I attempt a post-mortem anyway."

"Okay, you win. What time shall I be there in the morning? Bear in mind, I have a funeral to attend at eleven on the other side of town." It was pointless to argue with him; she could feel exhaustion tapping at her bones.

"If you promise me you'll go straight home, then I will consider an early start. Shall we say about seven?"

"That's fine. I'll see you bright and early at the mortuary."

He walked off without saying goodbye and for some reason she felt abandoned by his departure.

"Come on, I'll drive you home," Pete said, his eyes burning through Arnaud's back.

"But your car is back at the station," she replied.

"I'll drop you off, take your car home, then pick you up in the morning, if that's okay?"

She was in no mood to argue with him as they got in the car. He cursed when he bashed his knee on the steering wheel. She was a good six or seven inches shorter than he was. His frustration increased when his belly prevented him from locating the knob that adjusted the seat.

Lorne found it hard to keep a straight face, and he shot her a disapproving look.

It was dark when they pulled up outside her house. Her heart pounded as she prepared herself for yet another of Tom's likely filthy moods.

Pete noticed her anxiety and asked if she wanted him to accompany her.

She smiled and placed a hand on his arm. "Would you mind, just for a minute? I know he won't argue if you're there. I want to see Charlie's all right before I thrash things out with him."

Tom's angry scowl changed to a loving smile when he spotted Pete lurking behind her.

"Is Charlie in her room?" Tom nodded and turned his back. "Get Pete a drink will you please, Tom?"

After checking Charlie was happy and had completed her homework, Lorne returned downstairs to find the boys debating football. *Of course; what else?*

"He's gotta be the best player Wenger has brought to the club in a long time, apart from Henry that is."

"Who are you talking about?" Lorne sat on the leather sofa next to her husband.

"Jose Antonio Reyes, the kid they bought in January. He's playing out of his skin at the moment."

"The cute one with the sexy smile, you mean?"

Both men looked at her in surprise. Tom asked, "But you don't take much notice of football when it's on. How the hell do you know who we're talking about?"

Her secret was out. How the hell was she going to get out of this one? "There was an article in Pete's paper the other day about a new player Arsenal recently signed. You don't have to be a flippin' genius to work it out. I am a DI, after all."

Pete and Tom eyed her suspiciously but decided not to challenge her. She stood and went through to the kitchen to fix something to eat. Not having much of an appetite, she settled on another cheese and tomato omelette. She poked her head in the lounge and asked Pete if he wanted to stay for dinner. He declined, and she felt the panic rise within. Her safety net was deserting her and heading for the front door.

"Thanks for paving the way for me, Pete," she whispered as he made to leave.

"See you in the morning, boss. I made Tom aware of the stress you've been under today," he assured her before closing the door behind him.

Lorne crept back into the kitchen and sat at the breakfast bar to eat her omelette. Putting the last mouthful of dinner in her mouth, she looked up to see Tom leaning against the doorframe watching her. Their eyes locked, searching for answers to questions that neither of them were prepared to ask.

In the sickening silence, Lorne washed her plate, placed the bottle of wine back in the fridge and tried to walk past him, but he refused to budge. She took a step back, pleading with her eyes to be allowed to pass. He stood firm, so she returned to her seat and waited for him to speak.

The tension was palpable. Neither of them knew where to begin. It was up to one of them to start a conversation that could either break or make their marriage. But which of them was it going to be? She was weary, exhausted beyond comprehension. His selfishness caused her blood to boil—all she wanted to do was curl up in her soft, warm, comfortable bed and go to sleep.

Instead, Lorne asked, "Did Charlie enjoy her stay at grandma's?"

"Yup."

"It's been one hell of a day," she said, hoping to gain a little sympathy.

It didn't come. "I know. Pete told me."

Her emotional state caught up with her, and tears welled in her eyes. "What do you want from me, Tom?"

"I want you to be my wife. Is that too much to ask? Apparently, it is."

"What's that supposed to mean?"

"It means, I want things back to the way they were before you got this fucking promotion."

The vicious impact of his angry words slapped her in the face. "Don't raise your voice. Charlie will hear."

"Your consideration for our child is touching, if a trifle false." His face was taut with an anger she'd never witnessed before. His handsome features became twisted and ugly.

"False. In what way is it false?"

"If you had any, *any* consideration for your child, you'd be here when she came home from school. Be here when she ate her dinner.

But it's more convenient for me to do it, isn't it? Saves you the trouble."

"That's not fair, Tom." His words twisted her stomach into knots.

"Life ain't fair. But you know that, don't you, Lorne? To you, life is about locking up criminals rather than spending time with your family. When was the last time you took your daughter swimming? Bloody months ago, that's when. When was the last time you sat down and helped Charlie with her maths homework? Months ago. But then you've got someone to fall back on, haven't you? Well, supposing I walked out on you tonight. What the fuck would you do then?"

His words frightened her—as was his intention, she suspected. He was right. It had been months since she'd spent any quality time with either of them. Maybe Charlie had received a bad report from school he wasn't telling her about? She couldn't rely on Tom to help their daughter with her homework because he wasn't the sharpest chisel in the toolbox—he'd always wanted to play with cars rather than take an interest in studying at school. The teachers at one point had thought he was dyslexic—in truth, he'd just been plain lazy—so they'd let him plod away at his own slow pace.

What the fuck would she do if he walked out on her and their marriage?

All these questions, and she didn't have a single answer to give him. "Tom...please, you know how difficult my job is. As I recall, you supported me in my application for promotion."

"That was before I knew how much time you'd actually spend at home. Do you have any idea what my state of mind is these days? These four walls, that's all I see twenty-four hours a day. And do you care? Huh, don't make me laugh. You couldn't give a shit about it. You don't even realise it, do you?"

She was too stunned to answer him. Too ashamed to look at him, and he was quick to point this out.

"What's wrong, Lorne? Hit the nail on the head, have I?" He took a big stride towards her, and she cowered. "Christ, did you think I was going to hit you?" he asked incredulously.

"I don't know."

"It proves we no longer know each other the way we used to. It's pointless going on." His shoulders slumped in defeat as he plonked down on the stool beside her.

"Please, Tom. Don't say that. I love you." She placed her hand on his arm.

"Do you, Lorne? Or do you just see me as someone you can rely on to take good care of your child?"

"You mean *our* child?"

"When it suits you, she's our child; other times, I just don't know what she is. A noose around your neck maybe?"

"How can you say that? I love her as much as I love you."

"Then for Christ's sake, start showing it. Show some interest in your family for a change. Take last night, for instance. I told you Charlie would be spending time with her gran. It was an ideal opportunity for us to spend time together. But no, you told me you *had* to work late."

"You said you were going out with the boys for the night," she cried in anguish.

"If you'd asked me not to go, I would have thought up an excuse to get out of it. I would have done that for you, Lorne. For you. What the hell do you do for *me* nowadays? Think carefully before you answer." A sneer came with the warning.

She wracked her brain and had trouble remembering the last time she had done anything nice for him. For how long had he bottled up all that anger inside? Was this what had been wrong with him over the last few months? Why hadn't he mentioned it before then? Was she that wrapped up in her work, that her family life took a poor second place to it?

"It's difficult, isn't it? I'll tell you when it was: four months ago to the day; you looked after Charlie while I went fishing with Dan. Four shitting months since I've had a single day off. Whereas you—well, what can I say? When was the last time you did the vacuuming, cleaned the bathroom, picked up a duster—"

Her hands flew up to cover her ears. "Stop it. Stop it, Tom. I'm begging you—"

He strode over to the cupboard above the breakfast bar and pulled out a tumbler, which he filled with whisky from the new bottle that had been sitting on the countertop beside him.

"That's your answer to our problems, is it?" Lorne asked, voice shaking with annoyance.

"Let me know if you can think of a better one," he shot back, and he emptied his half-filled glass in one gulp.

"I'm tired. I'm going to bed now, Tom."

As she walked out of the kitchen, she heard the chink of the bottle hitting his glass. *Let him get on with it. Let him drown his sorrows. What do I care, anyway?*

Weary, she climbed the stairs to her bedroom. The trouble was she *did* care, but she was also confused. Did she care enough to save her marriage? And what part did Jacques Arnaud play in her confusion?

She found an old pair of pyjamas to wear, just in case Tom had any intention of making up with her when he finally came to bed.

Sleep evaded her. Every time she attempted to close her eyes, the terrifying images of the charred body burned her eyelids. Beads of sweat seeped from every pore. Guilt-ridden, that was what she was. "What if?" was a terrible question to ask, but it was a question she punished herself with, over and over again. *What if* she had been there to take the killer's call? *What if* they had at least started bringing in suspects? *What if* she didn't have this fixation with Jacques? *What if* she was the next name on the killer's list? And finally, *what if* he did eventually kill her, and she never got to see her daughter grow up?

She held her breath, pretending to be asleep when Tom staggered into the room and got into bed beside her.

"Lorne, sweeyheart, are you ashleep?" he slurred as he leant over her.

Rigid with apprehension, she dared not wiggle her big toe, in case he realised she was awake. Before long, his snoring kept her awake, instead of the vivid images of the mysterious woman's charred remains.

Chapter Thirty-Four

The alarm went off at six fifteen, and Lorne turned it off before Tom had time to register what the noise was. Creeping around the bedroom, she gathered clean clothes and closed the door behind her. After grabbing a quick shower, she dressed and was ready for Pete ten minutes later.

Pete pulled up and found her standing in the porch, shivering, her hair soaking wet.

"Don't say a word," Lorne warned, jumping in the passenger seat. She leaned forwards and turned the heater on full blast.

"But Tom was fine when I left. You must've rubbed him up the wrong way or somethin'."

"Let's just say he knows how to put a brave face on things when company is around. This is hopeless. I'll dry my hair in the ladies' at the mortuary. Put your foot down, Pete, before I catch my death."

"And you wonder why I ain't married?" he mumbled under his breath.

When they arrived, the mortuary only had a couple of lights on. Pete shook the front door until Jacques appeared.

Taking in her appearance, Jacques looked up at the sky. "I wasn't aware it had been raining."

"It hasn't," Pete retorted sharply as Lorne rushed off to the ladies' room.

Once the pair of detectives had changed into the required protective clothing, they joined up with Arnaud in the mortuary. Pete stayed in his usual position, and Lorne stood beside Jacques like she always did.

"No Bones today?" Lorne asked.

"I told him to come in later; he'll be here about nine. There was a motorway pile-up to deal with last night—we didn't leave here until about two this morning."

"You should have rung me. I would've come in later. What's that look for?"

He eyed her suspiciously as he pulled on a pair of latex gloves. "I told you to go home and rest. If that's what rest does for you, I can see why you are a workaholic."

"Thanks. Didn't realise I looked that bad. Leave it, Jacques. Please." She glanced over at Pete, who was watching them through slanted eyes.

Jacques understood what she meant, and he whispered out of the corner of his mouth, "We'll talk about this later, when the evil eye is not watching our every move."

The post-mortem commenced. "The body is that of Sandra Crayford, aged fifty-eight, five feet five inches in height," Jacques said.

"How do you know who the victim is?"

"At the scene, we found the woman's handbag. Her driving licence and other ID were inside. It's over there on the bench."

The bench in question was within Pete's reach, and Lorne motioned for him to take a look. It was understandable that they hadn't noticed the bag at the scene; they'd been otherwise engaged, trying to put the fire out.

Jacques went on, "She has an ID badge that indicates she was a social worker." He examined the body, noting out loud all the bruises he found, for the tape's benefit. "Ah, this is strange. There are a series of indentations like this one here." He pointed to a mark on the woman's chest.

Lorne leaned over the charred remains to take a closer look.

"Two marks about a centimetre apart. What do you make of that, Inspector?"

"He used an implement that has two points. What about a garden fork, maybe something like that?"

"You mean like this?" He held up an evidence bag with a garden fork inside. "It has three prongs, which are pointed. They would have pierced the skin."

"Dare I ask? Did you find that near the body?" She knew what his answer would be before he even said it.

"Not near the body—*in* the body, just like the others. It was embedded in her vagina. The marks I have here would have been made by a blunt object, not one that is pointed."

"What about the end of a crowbar?" Pete asked as he sorted through the contents of the woman's bag.

"Come over here and take a look," Lorne said.

"I'm fine where I am, thanks!"

Lorne tutted. "Make yourself useful. Go and see if there's one in the boot of my car?"

"What the heck are you doing with a crowbar in your car?"

"It was precautionary. You know, the Gripper Jones case? Why the hell am I explaining this to you? Get it now, Pete. Please."

"Okay, okay. Keep your knickers on." Pete blushed when he realised what he'd said, and in whose company. He quickly left the mortuary in embarrassment.

"Don't go outside in those clothes," Jacques shouted after him. He turned to Lorne. "Now we're alone. Tell me what happened to you last night?"

Lorne tried to brush it off as just another sleepless night that went hand in hand with the job, but Jacques was having none of it. He pressed her for an answer.

"A mixture of things I suppose. Having to put out a burning body affected me, badly. Guilt, because I think I could have prevented this or at least delayed it. The fact that I could be the killer's next victim, or there's always the argument I had with my husband when I got home. Take your pick. Does that add up to a sleepless night in your book?" She managed a weak smile.

"Did you make it up with him?"

"No. Pete picked me up before he woke from his drunken stupor." She shrugged. Her eyes darted around the room, looking anywhere but at Jacques.

"Does he have a drinking problem?"

"Only after an argument. He thinks it solves his problems."

"And does it?"

"I wouldn't know. I'm not around him that much. He's just feeling sorry for himself and chose to take it out on me. Don't worry. I have broad shoulders. It'll blow over; it usually does."

"You shouldn't have to put up with that. Does he know how demanding your job is?"

"That's the problem—the job, I mean. Because I accepted promotion, I spend less time at home with him and Charlie. I think the crux of the matter is that he feels isolated. He spends every waking minute of the day at home. He gave up work years ago, and now it's proving impossible for him to find a job. It was his decision to become a house husband. My workload won't allow me the time to sort things out at the moment. He'll be fine when I get home tonight, I'm sure."

"I might speak out of turn here, but to me he sounds selfish. Especially when it was his decision to give up work."

"That's right, but look at it from his point of view. You'd go mad if you were confined to four walls most of the day, cleaning up after two women."

"I'm afraid, *ma chérie,* I wouldn't have allowed myself to get into such a position in the first place. I repeat it was *his* choice. I have plenty of married friends where the wife is at home all day. They appear to survive better than your husband does. Life is, after all, what you make it. Tell him to get a hobby or do some decorating if he's that bored."

It was pointless making excuses for Tom to a person she barely knew herself. She quickly changed the subject. "Was it a big pile-up?"

"Sorry, I don't understand?"

"Last night. Was the motorway pile-up a big one, many fatalities?"

"Ah, the typical swift change of subject. I thought you were better than that, Inspector?"

Lorne noticed how hurt he looked and wondered why he would be interested in her dull marriage. *Or does he take pleasure in hearing about my husband's inadequacies?*

"It's a sore subject, that's all, Jacques. If you want me to start blubbering like a child then fine, but if it's all the same to you, I'd rather not let my sergeant see me with my defences down."

Before he could answer, she was relieved to hear Pete's heavy footsteps trotting up the corridor.

"Here it is." Pete held the crowbar in his outstretched arm. Lorne blew out a frustrated breath as she went to fetch it.

Jacques' hand brushed against hers as he took it from her. Their eyes met, his sparkled with amusement.

"If this matches, then we better start taking our psychic Miss Lang seriously," Lorne said. Jacques raised an eyebrow. She explained, "She thought the weapon was a bar with a hook and a point."

"It's a perfect match to the injury. I'll compare the other cases after I have finished the post-mortem. Now, where was I? Oh yes, the right ear is missing. I think we can assume it will reappear shortly through the post."

Jacques completed the post-mortem by ten thirty, giving Pete and Lorne thirty minutes to get to the funeral.

Chapter Thirty-Five

A van making a delivery to Sam's electrical store blocked the shortcut they wanted to take up Miller Street. Lorne tooted her horn, and the driver rudely aimed a V-sign at the car. Pete pulled the door handle, but Lorne managed to restrain him. In the end, she was forced to back up and go the long way round. They arrived at the church with only minutes to spare.

A large crowd was winding their way up the path to the entrance of the church. Oliver was just inside the door on the left, welcoming mourners acquainted with his mother. The upper-class were well represented amongst Belinda's friends. On the right, Colleen and her husband were greeting people paying their respects to Doreen. The pews on the left were already full, a stark contrast to those on the right—a reflection of the divide there'd been in the two women's lives.

Oliver smiled at Lorne and Pete as they approached. "Nice of you to come, Inspector, Sergeant." Oliver greeted them each with a firm handshake. "A place has been saved for you at the back." He pointed to a pew on the 'posh' side of the church.

"Thanks, Oliver. We'll talk later."

Once they were seated, Lorne and Pete started people watching. "Those two look totally out of place," Pete whispered. He nodded towards a couple in their fifties, sitting in the second row at the front—the wife was the only woman on the 'posh' side not wearing a hat. The other women in the congregation looked as if they were trying to win first prize on Ladies' Day at Ascot.

"They must be the Halls. Keep an eye on them. We'll have a word with them after the service."

During the service, friends of each twin read several touching eulogies before Oliver stood to make his speech. After thanking everyone for coming, he turned his attention to the investigation. Lorne thought he was about to slag off the police for not coming up with any significant clues yet, but to her surprise, he praised her team for doing their best with their enquiries. He finished his speech with a plea from the heart, urging all those gathered to help the police find the culprit who'd killed his relatives and bring them to justice.

Lorne even spotted Pete wiping away a small tear when the coffins were lowered into the family plot alongside Oliver's father.

"Mr. and Mrs. Hall, can we have a quick word?" The pair clung to each other as the detectives walked towards them.

"Who are you?" Mr. Hall demanded defensively.

Lorne flashed her ID. "We'd like a few words about your roles within the Greenaways' household, if you don't mind?"

"I see. I told a colleague of yours we don't know anything about Mrs. Greenaway's murder." Mr. Hall threw a protective arm around his wife's shoulder.

"Yes, but you neglected to tell her you'd had problems with a previous employer, didn't you, Mr. Hall?" Pete said.

"Can we talk about this somewhere else?" the man said, nervously glancing around.

Lorne nodded, and the couple followed the detectives to their car.

"So?" Pete asked.

"We were forced to leave our previous employers because Mrs. Mountbatten, the lady of the house, became neurotic. She was prescribed some new tablets for her nerves, and her mind started to play tricks on her. Her husband was an explorer and went away on expeditions for months at a time."

"What sort of things did she start imagining?" Lorne watched the colour drain from Mrs. Hall's gaunt face.

"It was a large house, and one night, just after midnight—we'd gone to bed hadn't we, love?" The woman nodded but her gaze remained lowered and focused on her lap. "Mrs. Mountbatten thought there was an intruder in the grounds. She'd seen a shadow from her bedroom window. I went outside to take a look but couldn't find anything. A couple of Dobermans roam the grounds, so if there'd been an intruder they'd have let us know. The dogs didn't even stir."

"What happened next?"

"When I went back inside, she offered me a glass of whisky, which I gladly took. It was a cold, frosty night in December. She was a bit agitated about something and told me she and her husband were experiencing…difficulties in the bedroom."

He gulped, then went on with his story. "Well, she started coming on to me. Playing with the hair on my chest, that kind of thing. I was uncomfortable and told her to stop. She took it as a come-on and started tearing at my dressing gown, trying to remove it. That's when Margaret came into the room. I think her scream startled Mrs. Mountbatten, and she tried to make out that I was coming on to her. It was a lie, and I told her so. She was ashamed, although she wouldn't admit it and ordered us out of her house. We left the next morning. We told the agency straight away. They queried it with the woman and called her bluff. They told her that if she wanted to press charges she would have to do it within seven days. She refused to get the police involved; the agency took that to mean she'd been lying and that we were telling the truth. That's why they kept us on their books. Then the Greenaway job came up, and we've worked there for over ten years. With no bother, I hasten to add."

"That must've been an awkward time for you both." Lorne suspected Mr. Hall was telling the truth, so her questioning went in another direction. "I wonder—did Mrs. Greenaway ever receive any strange phone calls or suspicious visitors that you can remember?"

"Not that I can recall. She was a nice lady, never uttered a bad word about anyone. Why would anyone want to kill a woman like that or her twin sister? They must be sick."

"That's what we intend to find out. Have you found another job yet?"

"The agency told us yesterday they've got another post for us. It's about ten miles from here. We start next week." The man sounded relieved as he squeezed his wife's shoulder. Mrs. Hall rested her head on her husband's chest and smiled at Lorne for the first time during their conversation.

"Keep us informed of your new address, won't you? You may be called as witnesses, if and when we catch the killer."

The Halls left the detectives at their car.

"They seem a nice couple," Lorne said, watching them walk away.

"I'll have to admit they do. They're damn lucky the agency stood by them. Usually, when toffs talk, people listen."

"Come on. I'll stop at the bakers in town and treat you to a baguette and a cream cake."

His eyes lit up. "Thought you were putting me on a diet?"

"Well, I need cheering up, and a chocolate éclair usually hits the right spot. What sort of boss would I be if I didn't get you one as well?"

The clock on the nearby church struck one as they arrived back at the station. Lorne noticed a note lying on her desk when she walked into her office. It was from the psychic, Carol Lang. It read: *Inspector, forgive me. Ring me if I can be of any further help with the case?* The women ended the note with her phone number.

"What's that?" Pete entered the room with two cups of coffee. He kicked the door shut behind him.

"A note from Carol Lang. I must give her a ring after lunch to see how she is."

"It galls me to admit it. But she was bang on with what she told us. A rabbit and a hat come to mind."

"Actually, I reckon she pulled the whole cast of *Watership Down* out of it. She was amazing. Don't tell me you've changed your mind about mediums?"

"Small, *medium*, or large, it would take a darn sight more than that to alter my views entirely. There's always the possibility of her working with the criminals." Pete smirked.

"Ever the cynic, Pete. I think we should continue hunting down the rest of the drivers this afternoon."

"Fine by me. I'll pull the file after lunch."

There was a knock at the door.

"Come in," Lorne shouted.

Tracy peeked in. "Sorry to disturb your lunch, ma'am. The chief would like to see you ASAP."

"Thanks, Tracy. How far did you get with the list of sex offenders?"

"About a third of the way through the list. Looks like the word has got around, though. Every time we knock on a door, the bloke seems to be expecting us. We're checking through some alibis, but so far, they're coming up smelling of summer blooms rather than shit. We'll keep on the trail until it goes cold."

"Keep me informed. By the way, tell Molly we've questioned the Halls and I'm satisfied we can scrub them off the list, too."

Lorne took a bite out of her éclair as she rang Carol Lang. "Hi, Carol. Sorry we had to run off the way we did. How are you feeling?"

"Inspector, how nice of you to call. Please tell me what you found?"

"I have some bad news. We found the woman we were after. Unfortunately, we couldn't save her. Carol, I was wondering if you've ever helped the police out on an investigation before?"

"No, never. I haven't had my skills for that long, you see. I was involved in a near-fatal car crash about three years ago. That's when I got the calling from God. When I was lying in my hospital bed, I saw a bright light. At one point I was levitating over my body. Obviously it wasn't my time to go because I was sent back. After that, I discovered my gift."

The psychic's tale fascinated Lorne. "Were you religious before the accident?"

"Not in the slightest." She laughed softly. "Never stepped foot in a church, apart from the odd wedding and funeral that is. They give me the creeps. It would mean a great deal for me to help on the investigation, especially as I'm having these visions. It would be good to make sense of them, Inspector."

"I'll have to find out what the correct procedures are. Obviously there's the matter of confidentiality to consider. The last thing we want or need is the media knowing details about the cases. It would be far too upsetting for the families of the victims. Give me a few days to do some digging, and I'll get back to you. Saying that, if you have another vision in the meantime, please contact me or a member of my team straight away."

"I will. Please pass on my condolences to the family of the victim. And sorry I wasn't able to help sooner."

"I'll be in touch." Lorne hung up the phone.

"Christ, I hope the new chief is okay with that." Pete shoved the last mouthful of cake in his mouth and swilled it down with a swig of strong coffee.

"That reminds me: I've been summoned by the old one." She brushed the crumbs off her face and lap, tidied her hair, then set off.

She heard the mumble of voices coming from the chief's office as she approached. His secretary opened the door to announce her.

"Ah, here she is. Lorne, come in; join us. I'd like you to meet your new chief inspector…"

The chief continued talking, but his words drifted past her. Lorne's mouth fell open. The man rose from his seat, his athletic frame blocking out the light filtering through the chief's window. His jet-black hair had wisps of grey running through it. His suit was obviously designer—proof, if any were needed, of how far he had climbed up the police ladder.

As he stretched out his hand to shake hers, she caught a glimpse of his immaculate white cuffs, fastened with gold cufflinks that glinted in the glare from the overhead light.

She felt anchored to the spot. Her reaction amused him, evident in the twinkle of his smoky-grey eyes. He cleared his throat, and she glanced down at his outstretched hand. Lorne wiped her sweaty palm down the front of her skirt before slotting her hand into his. He squeezed it, crushing her fingers so they overlapped. He smirked, but she was determined not to wince or cry out in pain.

"…Sean will be taking over from me on Monday. Sorry, do you two know each other?" the chief asked, watching the sparks fly between them.

"Let's just say our paths have crossed once or twice before— haven't they, Lorne?" He winked, and an ominous shiver shot up her spine.

She was relieved when he didn't let on to the chief just how *well acquainted* they'd been in the past. "It's been a while, Sean," she said.

"Ah, times have certainly moved on. I'm afraid you'll have to call me 'boss' or 'Chief Inspector' now, Lorne. It's a little less familiar, don't you agree?" His smirk deepened as her cheeks turned pink.

"Of course. I won't make the same mistake twice."

"We've just been discussing you, Lorne," the chief said as they all sat down.

Lorne focused on her current chief and raised an eyebrow. "You have?"

"Yes, I've been filling Sean in on your latest case. Told him how the killer has been contacting you and that you believe he's watching you. We've decided it'd be best if you took the weekend off. Have some 'R&R', and then start afresh on Monday. Let's be fair: It's been a while since you had any time off; you'd certainly benefit from it. What do you think?"

"With respect, sir, I think I'd rather stay on the case over the weekend. Try and catch the killer before he targets someone else. Correct me if I'm wrong, but that'd be extremely difficult to achieve if I'm sat on my backside at home."

Roberts broke in before his counterpart could speak. "I'm afraid it isn't open to discussion, Lorne. I need my best DI in *top form* when I take over on Monday. I heard on the grapevine that you did an excellent job on the Gripper Jones case. When did you last have a day off?"

"I can't remember." Lorne's heart raced in annoyance.

"I'm sure—Tom, is it?—would be happy to spend a weekend with you for a change?" His eyes challenged her, and Lorne's gaze dropped to the floor. *How dare he mention Tom!*

A forgotten hatred she'd successfully kept buried for the past thirteen years bubbled to the surface. *Is this Sean's chance to get revenge?* Was he about to make her life a misery, the way she and Tom had once made his? She could feel the thumbscrews turning already. Maybe she should throw in the towel now, before she gave Sean the opportunity of sacking her?

"When you know me better, *Chief,* you'll realise I'm a workaholic. I tend to do my best police work when I'm under pressure. Tom accepts that my career comes first," she said, trying to disguise her temper.

"I've heard all I need to hear about you, Lorne. I've followed your career closely over the years. I *insist* you take the weekend off to replenish your resources, then we can tackle the case on Monday, together."

Lorne backed down, realising it would be pointless to argue further.

"I know when I'm outnumbered. You win. I'll knock off at five tomorrow and return for duty at eight on Monday morning." She exhaled a deep, irritated breath and got to her feet.

Roberts' voice followed her to the door. "Have a long weekend, Inspector. Finish at five tonight and report back at nine on Monday, not eight. I look forward to working with you, *Inspector*."

Lorne was seething but determined not to show it. Turning, she smiled at the man who'd been her mentor over the years. "Are you having a farewell drink, sir?"

"I'll come back after you've solved the case. I know that won't be long. Take care, Lorne. Regards to Tom and Charlie." His smile was full of regret. *Is he sad he's going or guilty about leaving me in Sean's tyrannical hands?* It was an absurd thought, because he didn't have a clue what Sean was like. She, unfortunately, knew Sean Roberts very well.

Chapter Thirty-Six

Lorne slammed the door to her office behind her. Pete entered moments later and found her sitting at the desk, her head buried in her hands.

"What's up?" he asked, dropping into the chair opposite.

"I need time to cool down, Pete, if you don't mind." She picked up some files, stomped over to the filing cabinet, thrust the files away and closed the drawer with a force that made the cabinet rock.

"I take it all this aggression is because you just met the new chief?"

"How do you know that? Have you been spying on me, too?"

"Don't take it out on me, boss. Hey, Molly and Tracy are in a right dither over him. Told me he's really good-looking. I can see Mitch's nose being put out of joint."

Her frustration grew. "You know what they say—never judge a book... I've got to get out of this place. Come on. Grab the taxi driver's file. I'll just nip to the ladies' and meet you at the car."

* * *

"Are you stupid? Why take unnecessary risks? You were an idiot to burn the body in daylight like that, do you *want* to get caught?" The woman nervously shuffled her feet.

"I wanted to show that Inspector I was angry with her. I'm sick of her not taking me seriously." The man rifled through the newspaper, agitated he couldn't find the story about him and his handiwork.

"She's just slow, that's all. I'm sure she's taking you seriously; she'd be foolish not to."

"Maybe we'll help things speed up a bit, then. What do you say?"

"How?" the woman asked.

"I'm gonna snatch that Sedark woman in broad daylight. Let's see what Simpkins thinks of that. And if that doesn't work, we'll *make* the inspector take us seriously."

"She's bound to make the connection soon, take things easy."

"I like playing with the woman." The corner of the man's mouth lifted.

"And if she catches you, where will that leave me?"

"I'll never leave you, love. A few more days, and it'll be over. Then we'll get our lives back. Time to start afresh."

The two hugged, and the woman sighed contentedly as the man kissed her forehead.

* * *

"Who's first on the list?" Lorne's foul mood lingered.

"Do you want to continue with the ones who were sent down on sexual assault charges, or do you wanna start at the top?"

"Sexual deviants *first*."

"Tommy Adams. Lives ten minutes from here on Dune Street, another rough area."

"Nice to see they stick to the same parts of town. Just like sewer rats, they seem to know their place."

"Forty-nine—here it is, boss."

The windows of the house were boarded up, and the front wall was crumbling. As they walked up the three steps to the door, Pete pointed to the drainpipe coming away from the wall, probably because someone had climbed up it to reach the first-floor flat.

A man in his mid-fifties, wearing a stained vest and jogging pants opened the door.

"Yeah, what d'ya want?" He took a drag from his cigarette and spluttered as he inhaled.

"We'd like to ask you a few questions about Kim Charlton." Lorne and Pete flashed their warrant cards.

"Who? Don't know anyone by that name."

The man tried to shut the door, but Pete thrust his foot in the way. "Listen, buster, it's your choice—either you answer our questions here, or we do it down the cop shop. What's it to be?" Pete sneered, pushed the door back, and burst into the hallway.

"Hey, you can't come bursting in here like some maniac. I got rights."

"Boss, have you got your cuffs handy? Guess we'll have to take this prick in after all."

"What the... There's no need for that. I told ya, I don't know any Kate Charlton."

"Kim Charlton. Her name's *Kim* Charlton. She's a regular punter with your firm," Lorne corrected him. She looked over her shoulder at the small crowd gathering in the street.

"I ain't never picked her up, I swear. Check with the friggin' firm; they'll tell ya."

"Last Thursday, one of your colleagues was supposed to pick her up, he couldn't make it. Did you pick her up?"

"What time last Thursday?"

"Sometime between eleven and half past, at night."

"Nope, I was one of the drivers that was told to stay in town. We usually stay outside the Rose and Crown pub. They start kicking out early down there 'cause they've had a lot of problems with customers getting rowdy after hours."

"How many of you were down there? Who were the others with you?" Lorne asked.

"Let me see. Len was there, and young Aiden," the man said, eyeing Pete warily.

Lorne consulted her list and verified the names in full with Adams. "Len Dixon and Aiden Cole?"

"That's them. I can vouch they were with me about that time."

"Did any of them pick up a fare from the pub around then?" Pete asked.

"Maybe. I can't be that definite."

"But they could've?" Lorne asked, and the man nodded. "If they had, maybe one of the fares wanted to go near the girl's address. They might've dropped by and picked the girl up—is that possible?"

"Not really. The boss tells us to drop off quick and get straight back to the pub."

"Okay, thanks for your help, Mr. Adams. If you remember anything else, will you give me a ring?" Lorne handed him a business card, and she and Pete left.

"Guess that just made the list smaller by three names." Pete grumbled to himself.

"Who's next?" Lorne checked her watch. Four o'clock. One more visit, then they'd call it a day. She had no intention of working a single minute past five, as instructed by her new boss.

Fred Falconer was next on the list. He lived in a better suburb and had a wife and two kids. He openly answered their questions in front of his wife. Lorne knew if he'd had anything to hide, he wouldn't have done that. They headed back to the station.

"It's time for me to knock off," Lorne told Pete as they pulled into the car park.

"Huh. It's only five o'clock. You never knock off at five. You feeling okay, boss?"

"Fine. I've been *ordered* to take a long weekend off. I won't be in again until Monday."

"Hmm... So that's why you've been grumpy all afternoon." Pete nodded slowly.

"I have not," Lorne bit back.

"Have too. What's going on? What's the story with you and the new chief then? Got a past together, have ya?"

"Yes, Sean Roberts and I have come across each other before."

"What's he like? You gonna tell me about him?"

"No, I think it's best if you make your own mind up about him. He'll show his true colours soon enough; I'm confident of that."

"You can be so bloody frustrating at times. What about the investigation?"

"I'm leaving things in your capable hands."

"Gee, thanks. Does that mean I have to deal with Arnaud?"

"Yup, you're the leading investigator, for the weekend at least. He's a softie once you get to know him."

"I'll take your word on that. One thing's for sure, though: I don't intend to spend the night with him like you did, just to get in his good books."

She refused to rise to the bait and issued him a warning glance. From Pete's expression, he knew he'd overstepped the mark.

Chapter Thirty-Seven

On her way home, Lorne stopped at the local off-licence. Her mood had already improved since saying goodbye to her partner. During the drive she'd been thinking how she, Tom, and Charlie could spend the weekend together. Maybe she'd take Charlie swimming or perhaps all three of them could go away on a spur-of-the-moment camping trip. *Hmm...wrong time of the year for that!*

The silence hit her as soon as she opened the front door. Maybe Tom had taken Charlie shopping or to the arcades as a treat. It wasn't as if he was expecting her home early. She wandered through to the kitchen and shivered at the coolness of the tiles on her bare feet. When she put the bottles of white wine in the fridge she noticed how bare it was. *That's strange. Tom always goes to the supermarket on Thursdays; complains the huge queues are hard to handle on Fridays.*

Opening the kitchen cupboards, she found them nearly empty, too. What was Tom playing at?

It wasn't until she placed the bottle of whisky she'd bought for Tom in its usual place that she spotted the note.

Lorne, I've taken Charlie to Mum's for a few days. Maybe the break will do us good. It'll give us the time we need to reflect on our marriage. I need to consider if it's worth the time and trouble anymore! Don't bother ringing; I need to see if I miss you. At the moment, I can't bear to be near you. I've told Charlie you're going away on a course for a couple of days, so she won't be expecting to hear from you either. Tom.

He must be joking. This can't be happening. For God's sake, Tom, don't abandon me now. Her hands trembled as she read the note five or six more times. Opening the whisky, she said aloud, "Oh my God. He's left me." She poured a large glassful.

What the hell was happening to her life? She felt as though she'd been dumped in the middle of an ocean, not knowing if she was going to drown or be able to stay afloat. Her chances of survival lay ominously in the hands of the people around her.

Why was life being so harsh to her? Why now? She didn't deserve this.

She needed a lifeline to reach out for. Taking a leaf out of her husband's book, she turned to the whisky for comfort, and collapsed into bed about ten.

Friday morning was a non-event. Eventually, Lorne stirred at one in the afternoon to the distant sound of the phone ringing. The answerphone kicked in, but the person calling didn't leave a message. Her head pounded as she struggled to the bathroom, then, standing under the cold water, she showered for a couple of minutes.

She couldn't face the thought of eating. What was she going to do for the next three days without her family around? She hated shopping at the best of times and couldn't stand the thought of traipsing round the supermarket by herself. What about doing some gardening? That was pointless, too. It was bucketing down outside, adding to her misery.

After tidying the house, she picked up a book and read for a few hours, only to give up on the latest blockbuster when she found the plot confusing.

During the afternoon, the phone rang continually, but she was in no great rush to answer it, and the caller stubbornly refused to leave a message on the machine.

She was in the kitchen deciding what to cook for dinner when the doorbell chimed. Before she'd shut the fridge door, the bell rang again.

"Give me a bloody chance!" She walked up her long narrow hallway.

Her scowl turned to surprise when she opened the door.

"I've been calling you all day, *ma chérie.*"

She felt a mess and hid behind the door. "Jacques! How did you get my address?"

"Ah, that is for me to know. Is there any chance of you inviting me in out of this rain?" His hair was plastered to his face, but it didn't detract from his boyish good looks.

"I'm not really up to receiving visitors," Lorne said, still shielding herself with the door.

"Would you like me to go?"

When she saw how hurt he looked, she relented, pulled the door open and walked back up the hall.

"Where do I put my coat?" He stood in the puddle he made on the Minton tiles.

"On the rack at the end of the hall. Come on through when you've done that." She pointed at the rack and disappeared into the kitchen.

"This is fantastic. Have you been here long?"

"A few years. It wasn't like this when we bought it. We've been busy renovating it—or, rather, Tom has. I was just about to make dinner. Would you like to join me?"

"Are you eating alone?" His right eyebrow shot up.

"Not if you join me. Yes or no? I can't promise a gourmet meal. It'll just be something quick and easy," she told him, mulling over the contents of the fridge.

"I would love to, *merci*. Can I do something to help?"

"Open the wine for me. I can manage the preparation. Anyway you've been at work, today." She handed him a bottle of Chablis and a corkscrew.

"And why haven't you been at work today? Are you ill?"

"I had a few days holiday owed me." She opened a tin of tomatoes and poured them in a pan. "Pasta and tomato sauce okay? I'm afraid the cupboards are a little bare. I planned on going shopping today but never got around to it." She watched him take in her dreary appearance and felt the colour rise in her cheeks.

"I love pasta. It will be good for my waistline. I'm afraid I eat far too many take-aways."

"You'd get on well sharing a place with Pete." Lorne laughed, surprising herself.

"I like it when you smile."

The colour in her cheeks deepened.

"I'm sorry. I didn't mean to embarrass you."

She peeled and chopped a couple of onions and threw them in a pan, then sliced up half a dozen mushrooms, adding them to the onions. Her eyes watered, and she reached for a tea towel to wipe them. It only made them worse. After removing the pan from the stove, she sat on the stool beside Jacques and sniffed, trying hard not to cry.

His arm draped around her shoulder, and she could no longer hold back her tears. "Forgive me, Jacques. I don't usually cry like a baby in front of strangers."

"Is that what I am? A stranger, Lorne?" His arm slipped from her shoulder.

Her eyes met his, and she could see the hurt her thoughtless words had caused. "No…I didn't mean to sound so harsh. Forget I said it. I'll get on with dinner; you must be starving."

She attempted to get off her stool but he stopped her. "Lorne, please tell me what is wrong. I might be able to help."

She felt soothed by the mellow, comforting tone of his voice. *What is it about his French accent that makes my heart race?* "My life's a mess. There's nothing you can do to help."

"At least let me try. Let me in to your confused world. My dear mother used to say it is far harder to help if a problem remains hidden."

Lorne smiled as she studied his face. She was tempted to run her hands through his soaking wet hair but managed to resist. "We have a similar saying in this country, too. A problem shared is a problem halved."

"There you go, then. So share with me."

"If I took the trouble to sit down and analyse my problems, they probably wouldn't seem half as bad."

"You're wasting time. Tell me."

His persistence paid off, and she told him what was troubling her, glad that she didn't break down again.

"So this Sean Roberts—you say you know him, but I don't understand why it should upset you so much. The old chief departing and the fact that the killer keeps ringing you—I can understand how those things might upset you. But why Roberts? What did he do to you?" One hand remained on his thigh and the other rubbed her arm, coaxing the troubles from her.

"It's not so much what *he* did to me. It's more what I did to him. We used to be an item, then I met Tom." Jacques looked puzzled, so she enlightened him. "An item—we were together, boyfriend and girlfriend."

"Ah, I think I know where this is going to now."

"We were together for two years—he wanted us to share a flat, but I couldn't. I told him I wasn't ready for commitment. He grudgingly accepted that, but soon after, we started drifting apart. One day, my car broke down, Tom was a mechanic at the local garage. We hit it off straight away. I dumped Sean that night, and within two weeks, I was living with Tom. That's why he was so angry. He'd found out about our living together from a mutual friend. He caused a stink at work, calling me all sorts. He was hurt and annoyed. I'd told him I wasn't ready to commit and yet..."

"So how was the matter solved?"

"The chief inspector at the time summoned us to his office, reprimanded us, and insisted that one of us would have to be transferred. Sean jumped at the chance to move on. It took me a while to get back in the hierarchy's good books. Eventually my hard work paid off, and I got my long-awaited promotion a few months ago. That's when the problems started with Tom." Her voice was tinged with sadness.

"Talking of which, why is Tom not here, if you don't mind me asking?"

"That's why I'm so upset. When I got home last night, I found this note." She flattened the balled-up note lying on the counter and handed it to him.

"It's personal. Are you sure?"

She nodded, and Jacques read the note. When he looked up, she had tears trickling down her face. He jumped off his stool, closed the gap between them, and gathered her in his arms.

"I'm so sorry, *cherie*. Now I understand why you feel so devastated. A good cry will get it out of your system."

Yes, but will it bring Charlie and my husband back? She rested her head on Jacques' shoulder. The smell of his aftershave made something stir inside. Slowly she pulled away from him, their faces a few inches apart. Her mind raced along with her pulse. His eyes glanced down at her lips. *Oh my God. He's going to kiss me.* Their lips met in the gentlest of kisses. But no sooner had it begun than did it end.

"Lorne, I'm sorry. That was selfish of me. I fear I have made your troubles worse."

"It's okay, Jacques. It's not like you forced me to kiss you. We'll forget it ever happened. I wouldn't want it to spoil our friendship."

He gave her a smile. "I thought you were in the middle of cooking a meal?"

She jumped off the stool and pecked him on the cheek. "Thanks, Jacques."

They consumed the two bottles of wine she'd purchased the previous night and sat on the sofa chatting and laughing like a couple of long-lost friends who hadn't seen each other in decades. She laughed outrageously at the tales of disastrous dates he'd had since living in England. He told her how most women were repulsed and scared off once he revealed his profession to them. Lorne told him how she regretted not spending more time with her daughter. The one subject they sidestepped was her marriage.

They were interrupted at ten thirty when the phone rang. Lorne answered it on the fourth ring. "Hello?" The silence troubled her. "Hello? Tom, is that you?"

"Inspector, you were absent from work today," her accuser said.

Lorne clicked her fingers at Jacques. Covering the receiver, she whispered, "It's him." Jacques joined her, and she held the phone away so they could both hear. "I've taken a few days off."

"So you're not bothered about catching me, then?" the muffled voice asked.

"Why are you killing these women? What have they done that's so wrong?"

"You have a good reputation, Inspector. Surely if it's that good, you'd have worked it out by now?"

"You said you want retribution, for what?"

"It was time for them to suffer, the way we suffered."

"Who's 'we'?"

"Does promotion suit you, Inspector? Perhaps too much paperwork has affected your crime-solving abilities." He laughed, goading her. "Have you lost your *killer instinct,* Inspector?"

"Who is the last person on your list?" she asked, trying to outmanoeuvre him.

"I have no idea how you know about that, Inspector, but yes, it's true. There is one more person on my 'hit list', if you like."

"Meet me. We'll discuss things." Jacques pulled at her arm and angrily shook his head.

"When the last victim is out of the way, then we'll meet, Inspector. You can be certain of that. Enjoy the rest of your evening with the doctor. Answer me this—did you intend to drive your family away?"

The killer hung up before she had a chance to respond to his cruel accusation.

Tyres squealed outside, and Jacques ran to the window. "*Merde,*" he uttered under his breath.

"What did you see?"

"A car disappeared round the corner before I could see the number plate."

She slumped down on the sofa and buried her head in her trembling hands. He rushed to comfort her. "Why is he doing this to me, Jacques? How did he get my phone number? How did he know my address?"

"Lorne, does Tom know the killer has been contacting you?"

"No, I didn't get the chance to tell him. I'd better ring him in case he's in danger." Her hands shook as she looked up her mother-in-law's phone number in the small telephone notebook on the shelf next to the phone.

"Hi, Janet. It's Lorne. Is Tom there, please?"

"Hello, Lorne. Do you have any idea what time it is?" her mother-in-law snapped.

"I know. I'm sorry to be calling so late, but it's really important I speak with him."

"Well I'm sorry, Lorne, but he doesn't want to talk to you. Did you get the note he left for you?"

"Yes I did, but something has happened that he should be made aware of."

"Oh really, Lorne. Tom said you would try every trick in the book to talk to him and Charlie. He'll ring you when he's ready, and by the looks of it, I wouldn't waste your time standing by the phone."

"He can't keep Charlie from me. I'll take him to court if necessary." Lorne felt crushed. Her mother-in-law appeared to be revelling in her family's disruption. She'd never approved of Lorne anyway.

"Do what you have to do. As far as I can see, you and my son are finished, I'm sure of that."

"Just tell Tom I called, will you?" she told the vindictive woman before hanging up.

"A pointless exercise, I take it?" Jacques asked when she threw herself on the sofa beside him.

"His mother has never liked me—never been scared to show it, either. By what she just said, I think Tom's left me for good." She shook her head and held back the tears threatening to fall.

"I'm sorry, *chérie.* That's terrible, especially at a time like this. Perhaps if you don't contact him, he will realise he misses you. I know I would."

"Oh, Jacques, you're so sweet. I'm afraid that's not Tom's style. He's stubborn and pig-headed. He'll expect me to suffer a lot before he's prepared to back down and come home, if he ever does."

"Well, I'm not leaving you. I'll spend the night here on the couch," Jacques whispered, wrapping his arms around her.

She pulled away and kissed him on the cheek. "Would you mind? I don't think I could bear spending the night alone, knowing the killer is watching my every move."

"No problem. It would be an honour."

Chapter Thirty-Eight

The face at the window watched her breathing. The moon's glare highlighted his gruesome features. He waited for the right moment before easing open the sash window, climbing through and stepping into her bedroom. She bolted upright. "What do you want?" she whispered in fear.

His goading laughter filled her ears before his vicious tongue replied, "I want you, Inspector. It's your turn."

A scream rebounded off the walls—had it really come from her? Jacques burst through the door, wielding a poker and switched on the light.

"What is it, Lorne? Was there someone here?"

Sitting up in bed with the quilt tucked tightly under her chin like a frightened child, Lorne's gaze swept the room. "Oh God. I must've been dreaming, but it seemed so real."

"You're safe. I'm here. No one will hurt you." They both looked at the poker. "If someone tried to get in, I'd poke them to death." The tense atmosphere lifted, and they both laughed.

"Will you stay with me?"

"Will I be safe? You might think I am here to attack you and kill me in my sleep."

"You idiot. Get in." She pulled back the covers to reveal thick pink pyjamas. Still fully clothed, Jacques climbed into bed. They fell asleep wrapped in each other's arms.

The sun found a slight opening in the curtain and woke them at nine the next morning. After eating a leisurely breakfast, they decided to take a stroll in the nearby park. Standing by the boating lake in the centre of the park, they watched the swans gracefully float past them. Lorne felt relaxed and trouble-free for the two hours they were there.

"I'd like to call in at the station, to pick up a file," she said as they strolled hand in hand towards the exit.

"I think you should sort out a trace for your home number while you're there."

They had discussed the matter at length after she'd received the call the previous evening, but the thought didn't sit well with her. She considered it an unnecessary intrusion, but Jacques had argued and pointed out they stood a better chance of catching the killer if he got involved in a longer conversation with her at home.

"Okay, I'll sort it out when I'm there. Actually, I'm kind of glad Tom and Charlie are staying elsewhere at the moment."

Pete was surprised to see her when she called in to the station. Jacques insisted on staying in the car.

"Hi, boss. What's up? Didn't expect to see you till Monday," Pete asked as she swept past him and into her office. It was silly, but she felt relieved not to see him occupying her desk.

"Anything happen that I should know about?" she asked, hunting through her filing cabinet.

"Nope. Hey, what's going on? Come on. I can tell when something's up. Tell me?"

"The bastard rang me last night. He was watching the house." She continued flipping through the files, avoiding his eyes.

"Shit, what did Tom say?"

"He wasn't there," she mumbled.

"Jesus. What time did the freak call?"

"About ten twenty. Why?"

"Stop it. Dammit, will you stop what you're doing and tell me what went on?" He grabbed her shoulders and guided her to the chair then sat opposite.

"When I got home last night, Tom and Charlie had gone. He's left me and gone back home to mummy."

"Shit, and the killer was watching the house. He knew you were alone?"

She sucked in a deep breath and considered her response. "Jacques was there. Now don't look like that. He was concerned because I wasn't at work yesterday and called round to see me. It's lucky he was there. I was crapping myself, Pete."

His face twisted with anger the second she mentioned Jacques' name. "So he stayed with you all night?" he asked, through gritted teeth.

"Yes." she admitted cautiously.

"What did he say? The killer I mean, not …"

"He confirmed he has more than one person on his list. Then he told me he'd be willing to meet me."

"You're not *considering* it?"

"If it's the only way we can nab him, then yes, it's something I'm willing to do."

"I won't let you."

"You won't have a say in the matter, Pete. I'm still your superior. I may be off-duty at the moment, but this is still my investigation. You'd do well to remember that!" she warned him.

"We'll see. I'll get a trace organised for your line at home. Do you want me to stay at yours tonight, or will you have company?"

"That's not necessary. Jacques and I will be going over the case. He might spot something we've missed. Don't give me grief, Pete. I have enough to last me a lifetime already."

Apologising, he insisted on walking her out to her car. Before she had the chance to stop him, he marched up to the passenger door and yanked it open. Sneering at Jacques, he warned, "You better take care of her or—"

"That's enough, Pete. That's uncalled-for."

"Maybe, maybe not. I'll see you Monday." Pete stomped away, still shaking his head as he disappeared back into the station.

Chapter Thirty-Nine

Lorne and Jacques were going through her files when her doorbell rang. Jacques grabbed the poker and followed Lorne to the front door.

"Who is it?"

"Inspector Simpkins, it's Colin Sharp from work."

"It's okay. He's come to set up the trace. You can put your scary weapon away now, macho man." Grinning, Lorne ushered Jacques back to the lounge before opening the front door for her colleague.

Thirty minutes later they were alone again, busy trawling through the files.

"Your sidekick is correct about one thing." Jacques reached for his cup of coffee.

Lorne frowned. "Oh? What's that?"

"The killer's crimes are escalating. I found smoke in Sandy Crayford's lungs, which can only mean one thing: She was alive when he set her alight."

"Jesus, that poor woman. No wonder Carol Lang passed out, if she saw the crime through the killer's eyes—it must have been a terrifying ordeal."

"Do you believe in psychics?" he asked.

"Don't you? I must admit, before I met Carol, I was undecided. But so far, the accuracy of her visions makes it difficult to doubt her."

"It would take a lot to convince me. What makes you think it's a taxi driver you're after?"

"We found a Toni's taxi card at Doreen's house and in Kim Charlton's handbag. It's the only thing we've found to connect the victims."

"Is it possible he could work for another firm? Perhaps planted the cards as a diversion?"

"It's an interesting theory, but…Kim Charlton was a regular with the firm."

"Have you questioned all the drivers yet?"

"So far we've only spoken to a couple of the drivers. The only ones left on the list are those with minor burglary and ABH charges and a couple with no prior convictions. I plan chasing up the rest on Monday, providing Sean Roberts doesn't interfere."

"Okay. Next we should examine what the psychic told you. She mentioned two of the women were a mistake, which two and why?"

"It's possible that one of the twins could've been a mistake, but which one? Belinda was wealthy, the more likely to have gained enemies over the years, whereas Doreen was a retired headmistress. Both of them were widowed. We investigated Belinda's husband's death and found nothing suspicious. Apparently helicopter crashes happen quite often in bad weather. Doreen's husband died of natural causes, nothing untoward there."

"And you investigated the son—Oliver—thoroughly?"

"Don't you start. He's Pete's prime suspect. He's clear of any suspicion in my book, though. Besides, how would he know Kim Charlton and Sandy Crayford? He lives in Cornwall?"

"Sandy Crayford, a social worker. Lived and worked in the area for years. They have dealings with heads of schools, don't they?" Jacques frowned.

"'Retribution', the killer said. He also said that it concerned something that happened years ago. There could be a connection through their work. Social workers usually have to work in conjunction with schools. I'll delve a bit deeper into that on Monday. Come on. I feel like cooking."

Lorne grabbed his hand and pulled him into the kitchen. On the way home from the park, they'd stopped off at the supermarket for provisions. It was the first time in weeks she could honestly say she was looking forward to a decent meal.

She cried again while she peeled the onions. Jacques laughed, but they both froze when the phone rang. Lorne picked up a tea towel and wiped her eyes as she ran through to the living room, Jacques close behind her. The same time she answered the phone Jacques began the trace.

"Hello?"

"So much for calling me back. What the hell is going on, Lorne?"

She felt relieved to hear her sister's voice, even though it was full of anger. "It's okay. It's only my sister," she whispered to Jacques who was listening closely beside her.

"Who's there with you? Have Tom and Charlie come home?"

"Calm down, Sis. No, they haven't come home, and how in God's name did you know they'd left, anyway?" Lorne asked, feeling put out that her sister knew everything about her marriage from other people.

"For Christ's sake, Lorne, stop answering a question with a question. If Tom's not there with you, then who *is*?"

"It's a colleague from work, if you must know." Lorne blew out a frustrated breath.

"Male or female?" Jade responded quickly.

"If you must know, it's a male. Before you start, this has *nothing* to do with why Tom left me."

"Oh really, just how naïve can you be?"

"Look I don't want to fall out with you about this, Jade, so why don't you just tell me why you've called and let me get back to work," Lorne said, struggling to remain calm.

"And to think we used to be so close. I was ringing to see how you're coping without Tom and Charlie. I even had a stupid thought that you might like a shoulder to cry on. But obviously not, stubborn as a bloody mule that's you, Lorne. Even when I offered to help with your little *predicament* last year, you threw it back in my face."

"Jade, you promised me you wouldn't keep harping on about that. I'm going to hang up now before we get into a slanging match. It's obvious whom your loyalties lie with. For your information, I've tried ringing Tom, but he *won't* take my calls."

"But—"

"For once in your life, Jade, will you *listen* to me?" Lorne paused, waiting for her sister to retaliate, but to her amazement, the interruption never came. "Currently, I'm dealing with the worst case I've ever had to deal with, so I'd be grateful, *extremely* grateful, if you'd back off and give me—"

Before she had the chance to finish her sentence, Jade hung up.

"Shit. That's all I fucking need, a wounded sister." Despondent, Lorne walked back into the kitchen, Jacques at her heels.

They finished preparing dinner in silence, and it wasn't until they were halfway through the meal that Jacques enquired about what he'd overheard.

"Tell me to mind my business if you want, but can I ask what your sister meant? What happened last year? It upset you when she brought the subject up." Jacques reached across the breakfast bar and placed a hand over hers.

She toyed with the idea of telling him but found it difficult to divulge such a personal secret.

After a few minutes' silence, Jacques spoke again. "*Chérie,* I'm so sorry. It was rude of me to ask."

He looked sad, and Lorne felt guilty. "No, Jacques. It's fine. I'll tell you, I'm just trying to search for the right words. I've fought hard to keep it hidden, and it's difficult for me to just blurt it out." She stared at the half-eaten plate of food in front of her.

"If it is too painful, then don't tell me. But if you think I might be able to help in some way, then please open up to me." He gently squeezed her hand.

What do I have to lose? She prepared to unburden her guilty secret to a man she hadn't been able to bear being around a few days before.

"A little over a year ago...I had an abortion." She searched his face though tear-filled eyes for any kind of reaction. There was none. No sign of hate in his eyes, and his smile was one of reassurance. He nodded for her to go on. "Tom doesn't know."

Again she paused, waiting for a repulsed response, and again he waited patiently for her to continue.

She swallowed noisily before continuing. It was proving to be harder than she imagined. "We had always agreed we were only going to have one child, but then Tom changed his mind. He went nuts when he saw a packet of contraceptive pills in my bag. He made me stop taking them and after a few months, wallop, I was up the duff."

He raised a hand to stop her, querying her terminology.

"Sorry, I fell pregnant. I was frantic, didn't know what to do. So I lied and told him I was having menstrual pains, and the doctor thought I had an ovarian cyst. I told him I had to have an emergency operation and that the doctor insisted it would be dangerous for me to even consider having another child. I hated myself for lying to him, but I was adamant I didn't want any more kids." Lorne again avoided his gaze.

"So you had the abortion. What happened next?"

"You're gonna hate me for this part. Tom—in his infinite wisdom—had a secret vasectomy. I was astounded when he told me that as I'd been forced to have an emergency operation it was only fair he should do his part in preventing another dangerous pregnancy."

"Ouch! So I guess you got the better end of the deal."

"Only a man could think that." She let out a breath and said, "An abortion isn't exactly a stroll in the park, you know."

"I know. I'm sorry to tease, *chérie*. How long was it before you returned to work?" He looked perplexed, and she knew exactly what he was getting at—if only Tom had been half as smart.

"I returned after a few days' bed rest. I know it's usually about two weeks recovery after having such an operation. Fortunately for me, Tom isn't that well-informed about woman's operations, or maybe he's just not that interested."

"You know something, *chérie*?"

"What's that, Jacques?" Lorne raised a quizzical eyebrow.

"The more I hear about this bloody husband of yours, the more I dislike him. He gives a new meaning to the word *selfish. Merde!*"

"I think you're being harsh there, Jacques. Putting himself through a vasectomy could hardly be described as an act of selfishness, could it?"

Jacques shrugged. "Point taken. I apologise."

Chapter Forty

October 11, 2007

The gloomy weather mirrored Lorne's mood. She'd said goodbye to Jacques at the gate. At five to nine, she pulled into the station car park. The rain had just started. *Five minutes to spare. Just enough time to get settled before Roberts introduces himself to the team.*

"Have any suspects been pulled in, yet?" Sean Roberts asked as she pushed through the swing doors to the incident room.

A long silence welcomed her, and six pairs of eyes studied her, waiting for a reaction. A flush worked its way up her slim neck. *What the hell is going on?*

Pete's cough broke through the tension-filled room. "Er... No. We haven't managed to bring anyone in yet, sir." He shifted awkwardly as his gaze met Lorne's.

"Ah, Inspector, a little late, aren't we?" The chief asked, noting the time on his watch.

What the fuck did he mean by that? He'd told her to be here at nine. According to her watch, and the large clock on the wall behind her new boss, it was three minutes to.

"You told me to be here at nine, so here I am."

"No, I distinctly remember telling you to be here at eight. I wasn't aware that inspectors kept office hours of nine to five. We'll discuss this in my office later." He dismissed her as if she was something he'd stepped in. "You were saying, Pete?"

Pete's awkwardness was plain to see as Lorne swept past everyone and into her office. He cleared his throat again and continued reviewing the case with the DCI.

Lorne was seething, but she should've expected Sean to pull a cheap stunt like that. *How dare he undermine me like that in front of my team? If his intentions are to try and get rid of me, he'll have a bloody fight on his hands. Bastard!*

On her way in, the desk sergeant had given her a Jiffy envelope. Before opening it, she pulled on a pair of gloves. She saw similarities to the others she'd received. The address was written in thick black marker pen, so she was under no illusion as to whom the package was from. She rang Jacques straight away.

"Hey, missing me already? It's only been an hour since I left," he teased, but she wasn't in the mood for laughing.

"I was wondering if you could send one of your guys over to pick something up?" Her voice matched her sullen mood.

"I'm assuming another package has arrived. Wouldn't you like to bring it over yourself? I'm sure I could find time for a coffee in my busy schedule."

"I can't. The new boss wants to give me a bollocking for turning up late this morning. Can you make the necessary arrangements?" She hung up and sat down heavily in her chair.

"The new chief wants to see you in his office right away, boss," Pete said from the doorway.

Without saying a word to her partner, she stormed past him and marched up the long grey corridor to the chief's office. A secretary she hadn't seen before gave her a practised smile and told her to take a seat. The secretary disappeared into Roberts' office and came out again ten minutes later, notebook in hand. "Chief Inspector Roberts will see you now, DI Simpkins."

The taut back of Roberts' black leather chair greeted her. She stood in front of his desk while he talked on the phone, then his chair slowly rotated, and his eyes locked onto hers. When she couldn't stand his glare any longer, she walked over to the shelves of books in the arched alcove of his office but felt his gaze follow her every move.

When he ended his call, Lorne returned to stand in front of his desk. A smile reached his eyes, and she shifted uncomfortably before him.

The bastard isn't even going to ask me to sit down.

"You're looking good after all these years, Lorne," he said, a smirk playing on his lips.

Lorne didn't answer. She knew she looked good after all these years, but then, so did he. It didn't mean she still fancied him.

"Not keen on returning the compliment, I see." He picked up a pen from his desk and twiddled with it.

"What did you want, sir?" She'd wasted enough time already waiting around for him to make time to see her.

"I'd hoped our bitter feuding could remain in the past, but the look on your face tells me otherwise."

"You've made it quite clear how you want our relationship to be. Undermining me this morning hardly shows me you're making an effort, does it? If you still have a problem with me, let's thrash it out here and now. My team's a happy one, and I'd like to keep it that way," she replied calmly.

"Inspector, you've lost me. In what way did I undermine you?"

"Return to work at *nine* on Monday—those were the final words you said to me on Thursday afternoon. And what do I find the minute I step through the door after my enforced weekend off? I find *my weekly team* meeting coming to a close and you reprimanding me, in front of my staff, for being *late*. What exactly did you hope to gain from that little display?"

"I'm sure you must have misheard me, I definitely said eight. Anyway, that's beside the point. We have other pressing matters to attend to. From what I can gather from talking to *your team,* they seem to think you are well out of your depth with your current case."

She found it hard to believe her staff would even insinuate such a thing—she knew Pete would jump on anyone saying a bad word against her. There again, after the traumatic week she'd just had, nothing would surprise her anymore.

"How *dare* you!"

He gave her his best poker face and said, "DS Childs tells me four murders have been committed and not a single person has been called in for questioning yet. Why is that, Inspector?"

"Are you aware of how much work is involved in one murder case, let alone four? The amount of paperwork needed to sort through? As SOI, I have to attend all the autopsies. They're at least four to five hours long depending how brutal the crimes are…" she reeled off before pausing to take a breath.

"I see your temper is as fiery as ever, Lorne."

"For your information, sir, we were just about to start bringing suspects in when I was ordered to take a few days off."

"Convenient."

"Convenient or not, it happens to be the truth, *sir*. What else did my team tell you?"

"Um, let's see," he rotated his chair around 360 degrees to annoy her. "Ah yes, something about bringing a psychic woman on board. I hope they were pulling my leg with that idea."

She gulped noisily, and he smirked. "Actually, they weren't. If it wasn't for Carol, we wouldn't have found our last victim as quickly as we did," she snapped again.

"Ah that's just it, Lorne—your last victim was still a *victim*. You weren't able to save her, were you?"

"No, but—"

"Don't use her again. Do you hear me?" His eyes widened, warning her not to defy him.

"Childs also told me he suspected Oliver Greenaway killed his mother, but you refused to bring him in. I might have misheard him when he said something about your women's intuition told you he wasn't responsible for his mother's death."

You bastard, Pete. Wait till I get my hands on you. She fumed inwardly but then wondered if Roberts was trying to drive a wedge between her and her partner on purpose.

Calmly, she reassured him. "That's me just winding Pete up. He's a bit gullible. I always tell him it's women's intuition when my instinct tells me something relevant. Every copper works on instinct—or 'common sense', I think you blokes call it."

"So why didn't you bring Oliver in for questioning?"

"Simple—because he lives over two hundred miles away. And, he's not the type to go around killing his family off one by one. You are aware his aunt was the next victim, aren't you?" He nodded and motioned for her to continue. "Kim Charlton was sixteen, I couldn't see how there was a connection there when they lived so far apart. Finally, Sandy Crayford our last victim, had lived in this area all her life, I doubt very much if he's ever been in contact with her."

"Call him," the chief said, shaking his head in disagreement.

"Whatever you want. Do you want me to question him, or would you like DS Childs to have the privilege?" She hoped she'd disguised her frustration.

"I'll do it, if that's all right with you?"

"Fine by me. You'll be wasting your time, though."

"We'll see. What about this taxi driver, Wacko, is it? Do you have any intention of bringing him in?"

"We're waiting to see if his alibi checks out."

"Bring him in, and let Childs question him."

"Okay and what do you want me to do?"

"You can sit next door while both men are being questioned and observe."

"That's it?" she said, her frustration finally getting the better of her.

"Do you have a problem with that, Inspector? You'll find I'm very much a hands-on type of chief, unlike my predecessor, who was willing to let things move along at a snail's pace. We'll achieve better results doing things my way, you'll see. Arrange for the two men to be picked up. I'll expect them here by lunchtime. Get the Cornwall boys to bring Oliver in."

"I'll organise it right away." She turned and headed for the door.

"And, Inspector, it'd be better in the long run if you didn't fight me. I intend staying around this time. I've missed the old place."

Without saying another word, she closed the door behind her.

* * *

"Pete, my office. *Now!*" She stormed through the swing doors and headed for her office. Lorne was staring out the window when he entered a few seconds behind her.

"Yes, boss?"

"Take a seat, *partner,*" she said, still looking out the window.

"Have I done something wrong, boss?"

"I didn't know back-stabbing was in the Guide to Being a Good Copper handbook?" she snapped, her gaze fixed on a woman pushing a pram. *God, I miss Charlie so much.*

"Now wait just a minute—"

"If you're not happy being my partner, it wouldn't take me long to sign the necessary paperwork to ship you out. You only have to say the word."

"Whoa! Where's all this coming from?" Pete's face reddened with anger.

"Sean Roberts. I've just had a very interesting meeting with him. According to him you think I'm not up to the job."

"Hey, I wasn't the one who strolled in late for work. Blame the doc for that one."

She turned and glared at him. "I wasn't late! I was *told* to come in at nine. Since when do I turn up for work halfway through the morning?"

He shrugged. "Anyway, you weren't here, and he wanted filling in on the case. So—"

"So you thought, while the cat's away—"

"That's bollocks, and you know it. If you've got a problem with Roberts, don't go taking it out on me."

"Oh, my mistake, Pete. You know what? I thought I had a loyal partner. Obviously I was mistaken."

"In my defence, I only told him what he wanted to know about the case. I ain't said anything about you, but you carry on accusing me, and I'll go down the hall and tell him how I think you're screwing your whole fucking life up!" He thrust his chair back and marched towards the door.

Her nerves were in tatters. "Stop. Pete, wait. Sit down, please."

Pete kicked the door and leant his forehead against it. Guilt wrapped around her for questioning his loyalty.

They sat opposite and glared at each other. A few minutes later they'd both calmed down enough to hold a civilised conversation.

"Are you going to tell me who this geezer is?"

"Nope. You know I'd rather you make your own mind up about people," Lorne said, shaking her head.

"Well to me he seems an okay kinda guy. But if he can cause this much aggro between us, then I suppose he's a force to be reckoned with." Pete ran a hand through his thinning hair.

"He has an axe to grind with me from a few years back."

He nodded. "Come on, tell me."

"I owe you that much, but don't spread it around." Then she told him about their colourful past.

Pete gave a shrill whistle. "Guess we're both in for a bumpy ride, me being your partner and all."

"I'm sure it'll be all right, providing we don't allow him to play us one off against the other. Now, what happened over the weekend?" she asked, pleased their little spat was now behind them.

"I carried on where we left off. Went to see a couple of Toni's drivers with Tracy. We tracked all of them down, except one, a John Scott. His landlord gave him notice about six months ago, doesn't have a clue where he's gone. I was gonna go back to Toni today to see if she's got a new address for him."

"Does he have a record?"

"Naw, he was one of the clean ones on the list."

"Right. We'll do that later. In the meantime, the chief told me to bring Wacko and Oliver Greenaway in, wants them brought in at the same time. The plan is for you to question Wacko, while he tackles Oliver."

"And what does he want you to do?" Pete scratched the side of his face the way he always did when he wasn't comfortable with an idea.

"He wants me observing both interrogations. He obviously sees me as some kind of wonder woman. By the way, I received another package this morning. Jacques' sending someone over to collect it," Lorne said, busying herself with paperwork on her desk.

"Jacques, ay? What was in it? No, don't tell me: Sandy Crayford's ear?"

"Yup. Along with a note saying it was another part of the puzzle."

"Have you had any other calls from the killer over the weekend?" asked Pete.

"No, thank God. Have any missing women been reported?"

"Nothing has come to our attention."

"I'll get in touch with Cornwall CID; they can bring Oliver in. They should be here by about two. We'll pick Wacko up after lunch; we'll find out that other driver's address at the same time."

"Righto. Mind if I ask a personal question?"

"Now we're back on speaking terms, you mean? Go on."

"Did Tom leave because you're having an affair with the Doc?"

"Pete you're so wrong. You of all people know that Tom and I have been having problems for the last few months. Jacques has nothing to do with this. Don't blame him for something that's been on the cards for a while. And *I'm not*—I repeat, am *not*—having an affair with Jacques."

"It's just that at the beginning of this case you couldn't stand the guy and weren't afraid of showing it, but now…"

"I know. I admit I was wrong. There's a Dr Jekyll beneath his Mr. Hyde exterior. That reminds me—we went through my notes over the weekend, and he came up with a theory I think we should follow up on."

"What's that?" Pete looked unconvinced by Lorne's statement.

"Going back to what Carol Lang referred to with regard to two of the murders being mistakes. We were working on the theory that maybe Kim and Belinda were the mistakes and that there is a possible connection between Doreen the headmistress and Sandy the social worker."

"Logical, I suppose. Any thoughts of who might be the last name on his list?"

"Don't know. We didn't get that far. Let's pull these guys in, then we'll start digging into the two women's backgrounds. See if we can come up with any possible links."

Chapter Forty-One

Wacko appeared to be the one most unnerved by being hauled into the station. Pete was doing his bad-cop routine and not getting very far. "So, Wacko, your mate Lampard told us you always made sure you were available for when Kim Charlton wanted picking up. He also said you could set your watch by her. Always eleven o'clock on the dot, although the days varied. Did her parents set her a curfew?"

"How the fuck would I know?" The scruffy, unshaven driver sat with his head bowed, focusing on the plastic cup in front of him.

Pete paced round the interview room. "Come on, Wacko. She must've told you that in one of your pally moments?"

Wacko lifted his head, and he watched Pete pace. "Nope. She was just a ride, that's all."

"In more ways than one, I bet?"

"No way, man. She was sixteen, for Chrissake."

"Friendly sort though, wasn't she?" Pete pulled out the chair opposite the driver.

"Yeah, I suppose so. She wasn't shy; that's for sure."

"Did she tease you a lot, Wacko? Did you ever pick her up when she was wearing her school uniform? That must've turned you on. I know it would me." Pete stood up again and walked over to the two-way mirror. He grinned at Lorne and waited for the man to answer.

Wacko wriggled in his seat. *Maybe Pete's picked up on something.*

Lorne went from one side to the other, first observing Pete in action, then Sean Roberts. She found the chief to be a cool character during interrogations, but then, so was Oliver. Secretly, she was willing Oliver to give him hell, and at times, he did just that. Roberts lasted thirty minutes with Belinda's son. After releasing Oliver and apologising for inconveniencing him, Roberts joined Lorne in the observation room.

"Anything from this guy?" Roberts asked.

"Pete's been playing with him up till now. He's just started turning the screws a bit tighter," she explained, without taking her eyes off the taxi driver.

"Well. Did she tease you?" Pete asked the driver a second time.

"Not that I noticed." Wacko looked and sounded agitated.

"Now, we have it on good authority that you were livid that night. You know, the night she went missing?"

"Whoever told you that must've been lying." Wacko twisted his coffee cup in his hand.

"Finished with that?" Pete tore the cup away from him and slammed it into the bin in the corner of the room. "You told us yourself you drove around searching for Kim that night. You kinda said it matter-of-factly to me and my boss, as though it was no big thing. The trouble is, Wacko, your mates tell us a completely different story. They reckon you were *livid* you'd missed her that night. What's the real story with you and *young* Kim?" He placed two hands on the desk and leaned menacingly towards the driver.

"We were friends. That's all."

"And what the hell would a man in his mid-to-late thirties have in common with a *sixteen*-year-old girl?"

"We didn't do anything. I...swear we just talked."

"When DI Simpkins and I questioned you at the taxi office, you made a song and dance about not knowing which fare we were referring to. You pretended to go through the dockets your boss handed you. What was all that about?"

The man ran a nervous hand through his already scruffy hair, contemplating his response. "It was for Toni's benefit."

"Why?"

"If she found out I was keen on a punter, she wouldn't have let me pick Kim up again."

"I'll ask you again, Wacko, and this time I want the truth." Pete slammed his chubby clenched fist onto the table. "Did you and Kim see each other when you'd finished work?"

"Yes," the driver admitted, in a whisper.

Pete's gaze flew up to the mirror. "What? I couldn't quite hear you?"

"Yes, all right? Yes. We went for a burger once. I picked her up from school one day."

"Was it the uniform that did it for you?" Pete asked, the contempt evident in his voice.

"What kinda sick bastard do ya take me for? I liked her for *her*, not for what she was fucking wearing, man."

"What about Belinda Greenaway, do you know her?"

The driver looked puzzled for a few seconds before answering, "The old lady you found in the woods? Yeah, I've picked her up with her sister a couple of times. What about them?"

"What about Sandy Crayford? Does the name ring a bell?"

"Yeah, I seem to remember the name from somewhere. Why?"

"They're all dead, Wacko. *D-E-A-D*, dead. And you were acquainted with all of them. Can ya guess where I'm heading, now?"

"Shit, I get it. They're all fucking dead, and ya think muggins 'ere killed 'em all. You're out of your fucking tree, man."

"Am I, Wacko? We'll see. I've got a few calls to make. Be right back. Don't you go anywhere," Pete said, over his shoulder, leaving Wacko with a uniformed copper watching him.

"Excellent, Pete." Roberts patted him on the back when he joined them in the observation room.

"It's gotta be him. He knew all the victims. Knew where they lived and if they had family living with them or not," Pete stated, a smug grin across his pudgy chops.

"If I might offer a word of caution to the proceedings. Don't forget I've actually spoken with the killer. I'd have no problem recognising his voice again, and he definitely didn't sound like Wacko." Both men looked at her, astonished.

"Be fair, boss. His voice was muffled. You can't be sure what his real voice sounds like."

"Agreed. Where does he live?" Lorne asked, her mind racing.

"In a block of flats in Hillty. Why?"

"What's all this about, Inspector?" Roberts arched an eyebrow.

"We've already established the killer lives in one of two roads, roads that specifically back onto the railway line. Correct me if I'm wrong, but as far as I know, Hillty is nowhere near a railway line."

"Damn, I forgot about that." Pete appeared to be crushed by Lorne's observation.

"I'm not interested in that. I want *this* man charged with all four murders. Pete, get in there and arrest him. I'll get onto CPS. Let's get this case wrapped up now," Roberts said, anger stinging his voice.

Lorne grabbed Roberts' arm as he turned to leave the room. "Chief, you're making a big mistake. He's not the guy. If you arrest him, his solicitors would be rubbing their hands together, waiting for compo."

He glared at her hand, and she let go of his arm.

"Are we back to your women's intuition again, Inspector?"

"No, instinct. Plus a fair amount of fact, sir," she said, her tone full of sarcasm.

"Arrest him, Pete," Roberts ordered, dismissing Lorne's reasoning out of hand.

A red mist shrouded Lorne as she watched Pete make a fool of himself, arresting the man she was sure was innocent. When Pete told Wacko he was being arrested for the murders of four women, the poor man was rendered speechless, and while some people would take that as being a sign of guilt, Lorne's thoughts were to the contrary. She kicked the chair leg and cursed Sean Roberts for being the most stubborn man she'd ever met.

Lorne was still fuming when Pete marched triumphantly into her office an hour later.

"A job well done, I'd say," he said, throwing himself into the chair.

"We'll see when the forensics come back. I can't say I've ever arrested someone without having at least some form of evidence against them. Still, if that's the way Roberts wants it, let him dig his own grave. The rate he's going, it'll be twenty feet deep in no time at all."

Lorne picked up her phone and dialled. "Hi, Jacques. It's me. Look we've just arrested someone for the murders—against my better judgement, I hasten to add. If I send over a copy of his prints, can you see if they match those found at Doreen's and in the shed?"

"Wait a minute. Slow down. I am confused. Why arrest someone you're not convinced has committed the crimes?"

"It's a long story. Basically, the new chief went over my head and ordered Pete to arrest him. When can we expect the results?"

"If you bring them over yourself now, we can compare them right away."

"We're on our way." She hung up, and adrenaline coursed through her veins.

"I'm going with you, I take it?" Pete said.

"Of course you are. After we prove the prints aren't Wacko's, we'll get back on the trail of the drivers."

Pete whistled, then said, "The chief ain't gonna like this."

Fuck the chief, she felt like saying but decided against it. Instead she said, "Let's get out of here."

Chapter Forty-Two

"There it is in black and white. Conclusive proof that the man you have in custody is *not* the killer who carried out these barbaric crimes," Jacques Arnaud declared, not long after Lorne and Pete arrived at the mortuary.

Lorne gave him a satisfied smile. "On one hand that's great news, but on the other, our workload has just doubled." She stared down at the two sets of prints that couldn't be more of a contrast.

"How's that?" Pete asked.

Lorne blew out an exasperated breath. "Because of the chief's actions, we'll have to postpone going after the real killer until we've cleared Wacko. As if time wasn't against us enough."

"I have an idea," Jacques said with a glint in his eye. "What if I ring him and give him the good news. Will that help? Any grievances he has will be with me." He rubbed Lorne's arm in support under Pete's glare.

"It's worth a try. Be warned, Jacques: He's set in his ways. He's like a hundred-year-old oak tree standing firm in a tornado."

Jacques grabbed her shoulders spun her around and gently pushed her towards the door. "Leave Chief Inspector Roberts to me. Now shoo. Get out there, and find us a killer."

Once they were back in the car and en route to see the final driver on their list, Pete admitted, "Maybe I was wrong about the doc after all."

Twenty minutes later, when they entered the putrid-smelling taxi office, Mary greeted them with a face like a guard dog. She was tucking into a doughnut and had jam and sugar all over her chin.

"Toni's not here," the fat woman said, through a mouthful of doughnut.

"We'll wait for her." Lorne wandered around the office. Pete stood by the window, looking out.

Toni marched in ten minutes or so later, looking surprised to see them.

"Inspector, Sergeant. What can I do for you?"

"We've arrested Wacko, but we're still continuing our enquiries. Pete called on John Scott the other day, only to find he'd moved on six months ago. It would be great if you had a current address for him."

"You can't be serious. I would never have thought that of Wacko. Jesus, that poor girl." Toni dropped in the nearest chair, and the colour drained from her face.

"We've actually arrested him on four counts of murder. What about John Scott's address?" Lorne said.

Shaking her head, Toni walked over to where Mary sat. As usual, the controller gave the impression she wasn't listening. Lorne suspected the woman was soaking everything up like a sponge.

"Mary, what's John's new address?" Toni said.

"Haven't a clue."

"How many times do I have to tell you it's vital to keep personal information up-to-date? Is he on duty at the moment?"

"No. His address is around here somewhere, I just haven't had time to update his file."

Toni shook her head as she hunted through the pile of crap on the controller's desk. "At last. Here it is: 26 Clearmont Rd."

Lorne picked up on the glare Mary gave her boss. After thanking Toni, the two detectives stepped outside and sucked in a lungful of fresh air.

They pulled up outside number twenty-six as a man came out the front door. He froze when he saw them coming up the front steps of the large bay-fronted Victorian house. *Hmm... Convenient. Has someone tipped him off?*

"John Scott, we'd like a quick word. Mind if we come in?" Pete asked, stepping to within inches of him.

The man appeared surprised by Pete's abruptness. His hand shook as he placed his key in the lock. The old Parker jacket he wore had a tear under the right arm. Once inside, he removed his jacket and laid it carefully along the edge of the sofa. His five foot nine inches seemed to shrivel under the detectives' gaze. His shoulders slouched, and he dug his hands deeply into the pockets of his jeans. He had on an old-fashioned woollen tank top, the type a devoted aunt would knit a favourite relative. Underneath the tank top, he wore a short-sleeved blue and white striped shirt with a threadbare collar.

While Lorne surveyed the room, Pete bombarded the man with questions. John Scott assured Pete that he'd never met Kim Charlton. Wacko had told the other drivers to back off, and only Wacko was to pick the girl up.

Although the furniture was old and worn, the flat was meticulously clean and tidy. Lorne tripped over a lump in the rug. John Scott's gaze travelled with her. When she ran an inquisitive finger across the highly polished mahogany mantel, she was amazed to find it dust-free. An old gas fire served as the only form of heating in the relatively large room. The large maroon-coloured rug she'd tripped over covered rough-looking floorboards that showed signs of careless decorating around its edges. A tatty old painting of a galleon ship hung proudly on the wall over the fire.

Under the man's scrutiny, Lorne picked up a cheap imitation brass frame that showed signs of discolouration along one edge. In it was a photograph of John Scott with a woman. The couple were cuddling each other on a pier somewhere. *Is she a girlfriend, wife, a relative, or just a friend?*

Scott looked about twenty years younger, and the woman looked vaguely familiar. Lorne studied the man and then the photograph. When her gaze returned to Scott, he was smirking. His eyes widened, daring her to challenge him. She didn't. She felt strangely unnerved by the encounter, but why?

Lorne shuddered when they left the flat, and a cloud of uneasiness lingered. "Jesus, what a freak. Did you see the way he was looking at me? You asked him if he lived alone, didn't you, Pete?"

"Maybe he fancied ya." Pete laughed, and Lorne shuddered again. "Yeah, he told me he lived alone. Why?"

She pondered before answering him. "That's strange, because there's evidence of a woman's touch in that room. How many guys do you know who dust every day or plump up the cushions on their couch after they've sat on it?"

"You've got a point: not many. I know I ain't got time to do it. Maybe he's got a cleaner."

"Highly unlikely. I don't suppose you noticed the scratches he had on his neck either, did you?"

"Don't suppose I did, no," Pete admitted, tartly.

Lorne's phone rang. "DI Simpkins."

"Hello, ma'am. It's Tracy."

"Yes, Tracy, what's up?" Lorne picked up how nervous her colleague sounded.

"Sorry to bother you, ma'am, but you're needed back at base ASAP."

"Enlighten me?"

"Umm… It's important, ma'am."

"I understand, Tracy. ETA ten minutes."

Lorne's heart raced, and an ominous feeling swept through her.

Chapter Forty-Three

They barged through the swing doors of the incident room, both gasping for breath. The two distraught children, aged around eleven, were sitting at Tracy's desk immediately caught Lorne's attention.

Tracy hurried towards her and filled her in. "They arrived about an hour ago, ma'am. We've rung their parents; they're on their way. We haven't asked any questions yet, not until the parents arrive."

"I don't understand, Tracy. What's going on?"

"Sorry, ma'am, I should've said. The little ones ran into the station screaming. Apparently, their teacher called for a cab. She was going to drop them off on the way home. Out of the blue, the teacher said something to the driver. The kids said he blew his top and struck out at her. The kids got scared and jumped out of the car when he pulled over. They started shouting to draw attention to themselves, and the driver sped off, with the teacher still inside. They knew the station was close by and came here straight away to tell us. Up till now we've given them a drink and called for a doctor to check them over."

"Jesus, have they said anything? Like what type of car it was?" Lorne looked over at the kids.

"I tried to ask them without it sounding like I was questioning them, ma'am, and the girl thought it was dark green, but the boy seemed pretty sure it was a black Peugeot."

"Good girl. Ring Toni's Taxis. Make sure you only talk to Toni, no one else. Ask her what type of car John Scott drives."

"Right away, ma'am."

Lorne wandered over to the children and smiled broadly at them. "How are you two doing? I gather you've had a bad day." She pulled up a chair and sat between them. Pete stood behind, notebook at the ready.

The girl had swollen red eyes and was fiddling with a tissue in her lap. The boy's gaze looked glazed, as if he was reliving his ordeal in his mind.

Before the kids had a chance to answer, a WPC brought in the girl's frantic parents. The mother hugged her daughter as tears ran down her face. "Sharon, my God... Thank goodness you're safe."

"Don't fuss, Mum. I'll be all right. But the man...he took Miss Sedark. What's going to happen to her?" The young girl's eyes pleaded with Lorne for the answer.

"The more you can tell us, Sharon, the quicker we can find Miss Sedark. Do you know why the man hit your teacher?"

"He picked us up from school. She lives around the corner from us and sometimes gives us a lift. At first, he was quite chatty, and he asked Miss Sedark how long she'd been a teacher at school. She said about thirty years. Then the man kept asking her questions like, did she remember this and that from years ago?" The girl paused.

Lorne said quietly, "Then what happened?"

The girl let out a long breath and said, "Miss Sedark said she remembered the man—that was when he hit her. Lee and I jumped out of the car when the driver pulled over. I made as much noise as I could, Mum, just like you told me to, and no one came to help us. We knew the station was just round the corner, so we ran all the way. But he's still got Miss Sedark, Mum. We couldn't get to her."

The girl's mother hugged her again. "There, there, love. You did the right thing. So you do listen to your old mum, after all? I'm so proud of you, sweetheart."

"I know this must be hard for you, Sharon, but was Miss Sedark still conscious—I mean, awake—after the man hit her?" Lorne leaned forwards and rested her elbows on her thighs.

"No. I don't know if she was unconscious or dead," the girl replied, and a sob caught in her throat.

The doctor performed a brief exam and concluded that both kids were suffering from a touch of shock but felt they were tough enough characters not to have any lasting side effects.

Lee's parents arrived soon after, which meant that Lorne could direct her questions to both children. "Can you describe the driver to us?"

Lee started, "He had brown hair—"

"No, I'm sure it was blond," Sharon interrupted.

"How old would you say he was?" Lorne smiled at the kids.

"I'd say he was about forty," Sharon said, and that time, Lee agreed with her.

"Did he have an accent, or do you think he was from around here?"

"He was definitely from around here, 'cause he said Miss Sedark taught him years ago." Sharon looked pleased with herself.

Lorne stood up and took Pete to one side. "Look into John Scott's background, find out which school he went to and when. See if he's got any siblings too, will you, Pete? Jesus, I've just thought of something, Scott lives in Clearmont Rd."

Pete looked puzzled, and then the penny dropped. "It backs onto the railway line. Shit. You're right. It's gotta be him."

Before Lorne could respond, Tracy interrupted them. "John Scott drives a black Peugeot, ma'am. He was due to start work at five. Guess what? He neglected to turn up."

"Is Wacko still in custody?" Lorne asked the sergeant.

"He is."

"Do you know if Doctor Arnaud rang the chief?"

"I haven't got a clue, ma'am. I could find out for you."

"No, it's okay, Tracy. I'll go and see the chief myself after I've finished with the kids."

"I'll crack on. See what I can dig up on J.S." Pete walked towards his desk.

"Tracy, you come with me. We'll take down the kids' statements. I don't want to keep them hanging around here any longer than necessary. They've had a traumatic day."

* * *

Chief Roberts arrived as Lorne was recapping Sharon's statement with her.

"Can I have a word, Inspector?" he asked abruptly.

"I'm just about finished here, anyway. Thanks for all your help, Sharon. Now go home and get some rest. I don't want you worrying about Miss Sedark. You have my word that we'll find her, okay?"

"What's going on? Why wasn't I informed of this incident the minute it occurred? Why did I have to hear about it from my secretary?" Roberts demanded, anger making his mouth twitch.

"It all happened so quickly, sir. I didn't have time to tell you."

"Forgive me if I don't believe you, Inspector. Was it your idea to rush Wacko's prints over to forensics? I've had an irate pathologist on the phone, some guy with a French accent. He told me in no uncertain terms, he believes we're holding the wrong man for these murders. I smell a rat. Did you have anything to do with that call, Inspector?"

"First of all, we found prints at a few the scenes. I thought it only right we should check those prints against Wacko's. They didn't match. I didn't think they would. We've carried out all the relevant background checks on the guy, and nothing untoward has popped up. His alibi checked out. This guy's so innocent he hasn't even had a shit in the wrong place. If he had, I'd know about it." Her voice rose out of frustration. "Secondly, I *didn't* tell Doctor Arnaud to ring you. It's his responsibility to ensure he gives us the evidence he finds. He also, presumably, wants to make sure *innocent* people don't get thrown in prison due to aggressive policing."

"When you've quite finished, Inspector. It'd be wise for you to adopt a more respectful tone when you're speaking to a superior officer. I realise our situation must be unsettling for you, but the fact remains, that's exactly what I am: *your* superior. Do I make myself clear?" His eyes widened, and the angry twitch grew more intense.

"As clear as a nun's conscience, sir." Lorne said.

"What happened to the kids?" the chief asked sternly.

"Before I answer that, I'd like to know if I'm still the leading investigator on this case?"

"Have I told you otherwise?"

"No, but you ordered me to take the weekend off at a crucial time in the case."

"I think you'll find that decision was down to my predecessor, although I did agree with his decision. We hoped giving you the time off would flush the killer out into the open."

Holding back her temper, Lorne said, "Are you aware he contacted me at home, and his car was seen driving away from my house? Had I remained on duty over the weekend as planned, maybe, just maybe, my family wouldn't have been put at risk."

Roberts, looking sheepish, cleared his throat. "It was a regrettable mistake, and I can only apologise for the way things have turned out. Are Tom and your daughter all right?"

"Tom and I decided it'd be better if he and Charlie stayed at his mum's for a while. At least until we've caught the killer." She hoped the lie convinced him.

"Good idea. Look, I'll let Wacko go, but you need to bring in other suspects. Have you got any solid ones, yet?" he asked, mellowing for the first time since his return.

"Just the one. Pete and I questioned one of the taxi drivers today, John Scott. Just being in the same room as him gave me the willies." Lorne explained what happened and how she felt when Scott's eyes followed her around the room. "Pete's in the process of looking into his past now." He nodded, and Lorne felt he was, at last, taking her seriously. "One final thing, when we were at Scott's house I noticed some scratches on his neck. One of the victims, Doreen Nicholls, fought with her attacker, the pathologist found samples of skin, from the assailant, under her fingernails."

"Does this guy have a record?"

"Nope. Like I said, Pete's carrying out a more thorough check now. The guy gave me the jitters. He's creepy. Pete didn't pick up on anything, but then he's not a woman, is he?"

"Well, if your instincts are that strong, pull, him in. Hold on a moment. What about his voice? You've spoken to the killer; did his voice sound familiar at all?"

She shook her head. "Hard to say. His voice has always been muffled as if he was holding a cloth over the mouthpiece. Can you organise a warrant to search his house?"

"Leave it with me. In the meantime, pull everything on him—bank details, previous employment, the lot. Wasn't there some speculation about him having an accomplice at one point?"

"Yeah, we've got no idea if the accomplice is male or female, though. As soon as you get the warrant sorted, we can bring him in."

"Find out about the missing teacher, too, will you, Lorne?" Roberts asked.

"I'd like to organise surveillance on his house while we wait for the warrant to come through." Lorne surveyed the room for Tracy and Mitch.

"I agree. But if he's abducted the teacher, do you really think he'd be foolish enough to take her back to his home?"

"I can't answer that, but someone should be on the scene if he does. I'll get Tracy and Mitch over there. Can you sanction some overtime?"

"Just do what you have to do, Lorne. Leave me to worry about that side of things."

Lorne watched Roberts walk up the corridor to his office, unsure what the future held for her. She stepped back into her office and rang home, hoping Tom would've changed his mind and returned, but the answerphone kicked in. She thought about ringing his mum's house, but decided against it.

She was just on her way out of the office when the phone rang. Fear gripped her insides as she answered the call.

"Lorne, how are you, *chérie?*"

When Lorne heard Jacques' voice, she released the breath she'd sucked in. "Bearing up. I was just about to call you." She ran through the latest developments.

"That poor woman. We must remain optimistic. His previous victims have not been killed immediately. Perhaps it's his way of prolonging their punishment. If the victims are from his past, the mental abuse he subjects them to would probably be more satisfying than the actual murder itself. As soon as you get the warrant, ring me. I'd like to help conduct the search of his property, if you're adamant he's the killer."

"I just hope we manage to locate him before Miss Sedark becomes victim number five. When the warrant's in my hand, you'll be the first to know."

"I guess dinner is out of the question tonight?"

It seemed to be a daft question under the circumstances, but one she appreciated, nonetheless. "I'll be here all night. You could pop by later. I'll have to grab something to eat at some point."

"I'll do that. Have you heard from Tom?"

"No. I've just rung home, and he's still not there. I better get on. I'll ring you later."

Chapter Forty-Four

"Find anything interesting, Pete?" Lorne stretched knots out of her back as she approached his desk.

"The school's shut, so not much. John Scott attended Ashleigh High between 1975 and 1980, along with a Katherine Scott. I take it she's his sister. That's all we have on file," he said, pushing his notebook away from him in disgust.

"Contact the headmaster. I don't care if it is after hours; I'm sure he'll want to know about Miss Sedark. We'll get him to give us access to the school's files."

"Right away, boss."

"Tracy, you and Mitch stake out John Scott's house. Just watch the place until we get our hands on that bloody warrant."

Covering the mouthpiece of the phone, Pete said, "Boss, I've got the headmaster, Mr. Warren, on the phone. He's willing to meet us at the school now."

Lorne checked her watch. "Tell him we'll be there in twenty minutes. Molly, you and John take over from Pete. Go through John and Katherine Scott's bank records. Pete and I will be back in a few hours."

"Bearing in mind what happened the last time he abducted someone, what if the killer tries to contact you, ma'am?" Molly asked.

"Try to get a trace. Spin him a yarn. We should be back by eight."

* * *

When Lorne and Pete arrived at the school, Mr. Warren waited nervously at the entrance.

The man, in his early-fifties, pulled the collar of his cream trench coat high around his neck to keep the rain out. "Any news?" he asked.

"Not yet. I appreciate your co-operation, Mr. Warren. Has Miss Sedark taught here long?"

"She joined us straight from teacher training college about thirty-five years ago. She gets on well with the students. The personnel files are in my office."

As they swiftly made their way through the deserted school, Lorne asked, "What about the student's files? How far do they go back?"

"During the war, the Germans bombed the school, and it had to be rebuilt. Our records are now kept in a different part of the building. The authorities didn't want a repeat situation, so they had a steel room built at the rear."

"Do you mind if we see the student's files first?"

"Not at all. It's this way. Let me turn on some lights." He went to the boxed panel on the wall, flicked several switches, and the area flooded with bright light. The sounds of Lorne's low heels click-clicking on tiles echoed loudly in the silence as they followed Mr. Warren down to the end of a different corridor. He stopped in front of a pair of steel doors. "Here we are."

Once inside, Mr. Warren inched his way along the rows of storage boxes arranged neatly on metal shelving units. "Let me see…1975, you said. John and Katherine Scott… Here we are. John Scott, but no Katherine Scott. What age was the girl? Do you know?" He blew the dust off a manila folder and opened it up on a table in the centre of the room.

"We don't know. My team is checking at the moment. Any help you can give us would be a bonus."

"Let's see. Um… The boy was eleven. Ah, Miss Sedark was his P.E. teacher… That's a shame, his parents died when he was twelve. Ah, here we are—a sister three years younger, that explains why we've no record for her in this year. She would've been at primary school. Hang on, there's a note here from the headmistress at the time. My God, it was Doreen Nicholls …" He stopped and stared at the two detectives. "Wasn't she found murdered last week?"

"Unfortunately, yes. Please, what does the note say?" Lorne asked, as the case slotted together in her mind.

"It says John Scott told Miss Sedark that both he and his sister were being abused. She called in social services immediately. They were abused by their parents. How awful."

Pete glanced at Lorne and nodded. "Don't suppose you have the name of the social worker in there, do you?"

"Yes, here it is …"

"*Sandy Crayford*," they said, in unison.

"How did you know that?" Mr. Warren asked, astounded.

"An educated guess. Miss Crayford's body was found last Thursday. Another grisly piece of this jigsaw."

"Oh my God and you think there's a connection with this man?"

"We're not sure yet. Is it possible to have a copy of the file, Mr. Warren?"

"Of course, I'll do it immediately. There's a copier in the office."

"So what do you reckon?" Pete asked, as they waited for the file.

"Two kids, abused by their parents—the first thing we need to find out is how the parents died."

"I'll make enquiries when we get back. Aren't abused kids supposed to be removed from the family home? If that's the case, did the parents die before or after the kids were shipped out? Could J.S.'s accomplice be his sister?"

"What if the kids were taken from their parents, forced to live apart in separate foster or adoptive families. You hear about it all the time, especially back then. *Retribution*. That's what the killer said. It's got to be him. He's killed all the people who he considers let him down as a kid. His parents—that's something we have to investigate—his teacher, the social worker, and the headmistress." Lorne drew lines to all the names she'd written on a scrap of paper while she spoke.

Pete nodded his agreement. "Why, why now? I mean after all these years?"

"I don't know. Do we know how long he's worked at Toni's Taxis?"

"Not sure, I'll have to check. What about it?"

"Let's assume he's only just joined the firm. Maybe he picked up Belinda or Doreen in his cab one day. Perhaps, if he recognised them it triggered a bad memory. All we can do is speculate until we get back to the station." Lorne's mind wandered for a moment as she thought about her own family's issues.

"You're off somewhere else, boss. You okay?"

"I'm fine." She smiled sadly. "Just thinking about Tom and Charlie."

"I'm glad to hear it. You'd have to be an idiot to chuck all that away just because of a crush."

"No matter how many times I tell you, Pete, you're still going to think the worst of me. Jacques and I are just friends. Maybe if circumstances were different... But I promise you, nothing improper has gone on between us!"

"It's that bloody frog accent that sends you weak at the knees, ain't it?"

"Give it a rest, Pete." *God, will he ever stop going on about me and Jacques? Maybe if I change the subject.* "Wonder how long Mr. Warren's going to be?"

Thankfully, the man appeared a few seconds later. "Here you are, Inspector. There's a copy of John Scott's file, and a copy of Miss Sedark's personnel file. What about her husband? Have you called him?"

"She's married? I'm sorry. I just assumed she was a 'miss'." Lorne took the manila folder from the headmaster.

"Jane is one of those teachers who prefers to use her maiden name at school. She got married a couple of years ago. We all thought she would be a spinster all her life." For a moment, his eyebrows met, and he pulled his lips into a thin line against his teeth and bobbed his head as though in deep sadness. "Her address is in the file, or if you like, I could call round and tell Gordon?"

"We'll send a family liaison specialist to tell him. We'll need to ask him some questions as well."

"I see," Mr. Warren said, a hint of worry in his smile.

"Here's my card. We'll do our utmost to bring her home safely, Mr. Warren."

"Let's hope you find Jane, and soon."

Chapter Forty-Five

Chief Roberts was waiting for them in the incident room when they walked in. He waved a piece of paper at Lorne. "One warrant, Inspector," he said, handing her the folded sheet of paper.

"How did you manage to get it so quickly?" She took the paper and checked the details.

"Don't ask. Let's just say someone owed me a big favour. Mind if I tag along?"

"I have a few things to sort out first. I need to speak with the team. Be with you in ten minutes."

She quickly filled the team in and told Molly to dig up what she could find on the Scotts' parents. Then she rang Jacques from her office.

"Meet me at 26 Clearmont Rd. I'll be leaving in about five minutes, and Jacques…"

"Yes, *chérie?*"

"Full professional etiquette required. Roberts, the new chief, will be there."

"Message received and understood. See you there."

* * *

"Pete, you ready? We'll probably go in the chief's car." Lorne slipped on her coat.

They took the stairs down to the car park and found the chief waiting for them by his car. Roberts drove.

They pulled up outside J.S.'s flat at just after nine PM. Lorne jumped out of the vehicle and went to talk to Tracy and Mitch.

"Anything happen?" Lorne asked, bending down to talk to Mitch through the open window of his car.

"Absolutely nothing, ma'am. His car ain't here. I took the liberty of checking with the neighbours. The bloke two doors down says the man who owns the flats lives in the first floor flat. He's been out of the country for three months, visiting relatives in Oz. He's due back next week. Apparently, Scott likes to keep to himself. But lately, he's noticed different women going in his flat with him. Thought it strange."

"What's strange about it?" Lorne asked, her eyes set on the house.

"The guy said that he was puzzled when the women never seemed to come back out. Except one, she was totally different to the others. When I asked what was different about her, he said he couldn't put his finger on it. The guy also said he didn't think J.S. seemed the type to have one-night stands. He couldn't understand what these 'respectable-looking' women saw in him."

"The odd woman could be his sister. Right-o, we've got a warrant. I want you two to keep an eye on the rear."

The two sergeants left the car to take up their positions, and Lorne headed back to Pete and Roberts. With reluctance, Lorne said, "Do you want to take charge of this, sir?"

"No, I'd like to see how you handle yourself out in the field, Inspector."

Oh great, I'm under observation. Bloody charming!

Pete rang the doorbell, and although they could see a glimmer of light poking through a gap in the curtains, no one answered the door. "Break it down, Pete."

Moments later, the three of them separated and searched every room in the flat. After several minutes, they met up again in the man's living room.

"Shh... Quiet, did you hear that?" Lorne whispered. They all stood still and tried to work out where the whimper came from. Lorne got down on her hands and knees and placed her ear to the floor. Quickly, she pulled back the rug she'd tripped over on her previous visit, revealing a trapdoor.

Pete nudged Lorne aside and released the catch. He pulled the door open to reveal a dark, damp room that had a ladder leading down into it.

The muffled cry forced them to hurry down the rickety ladder. Lorne swung her flashlight around the makeshift cell. Terror-stricken eyes caught in the glare. The woman was stripped naked, sitting tethered to a wooden chair. "Get me a blanket, Pete!" Lorne shielded the woman's body from her partner. The chief rushed back up the ladder to call an ambulance.

Tears streamed down the woman's blood-soaked face. "Jane Sedark?" Lorne tore the tape from the woman's mouth. The woman gasped for air and nodded. Lorne took off her jacket and draped it carefully around Jane's shoulders to cover as much of her front as she could. Lorne tried to free the woman's hands and feet from their bindings, but her own hands shook too much. Just then, Pete returned with a blanket and untied the woman.

Blood had seeped into the small crevices age had worn in her skin. Her greying hair had large stripes of red running through it. The woman sobbed as it dawned on her she'd been found and was no longer in danger.

When she finally recovered her voice, the woman cried out, "Why …Why me?"

Thank God, we found her before he… Lorne's eyes stung, and she swore to herself she'd get the bastard, no matter what it took.

"We'll talk later, Jane. For now, let's get you to hospital, love. You're safe. That's all that matters. He can't hurt you anymore."

"Hello? Inspector, are you here?" A familiar voice called from above.

"Down here, Doctor Arnaud. We've found her. She's alive."

"Thank God. Have you called for an ambulance?" Jacques descended the ladder to the cell.

"The chief's just doing it. Can you check Jane over in the meantime?"

"Of course, of course. Now don't worry, madam. We'll soon have you out of here."

Lorne smiled at the gentle way Jacques treated the woman. His bedside manner touched her, considering how he was used to dealing with patients who generally lacked a pulse.

The ambulance arrived ten minutes later. Jacques found a possible fracture in Jane's skull from where J.S. had hit her in the car. She'd also sustained a couple of cracked ribs that the paramedics strapped up before they manoeuvred her up the rickety ladder on a stretcher and, whisked her away.

Roberts eventually joined them in the cell, again, and took in his surroundings. "Jesus, what the hell…"

To the rear, out of the tied woman's reach, was a dog bowl containing the smallest amount of thick porridge.

Inches away from the bowl were human faeces and a pile of women's clothes, including bras and panties, which Lorne assumed belonged to the previous victims. The beam from Lorne's flashlight highlighted the vast amounts of blood on every surface of the hellhole.

"They were kept like animals. Obviously stripped and, by the looks of things, beaten regularly," Jacques told the three detectives as he rigged up better lighting and took photos of the crime scene.

When Lorne spotted the way her boss was eyeing the Frenchman, she said, "Sorry you two haven't met. Jacques Arnaud, Home Office pathologist, this is Chief Inspector Sean Roberts."

"I believe we spoke on the phone earlier," Jacques said, offering his hand.

Sean gave Jacques' hand the briefest of shakes before he said, "We did indeed, Doctor. Can I ask how you managed to get here so quickly?"

"I have contacts who keep me abreast of certain situations, shall we say?" Jacques replied, holding Sean's stare.

"I see. Well, don't let me hold you up any longer. Inspector, a word upstairs, if you don't mind."

Sean shunted up the ladder ahead of her. Jacques chuckled, made a fist with his right hand, and mouthed, 'Give him hell.' She struggled to suppress a smile as she climbed the ladder.

Instead of reprimanding her for contacting Jacques, as expected, Sean surprised her. "I've notified the station. All cars are on the lookout for Scott's vehicle. Is there anywhere else he's likely to hide?"

"I haven't got a clue, as yet. First we need to find out where his sister lives. Did you instruct the team to notify Jane's husband?"

"Yes, I told them to send a car to take him to the hospital to be with her. I'll start the search around here. Contact your team, see what they've uncovered with regard to the sister."

"Excuse me, ma'am," Mitch interrupted. "There's something you should see next door."

They both followed Mitch into the bedroom off the hallway. The room was a throwback to the Sixties, dominated by large dark veneered furniture. The mattress was dipped in the middle and dressed in a quilted, old-fashioned, lime green eiderdown. Cork memo boards dominated the far wall. In hushed disbelief, Lorne said, "Oh my God!" Her eyes scanned the board, darting from one to the other. Pinned to them was an array of newspaper articles referring to the cases, meticulously lined up in date and crime order. *If only I'd had access to this room this afternoon...*

Sean stood alongside Lorne and pointed to a section of the newspaper cutting. "Jesus, the bastard's been laughing at us. See? The print is highlighted here, and he's written *ha ha* beside it."

Weary after the day's events, Lorne turned to him. "Mind if I make a suggestion?"

"Go ahead."

"We've recovered the woman, which was our main priority, and SOCO will be here soon to rip this place apart. We might as well call it a day. There's not a lot we can do until they've finished, anyway."

"Sounds like a good idea. It's approaching ten thirty, and we've got everyone searching for the bastard. Let's call it a day." Roberts headed towards the front door.

"I'll see you tomorrow, sir. I'm just going to check on the doc before I leave."

Pete and Jacques were just coming up the ladder when she returned to the living room.

Lorne walked over to the mantelpiece and studied the photograph that had caught her attention earlier. Jacques crept up behind her. "What can you do with this?" she asked, thrusting the picture at him.

"In what respect?" He took it from her.

"I need to know who the sister is. Any possibility your team could enhance the image by about twenty years?"

"Leave it with me. I'm sure my guys can come up with something."

"We've decided to call it a day. Have you finished down there?" she said, her eyes on the trap door behind him.

"Yes. Before I leave, I'd like to examine his clothes. See if there's a possible match to the fibres found at Doreen's house, if that's okay?"

"Sure, I'll help you. Pete, hitch a ride back with Tracy and Mitch, will you? I'll see you bright and early tomorrow."

Pete shrugged and appeared to be bothered by his dismissal, but Lorne could tell he was also dead on his feet.

Not long after, she found a grey tank top and handed it to Jacques.

"This could be just what we need." He tucked the garment into an evidence bag. "I'll get it examined first thing, make it top priority along with the photo. The results should be back around lunchtime tomorrow. Talking of food."

"Indian or Chinese?" Lorne asked, her stomach groaning on cue.

"You go home. I'll stop off at Mr. Wong's for a Chinese banquet and join you in about half an hour."

* * *

The answerphone was blinking impatiently when she arrived home. "Lorne, it's Tom. Could you pick Charlie up after school tomorrow from netball? Mum's got a doctor's appointment at four thirty and doesn't know how long she'll be. I've got a job interview on the other side of town at four. Ring me *only* if you can't make it. Netball finishes at five thirty, in case you've forgotten. Thanks."

Lorne was subdued when she opened the door to let Jacques in a little while later.

Jacques looked concerned. "Tough day, huh?" He took a few steps towards her, and Lorne backed away. He froze, but rather than look disappointed, he collected the plates and dished up their meal.

She let out a deep sigh and confided, "Tom rang. He left a message on the machine."

"Oh." Jacques waited for her to continue.

Lorne spoke, sadly, "Hearing his voice made me realise what a mess our marriage is in. He's asked me to pick up Charlie after school tomorrow. On one hand, I'm grateful he thought to ask me, as it gives me the chance of seeing her, but on the other, it's annoying how he regards me as a last resort. Neither Tom nor my *lovely* mother-in-law can be there when she finishes netball, so good old Lorne will fill in as a poor substitute." She poured them both a whisky.

"I'm sure you're wrong. You've had a tough day. The slightest problem will almost certainly magnify when you're tired. Think positively, *chérie*—at least he's asked for your help. To back down and call you like that must've been difficult for him, if he's still angry with you. Cut him some slack, is that what you English say?"

"Yes, that's right." A smile softened her worried features. "How come you're always so damn objective?"

"It comes with the job, *chérie.* Come on. Let's eat before that nasty MSG starts to solidify."

"You doctors certainly know how to put a girl off her food, I'll give you that." She picked up her fork and messed about with the sauce he'd dribbled over her prawn balls.

* * *

"Sis, it's me."

"John, thank God. Where are you?"

"Don't worry about me. I'll make this quick. I've arranged for you to stay at the *Swallow Hotel* for tonight. Don't go back to the flat. Do you hear me? The cops'll be swarming all over it by now."

"What about the woman?" she asked, voice hushed, aware that her colleague was within earshot.

"My guess is they've already found her. They'll have no idea she's not the final one. I'll prove 'em wrong soon enough, you'll see. Stay safe, Sis. We'll be together again soon."

Chapter Forty-Six

When Lorne arrived at work the next morning, it was still dark. Some of the team were missing, and she presumed they were already at Scott's house going through the evidence.

"Nice of you to join us, Inspector," Sean Roberts said as she burst through the door.

Glancing at her watch, she saw it was only seven thirty. The clock on the wall above Pete's head corroborated the time. Pete shrugged when she glanced at him.

"As I was saying," Roberts carried on, addressing *her* team. "Yes, we found Miss Sedark relatively unharmed. That doesn't mean we can start congratulating ourselves on a job well done. Until we have John Scott sitting in a cell, our job is far from over."

"Molly, step forwards and tell the team what you dug up on J.S. and his sister."

Molly stood in front of the group. Nerves got the better of her, and she dropped her notes on the floor. Motherly pride swept through Lorne as Molly prepared to speak. Despite their recent differences, Molly had shone the past week, and Lorne regarded her as a key member of the team.

"First of all, I checked into John Scott's background using the information Pete and the inspector obtained from the school. When J.S. was eleven, a games teacher—that would be Jane Sedark— noticed bruises on his arms during a PE lesson. She queried him about the marks. At first, he was reluctant to tell her, but finally broke down and admitted his parents had been abusing him and his sister. She took the complaint to the headmistress, Doreen Nicholls, who passed the complaint on to a social worker, Sandy Crayford."

"Yeah, me and the inspector figured all this out, Mol. Tell us something we don't know, will ya?"

"Well," Molly continued, embarrassed. "J.S. and his sister were removed from the family home and placed with separate foster families. He begged the authorities to keep them together, but they ignored him. Back then, it was almost impossible to place siblings together. Before the disruption, he was classed as a mediocre student, with middle-of-the-road marks.

"However, after he was placed in foster care and separated from his sibling, his grades went downhill fast—he went into a shell. He was sent to a counsellor. After a few months, his grades picked up. About this time, a fire broke out at the Scott's family home. His mother and father were both killed in the fire. I managed to trace the post-mortem reports. His parents were inebriated and incapable of escaping the fire.

"The fire was deemed to be an accident, but again, J.S.'s school work appeared to improve just enough to deflect the school's concerns. Then I researched the foster families. The kids were never adopted. Both families said they were good kids and spent every weekend together. They were quiet and withdrawn during the week, but when the weekend arrived, they'd come alive."

"Is it possible for an eleven-year-old boy to commit arson like that?" Lorne asked, perplexed.

"Take the Jamie Bulger case—eleven-year-olds are capable of a lot worse than arson," the chief replied, referring to the gruesome murder of a toddler by two pre-pubescent boys a few years earlier. Roberts urged Molly to carry on.

"That's about it, apart from one more thing. I rang Social Services and asked if they knew what happened to the kids after they left school. At eighteen, J.S. fought for months to get custody of his sister. Katherine was fifteen at the time. He became her legal guardian, and that's as far as their file goes."

After Molly finished, the chief said, "I've asked a friend of mine to pop by this morning. She's due about eleven. I'd like *everyone* to hear what she has to say."

"What exactly do you mean by *friend?*" asked Lorne, puzzled.

"She's a criminologist. She's coming in as a favour to me. I've given her the case facts, and she's come up with a profile of the killer."

Lorne folded her arms across her chest. "With respect, sir, isn't that like locking the stable door after the horse has bolted? We already know who the killer is. We've just got to track the bastard down."

"Maybe, maybe not, Inspector. Just remain open-minded when she arrives. Using the services of a criminologist is more plausible than using a psychic in a murder investigation, don't you think?"

Condescending bastard. Lorne narrowed her eyes, as he turned and headed out of the room. She pushed back her chair and went to follow him to his office.

Pete blocked her path with his large frame. "Leave it, boss. Come on. I'll buy you a coffee."

Lorne's frustration mounted as the morning dragged by. She thumped her hand on the desk, *I should be out there, going through the bastard's flat.* Instead she'd been ordered to stick around and wait for some shrink to tell her facts she already knew about a killer on the loose. A pointless exercise to accommodate one of Roberts' *friends.*

Eleven o'clock arrived, and along with it, a smartly dressed Susan Bywater. The woman, slim with high cheekbones that emphasised her good breeding, oozed confidence as she strode across to the chief. Lorne rolled her eyes as he welcomed her with a sickly show of affection. Lorne wondered if the over-the-top way he welcomed Ms. Bywater was for her benefit.

"This is Susan Bywater. You have everyone's attention, Susan, so when you're ready."

"Thanks, Sean." She gave him a smile that had an unspoken message attached to it. "After studying the notes, my profile for the killer is this. The man has a great deal of anger. He absorbs hostility until he can take no more. Then he kills the women in the midst of a violent rage." Ms. Bywater looked down at her notes and then continued.

"To look at him, he gives the impression he's a loner. Dresses in clothes that relate back to his childhood, shying away from today's fashionable trends. Sexually abused by a female member of his family, probably his mother. He's punishing his victims for their gender and for letting him down in the past. It's possible his anger killed his mother, and this served a purpose for a number of years. Recently an incident has brought the anger to the surface again. Something has triggered memories from his childhood, unwanted memories. They're causing pain that he's determined to prevent from destroying him again." She cleared her throat.

Roberts handed her a glass of water and she went on.

"He's anti-social. Gets all the companionship he needs from a sibling, maybe a sister. She's the key. Bring the sister in, and you reel him in. He's a protector, her protector. His home is meticulous—he's probably OCD. He has little or no sexual interest in women. Possibly impotent, unable to perform…"

The phone on Tracy's desk interrupted the woman's evaluation.

"Just a minute. Ma'am, it's Doctor Arnaud for you."

"Hello, Doctor? You're kidding… That's fantastic. We'll be right over." When she replaced the phone, she ran into her office and emerged seconds later, shrugging her coat on.

"Inspector, where do you think you're going?" Roberts frowned and walked towards her.

"It's urgent, sir. Doctor Arnaud has the results of a test I asked him to carry out. His team have enhanced the photograph of J.S.'s sister for me. Ms. Bywater just told us if we pull the sister in, we hook Scott. So I'm going to the path lab to see who the woman is. Then I'm going to bring her in for questioning. If that's all right with you?"

Blowing out a breath, Roberts relented. "Very well."

Yes, result! "Let's go, Pete."

When they were settled in the car, Pete said, "What a load of bollocks that was."

"I thought it might be. Give me Carol Lang any day. Hey, at least she led us to a murder scene."

"Did the doc give you any clues about the woman?"

Lorne shook her head as she changed down a gear. "He just said the results were back, and the picture was excellent. Let's hope we can identify the woman."

Jacques was waiting in the hall outside his office when they arrived. Lorne's heart pounded, and she couldn't tell if it was because of the sight of Jacques or because of the possibility of closing in on Scott's sister.

"The image is in my office," Jacques said, nodding at Pete and smiling at Lorne.

Lorne's hand shook when Jacques handed her the photograph. "Jesus, I *knew* it. I had a feeling about her. Thanks, Jacques, you've done it again." She pecked him on the cheek and sprinted up the hallway, with Pete close behind her.

"Good luck, Inspector," Jacques called after her, in amusement.

"Hey, hold up, boss. Are you gonna tell me who this woman is?" Pete called after her, breathlessly trying to keep up.

"You'll find out soon enough. Come on, chunky."

Chapter Forty-Seven

The rain lashed quicker than the windscreen wipers could cope with, and in her haste to reach their destination, Lorne manoeuvred the car through deep puddles on side streets and back lanes.

When she pulled up on the double yellow lines a few yards from the building, Pete quipped, "Hey, you begging for a parking ticket?"

"Ha bloody ha. You want to park a mile down the road and battle this bloody weather without a brolly?" She poked his upper arm. "As if *you've* never pulled a yellow double-liner."

"Okay, okay, point taken," he mumbled, head moving side to side like a metronome. When she turned off the engine, he said, "So when *are* you going to tell me who you think J.S.'s sister is? The suspense, as they say, is *kill*ing me."

"You'll find out soon enough. First, I need to ask a few questions, find out who took the call when Jane Sedark ordered the taxi for her and the two children." Lorne unzipped her bag and plonked her keys into it. "C'mon. Let's make a run for it." She stepped out of the car.

Holding her bag above her head, she ran to the front door of Toni's Taxis.

Pete stayed by the door, while Lorne ventured farther in to the office.

The two women seemed surprised to see them, but Toni managed to smile, while Mary peered at Lorne and her partner. *She sure doesn't like officers of the law, that one.*

"Hello, Inspector. What can we do for you this time?" Toni asked, pouring herself a coffee.

"We thought you might be able to help us locate one of your drivers?"

"Oh. Which one?"

"John Scott," Lorne said, in a calm voice, despite the adrenaline pumping round her system.

"He rang in yesterday, said he wanted to take a few days off. Has he done something wrong?" Toni's eyes drifted between Lorne and her employee, who was fidgeting at her desk.

"I don't know. Maybe, we should ask Mary?"

"How the hell should I know?" the overweight controller snapped back.

Lorne's eyes narrowed, "Surely, as radio controller, you should be aware of his every move, shouldn't you?"

"What's going on, Inspector?" Toni said.

"Why don't we ask Mary—or, should I say, *Katherine Scott*—about that?"

"Bloody hell!" Pete's voice bounced off the walls.

Lorne turned and, for a minute, wanted to laugh at Pete's gobsmacked face.

Toni shook her head, confused. "Mary, are you related to John?"

"What about it?" the woman shouted, her upper lip raised, baring her uneven teeth.

"You told me your name was Matthews. Why would you do that?"

"I think I can answer that one for you, Toni," Lorne told the bemused woman but kept her gaze fixed on the controller. "It was much easier for her brother to abduct the women on his hit list," she said, then looked at Toni, "if they deceived you." She addressed Mary again. "You doctored the dockets, made sure another driver's name was on the docket instead of your brother's. Am I right?"

"I don't know what you mean," Mary snarled.

"Where are the dockets from yesterday, Toni, and I'll show Mary *exactly* what I mean?"

"I'll get them for you. I put them away this morning."

While Toni located the dockets, Lorne glanced back at Pete, whose eyes and facial gestures told her he was itching to come through and question Mary, as well. She threw him a *Don't you dare* stare.

Toni removed the final shoebox from the top shelf of the unit behind her and handed it to Lorne. "Here you are. What specifically are you after, Inspector?"

"There should be a pick-up from Ashleigh High School at around four, maybe four fifteen, in the name of Sedark. Can you tell me who the driver was?"

"Let's see. Ah, here it is. The call came in at four ten, and the driver who picked her up was Wacko." Toni studied the docket and frowned.

Lorne tilted her head. "Something wrong, Toni?"

"You could say that, Inspector. Wacko wasn't on duty until nine o'clock last night."

"Perhaps you can tell me who was on control when the call came in?"

"It was you, Mary, wasn't it? What the hell is going on? Why would you put Wacko's name on a docket, when he wasn't even on duty?"

"I can answer that one for you, too, Toni. It was intentional. John Scott picked up Jane Sedark and two kids. Thankfully, the kids managed to escape, but Miss Sedark wasn't so lucky. We discovered her a couple of hours later in the cellar of his flat. Naked and tied to a chair. She suffered multiple fractures but is relieved to be alive. Unlike John Scott's previous victims. That's right, isn't it, Mary, er…I mean, Katherine?"

The controller glared at Lorne but remained silent.

"I'm so sorry, Inspector. I had no idea. Get your things together, Mary. You're finished here, and that goes for your skanky brother too."

"Yes, Mary, gather your things, you're coming down the station with us. Pete? Will you do the honours of escorting this person from the premises?"

"Will do, boss …"

"Just one more thing, Toni. Is the car Scott drives a company car or his own?"

"They all have their own vehicles, Inspector. I'd soon go out of business if I had to supply the cars."

"Thanks for your help, Toni. I hope you find a new controller and driver soon."

The colour continued to drain from Toni's face, and she asked, "Do you have any idea where Scott is?"

"Let's just say we're closing in on him."

A loathsome smirk appeared on Mary's face and remained there throughout the journey back to the station.

* * *

They put the woman in interview room one. Pete and Lorne nipped next door and observed her through the two-way mirror. The whole time she glared at the uniformed officer guarding the door.

"You were right. You said there was something fishy about her. She's one hell of an evil bitch."

"Let's hold fire on the congratulations. Wait till we've got her brother in custody, shall we? I'm chancing my arm here, Pete, but you know your mate, 'Stinger', on the local paper? Do you think he could run a story for us? Maybe he could let it slip that Mary was being held for questioning. If J.S. knows we're holding her, it might bring him out in the open, or at least force him to contact me."

Pete glanced at his watch. "If I'm quick, the story could make the late edition. I'll see what I can do. What about *her*?" He jerked his head in the direction of the interview room.

"I'm going to let her stew in there for a few hours. It might make her crack quicker."

* * *

Lorne replaced the receiver as Pete marched into the office twenty minutes later.

"Phew, that was a close one. Half an hour to spare. Stinger lapped up the story. They want to see this bastard caught as much as we do. Who were you on the phone to?"

"Gordon Sedark. Checking to see how Jane is. She's out of hospital, still shaken up, but she's coping remarkably well, considering what has happened to her. He wanted me to pass on his thanks to the team."

"Did you tell him about Scott's sister?"

"Not yet. So, now we sit and wait. Scott will be in touch soon, I have no doubt about that. Fancy grabbing a quick bite before we try and break down mardy Mary?"

"Did you tell the chief we've brought her in?"

"I have. He's still in a mood. Insists you should question her while I observe."

Pete pulled a face at the suggestion.

"Don't worry, I'll prompt you through the earpiece if needed, but I'm sure you'll be fine."

"Oh great. It'll be like Big Sister watching over me while I'm questioning The *Big* Sister," Pete grumbled on the way to the canteen.

Half an hour later, after draining the last of their coffees, Lorne asked, "Are you ready for this? We'll take her a sandwich. I'm feeling generous."

"You'd need a truckload of sarnies to satisfy her appetite, boss, by the looks of it."

An old saying popped into Lorne's mind, something about a pot and a kettle. She chuckled.

Chapter Forty-Eight

Pete flicked the switch on the recorder as soon as he entered the interview room. He cautioned her, using her real name of Katherine Scott, then fired questions as if there was no tomorrow.

"Hey, slow down, Pete. Give her a chance to answer." Lorne's voice came through his earpiece. "Ask her where she stayed last night?"

Pete did, and the woman refused to answer. He had placed the sandwich in the middle of the table, and her eyes focused on that rather than him.

Hours dragged by, and the response remained the same. Silence with a capital S. Needing a break, a frustrated Pete left the room every hour. After a quick chat with Lorne, he returned to try again.

At four forty, Tracy brought Lorne the early edition of the evening newspaper. On the front page and in thick bold type was the headline:

SUSPECTED SERIAL KILLER'S SISTER HELPING POLICE WITH THEIR ENQUIRIES.

"If this doesn't bring the bastard in…" Lorne said, satisfied by the piece Pete's mate had written. Tracy played with her watch as if the strap had pinched the hairs on her arm, and Lorne noticed what the time was. "Shit, is that the time? I'm supposed to be meeting my daughter from school. I'll have to ring my sister—see if she'll do it for me. Pete, I'll be right back," she said, before running out the room.

Her mobile was upstairs in her bag so she rang her sister from the nearest phone. "Jade, thank God. I'm supposed to be picking Charlie up after netball practice, but I'm stuck here—"

"You're kidding me? Again, you're putting work before your family." Her sister sighed loudly. "What time?"

"Thanks, Jade. You're a treasure. Now, if you can?"

"You owe me big time, Lorne," Jade shouted down the phone then hung up.

Lorne returned to the observation room. Pete looked as though he'd had enough of Ms Scott's 'no comments' and dodging the daggers shooting from her eyes.

About twenty minutes later, Tracy rushed into the room. She coughed to clear her throat.

"What's up, Tracy?"

"Ma'am, the phone was ringing in your office…and, I answered it."

Lorne could tell she was struggling to give her some bad news.

"Spit it out, Tracy, you're beginning to worry me."

"Sorry, ma'am. The call was from your daughter."

Lorne frowned. "And? She can't be home already?"

"Oh God, ma'am… She was still at school. She was hysterical."

"Tracy, for fuck's sake, tell me what's happened?"

"Your sister has been…abducted, ma'am."

Lorne's knees buckled, and she fell against the two-way mirror. "Pete, get out here. *Now!*"

"What's going on?" Pete asked, barging through the door. He looked at Lorne and then at Tracy.

Tracy continued, "Charlie saw her being bundled into the back of a taxi. A black Peugeot."

Pete shook his head. "Who was?"

"My sister, Pete. Scott has my sister."

"Oh, Jesus fucking wept. Tracy, get the chief. Now."

Tracy ran from the room, and Pete stepped forwards to comfort Lorne. The words echoed round her head. *My God, John Scott's got my sister. Don't lose it now, girl.*

The chief joined them as Lorne was issuing Pete with instructions. "Ring the school, tell them to keep Charlie, then ring Tom and *order* him to get to the school and pick his daughter up. Interview or not, got it?"

Pete nodded and left the room.

Roberts' features showed how worried he was. He handed Lorne a glass of water. "Tracy filled me in. Lorne, I'm so sorry. Come on. Let's get back to your office."

Lorne glanced down at his hand tucked under her elbow then, when she saw such sadness and concern in his eyes, she remembered he'd once thought the world of Jade, too. "What about *her*?" she asked, nodding towards the woman on the other side of the mirror.

"I'll get the desk sergeant to lock her up."

They had not long arrived at the incident room when the phone rang. Everyone stared at it before Mitch finally picked it up. "Just a minute. I'll put you through."

He held out the phone to her and mouthed. *It's him!*

"Let me take it, Lorne," Roberts insisted.

But Lorne hit his outstretched arm away. "No," she snapped. Her pulse quickened as she prepared herself for a confrontation.

"Lorne, listen to me. It's imperative that you remain calm, don't let him goad you."

"Christ, I know how to handle this, sir," Lorne said through gritted teeth. "Hello, this is DI Simpkins," she said, fighting to keep her voice normal.

"Lorne... It's me."

"Jade, sweetheart, are you all right? Where are you?" Lorne asked, tears burning her eyes.

"Ah, Inspector. Questions, questions, always questions. Did you forget to pick your daughter up? It's a good job your sister thinks more of her than you do." His hollow laugh filtered down the line.

"You bastard."

"Now, now, Inspector. If you want to see your sister again, you really should be nice to me." His voice was low and threatening.

"Just tell me what you want, Scott?"

"Keep him talking, we'll try and trace the call," Roberts mouthed to her.

"I'll consider doing a swap with you, my sister for yours. How about that?"

"I'm sure that could be arranged. I'll have to talk to my superior, see if he'll agree to it."

"Why don't you ask DCI Roberts now, that *is* him standing beside you, isn't it?" J.S. laughed in her ear.

Lorne twisted and peered out the window at the offices opposite. *Is he there, watching me?*

"He'll agree to it. Just tell me when and where?"

"I'll call back. My time's almost up, I'm sure you've got people beavering away tracing this call."

"Please, let me talk to Jade." But he'd hung up, leaving her listening to the dial tone. Her knuckles tensed and whitened as she gripped the phone. Roberts had to prise it from her hand.

Pete walked into the silence of the incident room. "What's going on?"

Lorne's explanation dried in her throat.

Confused, Pete asked, "Boss? No worries, Tom's gonna pick up Charlie."

"Scott just made contact," Roberts said.

"Shit. That's it. The bitch better start singing now or ..." Pete spat out in anger.

"That's enough, Pete. I don't want her knowing about Jade. We'll keep her banged up overnight, see how she likes that." She glanced at Roberts, and he nodded his approval. If she was going to meet with Scott, there was no way his sister would be handed over.

"I'm going over to Scott's place to see how SOCO are getting on."

"Are you sure you're up to it?" asked Roberts.

Lorne stared at him and shook her head. "I'll just make a quick call and get over there." She walked into her office and closed the door behind her. "Jacques, it's me."

"*Bonjour,* Lorne. What can I do for you?"

"I needed to hear a friendly voice," she told him, her own wavering slightly.

"Is everything okay, Lorne?"

"No. John Scott has found another victim..."

"What! Oh no. I read in the paper that you have his sister in custody. Do you think that forced his hand?"

"Oh, there's no doubt about that. I just hope he doesn't harm Jade. She sounded okay when I spoke to her earlier ..."

"Lorne, I don't understand. You're babbling… Oh my God, did you say Jade? Lorne—has he abducted your sister?"

"Oh, Jacques, it's all my fault. Tom asked me to do one simple thing, and I couldn't even manage that. Work got in the way as usual. Now she's gone. Gone forever, for all I know." Tears slipped down her cheek, and filled with anger and dread, she wiped them away.

"Lorne, you mustn't blame yourself. I'm sure she'll be fine. Think positive. What can I do to help?"

"There's nothing anyone can do. He's hinted that he'd be willing to swap his sister for mine, but I can't see the boss going along with that scenario. I'm just on my way to Scott's flat now. See what SOCO's turned up. That's if they haven't taken it all away already for examination."

"I've got a couple of posts still to do. When I've finished, I'll track you down. Till then, chin up and stay strong."

Chapter Forty-Nine

Around dusk that evening, Lorne, Pete, and the chief turned up at J.S.'s flat. The rain had stopped, but now, cold air swirled leaves close to the ground, forming mini tornadoes as the team gathered outside the property.

Before entering the flat, Lorne asked, "Has everyone got a pair of latex gloves?"

The SOCO team were just winding things up.

"Bloody hell, Pete, what a tip this place is," Lorne said, eyes scanning the clutter, then she approached the head of the team. "Hi, Jack. What've you got?"

The tall middle-aged man, still in his white suit, sidestepped the boxes of paraphernalia as he made his way through to the lounge. He pointed at the evidence they'd gathered. "Items of interest are a scrapbook and a shoebox we found in a wardrobe, containing some old pictures and a set of keys."

Lorne checked inside the shoebox. She viewed the photos one by one and passed them to the chief and Pete to examine. The pictures were pretty dark memorabilia from a troubled and traumatised past. In one photo, a raging fire engulfed a house. *What kind of warped mind films something like that? Is this his family home? Did he watch it burn to the ground?* Also in the box, she found a few Polaroid pictures of two gravestones. The inscriptions read Grace Scott and Geoffrey Scott. 'Good riddance' was written in capitals across the Polaroids in felt-tip pen.

The final item in the box, a black cloth wrapped around two playing cards—the king and queen of spades—and a Tarot death card.

"He's one dark, mixed-up cookie," Pete said. He gulped noisily when it dawned on him what he'd just said. "Sorry, boss, I shouldn't have said that."

"That's okay, Pete. It's nothing we didn't know already." Lorne sat on the sofa and flicked through the scrapbook.

Pete sat alongside her and whistled. "Jesus, the guy's been watching you for ages." He glanced up at her and then back at the scrapbook.

As she stared at hundreds of photos of herself, she remained speechless. Pictures of her with Tom and Charlie. Even a recent snap of her holding hands with Jacques in the park was included in the collection, along with lots of dull everyday photos of Lorne with Pete coming and going to work. But the most upsetting photo, in her eyes, had to be the ones he'd taken of Charlie in the school playground. John Scott had been stalking, not just watching her for days.

"Why? Why me?" she uttered the same words Jane Sedark asked when they'd found her earlier.

"Because you're the leading investigator on the case, one would presume," Roberts suggested, looking over her shoulder.

"Hey, take a gander at this," Pete said, turning to the penultimate page of the book. Neatly arranged were pictures of a smiling, young J.S. standing next to an elderly couple. On the final page were grainy pictures of a little girl, aged seven to eight—Lorne presumed it was his sister—with the same couple. "What do ya think? Could be the grandparents."

"Surely, if their grandparents had been alive, the kids wouldn't have been put into care. Maybe they died before the abuse scandal broke. Pete, ring Molly, see what she can dig up?"

Pete stepped out into the hallway, and Roberts took his seat beside Lorne. They browsed through the scrapbook again. "Maybe this place was some kind of holiday home. It looks in the middle of nowhere, surrounded by trees." Roberts picked up the scrapbook to examine the picture more closely. "It's some kind of cabin, nestled in a wooded area."

"A wood. I can see hills or mountains in the distance. In this picture, it looks like the same place. You can see the edge of the cabin here. There are acres of gorse and thistles. I'm thinking Scotland—the Highlands, maybe?" Lorne turned to her boss. He seemed distracted by something. "What's up?"

"Just a suspicion." He picked up the set of keys, one chunky and four Chubb keys.

"Are you thinking what I'm thinking?" Lorne glanced down at the keys.

"Find the log cabin and see if these fit. But if he's already on his way there with Jade, wouldn't he have taken these with him?"

Lorne shook her head. "Not necessarily. What if they're a spare set, in case the siblings got separated?"

"It might be a red herring of sorts, too. He's a canny character."

"That's true. So you think it might be some kind of decoy, left here on purpose for us to find?" Lorne nibbled the inside of her cheek, deep in thought.

"We have no way of knowing what goes on in his warped mind. We're talking about someone who waited almost thirty years to get revenge. And watched as his parents burned to death in a fire he, no doubt, set."

"Come on, Pete, where are you with that info?" Lorne called as Roberts' words sunk in. The insecure, unstable man he'd just described had her sister's life in his hands.

Pete marched back into the room. "Here we are. Apparently, while the decision was being made whether to place the kids with the grandparents or not, they were involved in a fatal car crash. Despite the grandparents begging the authorities to let the kids live with them, the couple's age was a contributing factor. Social Services thought the couple would find it a struggle bringing up two kids so young. Yet another reason for J.S. to blame the women who tried to help them."

"Those kids certainly went through the mill. I don't suppose Molly had an address for the grandparents?" Lorne asked her partner.

"She gave me two addresses, one near Leeds and the other a holiday home in Scotland."

"That's it. It *has* to be. I bet he's taken Jade there." Lorne handed Pete the photo they'd found of the Scottish hideaway.

"Did Molly have an address on file for the holiday home?" Roberts asked.

"Yeah, it was a bit of a mouthful. I didn't bother writing it down though."

Roberts patted Pete on the shoulder. "Not to worry. I think we better get back to the station anyway, just in case J.S. tries to contact you again, Lorne. We can study maps of the area there."

* * *

"Anything, Tracy?" Lorne asked, when they arrived back at the incident room.

"He called a couple of minutes ago, ma'am."

"What did he say?"

"He was angry, asked where you were. When I told him I didn't know, he became irate—started calling you a lousy mother, ma'am. I couldn't understand why and didn't know how to respond. I told him to call back in half an hour."

"And what was his response?"

"He said he might call back, or he might not. It depended how he was feeling. I'm so sorry, ma'am."

Lorne touched the young sergeant's arm to reassure her. "That's all right, Tracy. He's obviously referring to the fact I neglected to pick up my daughter. I'm the only person to blame for this cock-up."

When J.S. called back, they were all standing around the desk studying the map of Scotland.

He was angry and sounded agitated. "Where were you, Inspector?"

"Out doing police work. Can I speak to Jade?"

"Only if you ask nicely."

"Please, Mr. Scott, can I speak to my sister?" She glanced at her watch, realising he'd held Jade prisoner for four hours already.

"Only if I can speak to my sister." He laughed malevolently.

"I've had a word with my boss, and he's agreed to the swap," Lorne lied under the watchful glare of the chief.

"Has he, Inspector, or are you playing mind games with me?"

"No, it's true. Just tell me where and when, and we'll be there?" Lorne hoped her voice sounded calm and in control, despite her inner turmoil.

"I'll call back in half an hour. You'd better be there this time or Jade might end up with a few bruises." He laughed again, and she heard Jade squeal in the background as if he had hit her.

"Please... Please, don't hurt her any more," Lorne pleaded, but J.S. had already hung up.

Roberts shook his head. "You're playing a dangerous game, Lorne. I haven't cleared it with my boss yet. Until I do, I can't agree to the exchange. Has he hurt Jade?"

"She cried out in pain just before he ended the call. I'm not saying we'll carry out an exchange, sir, but we have to dangle some carrot. How would you feel if it was your sister he was holding?"

"I can't begin to understand what you must be going through, Lorne. But I must reiterate: You shouldn't be making him promises you cannot fulfil."

Lorne had no intention of listening to her boss. She was too busy hatching a plan of her own.

The chief grew tired of waiting for Scott to make contact and returned to his office.

When the follow-up call came in, Lorne asked Tracy to put it through to her office, where Pete joined her.

"Yes, I know it. What time? We'll be there. No, I swear it won't be a trap. Just my partner and Katherine will be with me. Can I speak to Jade? Be brave, Jade. I'll get you out of there."

"Where does he want to meet?" Pete asked.

"Keele Services on the M6. Pete, I'm going to put you in an awkward position. It's entirely up to you if you want to go through with this or not. I won't hold it against you if you disagree with my plan."

"Hey, we're partners, ain't we? Come on. You can fill me in on the way. I take it we ain't dragging his sister along for the ride?" Pete held out her coat.

Lorne smiled affectionately at him and slipped it on. "You're a good man, Pete. We've got to get out of here before Roberts spots us."

"Give me your keys. I'll pretend I'm nipping to the loo. I'll bring the car round the front so we can make a quick getaway."

"Okay, and I'll tell the team I'm going home to check on Charlie. That should lay a false trail for a little while."

* * *

An eerie fog stretched before them as they headed north on the motorway to the meeting point. Pete insisted on driving. Lorne's mind was full of *What-if?* scenarios. Her thoughts remained negative as the service station slip road loomed ahead of them.

"He'll be in the lorry park. It's over there. I don't want any heroics on your part, Pete. Let me do things my way, do you understand?"

"Yeah, I understand. It doesn't mean I have to agree with you, though, does it?"

"Don't jeopardise this for me, Pete. I just want my sister back." She spotted the only car parked amongst the lorries. It was a white VW Golf—he'd changed cars. "When I get out, take down his registration number. It'll help you later on."

"Will do, boss. Don't take any unnecessary risks," Pete said, gripping her forearm.

Lorne covered his hand with hers. "I won't, if all goes well. Take care of Jade, and I'll see you soon."

"I'm holding you to that. I could do without having to mould another partner into my way of thinking at my time of life."

"See you soon, partner." Lorne pecked him on the cheek, pulled the collar of her coat up around her ears, and got out of the car.

The cold air made her shiver as she crossed the tarmac to the parked vehicle. Pete got out of the car and rested his arms on top of the open door.

John Scott appeared and placed Jade in front of him. He held a knife to her throat and anxiously searched around him. "Where's Katherine?"

Lorne stopped ten feet away from him. She swallowed, hard. "She's in the car."

"Don't mess with me, Inspector. I can see your partner's alone." He pressed the point of the knife into Jade's throat, and she yelped as the blood trickled from the wound. Her bright blue eyes expanded in fear.

"Okay, okay. Please, don't hurt her any more. I'm begging you."

"You've tricked me. Give me one good reason why I shouldn't kill her?"

Keep your head, Lorne. Don't rise to his threats. "If you do that, you definitely won't see your sister again. I had trouble persuading my boss to swap sisters." Scott opened his mouth to challenge her, but she raised a hand to stop him. "I have a possible solution for that."

"Yeah, and what's that?" Scott tightened his grip around Jade's throat.

Lorne exhaled nervously. "We'll do a swap of our own."

He tilted his head, apparently puzzled by her suggestion.

She continued, "Set my sister free, and have me as your hostage. What do you say?" Lorne fought back the bile rising in her throat.

"Who's to say he'll go for it, this boss of yours?"

"If they don't meet a deadline of seven o'clock tomorrow evening, you can kill me."

"Lorne, no!" Tears trickled down Jade's cheeks.

"Hush, Jade. I know what I'm doing. Sean won't let me down."

"Only one way to find out, Inspector. One false move, Jade, and I'll slit ya bloody throat, you hear me?" Scott snarled, reaching out his right arm. "I'll let her go when I've got you by my side."

Lorne went to him. She kissed Jade on the cheek as she passed. "Run, Jade." Scott grabbed Lorne in a chokehold and carried out a body search for a possible concealed weapon. She went rigid under his touch and her heart sank as she watched her sister run into Pete's outstretched arms.

After finding nothing, Scott guided Lorne roughly to the Golf and threw her on the back seat. He put his knee on her tailbone and tied her hands behind her, then pulled a cloth bag over her head. The bag smelt of petrol and made her heave.

* * *

Pete dialled the office. "Tracy. Yeah, it's Pete."

"Hold on a minute, boss," the sergeant said.

"Where are you, Pete?" Roberts bellowed.

"I have Jade. I'm on the M6 at Keele Services. Send a vehicle to pick her up ASAP. I need to stay on Scott's tail, sir."

"Pete, where's Lorne? What the bloody hell are you playing at?"

"With J.S. I'll fill you in when you get here, Chief."

"Stay where you are," the chief ordered sharply. "We'll be there in a couple of hours."

"With respect, sir, we'll be inside, in the warm. I've got a young lady who's cold and hungry." Pete smiled at Jade and patted her hand.

"Okay. See you soon." They hung up.

"Come on, Jade. Now stop worrying. That sister of yours is made of strong stuff. It's not like we don't know where they're heading."

Jade gave Pete a weak smile before they both turned to see the white car exiting the car park.

Chapter Fifty

A few hours into the long trip, Lorne drifted off to sleep.

"Wake up, Inspector. We're here," Scott whispered in her ear.

The cloth bag remained over her head until they were inside the building. An orange glow lit the room and cast shadows off objects she guessed were furniture. When he tore off the bag, her eyes stung and were slow to adjust.

At first glance, the cabin appeared primitive, but on further inspection, it had everything they needed. Threadbare blankets layered a hand-carved bed. A two-seater sofa was positioned next to the tiny cast-iron wood-burning stove. A small slatted table with two dining chairs sat in the centre of the room. A small kitchen—if Lorne could call it that—was at one end, a two-ring stove running off a propane gas bottle, the only form of equipment in the tiny area. An old earthenware sink was precariously propped up on two wooden pillars.

A curtain had been pulled across one wall, which Lorne presumed hid the bathroom or toilet. A few red scatter rugs added warmth and comfort, while velvet curtains, more suited to a Victorian parlour, hung at the two windows.

"Welcome to your temporary new home, Lorne." Scott laughed nastily and untied her hands. He forced her into one of the two dining chairs, then retied her hands around the back of it.

"Where are we?" Lorne asked, feigning ignorance of their location.

"In a forest, north of where we started off from, that's all you need to know, Inspector." J.S. headed out the door.

Lorne frantically played with the ropes around her wrist, wriggling first one way then the other, but it proved hopeless. Her skin shredded painfully at the slightest movement.

* * *

Pete prepared himself for a dressing-down when he spotted the chief enter the café. "Hello, Chief. You made good time."

"We'll talk about this later, Pete. Let's get Jade out of here. Tracy's waiting outside to take you back to London. Did he hurt you, Jade?"

Her hand touched her throat where the knife had cut her, but she pulled her shoulders back, and her gaze met his. "It's good to see you again, Sean. Lorne said you were back. No, he just nicked the skin, I think. But I doubt if Lorne will be so lucky. Please, get her back quickly."

"Jade, I don't often say this, but you have my word on that." Roberts cleared his throat and escorted Jade out to the waiting vehicle.

When Roberts returned, he turned on Pete as they watched Tracy drive Scott's latest victim away. "Right. Now she's out of the way. Do you mind telling me what the hell is going on?"

"It's easy, really, Chief. Lorne felt she'd have more control over Scott if she was with him."

"And you went along with that? I can't believe you did that, Pete."

"You don't know how persuasive the inspector can be, sir. I've got every confidence in her negotiating skills."

"Fill me in. There's not a lot I can do about it now, but I'm warning you, when this is all over, you and Inspector Simpkins will regret leaving me out of the loop. It was a reckless course of action and totally against procedure."

"Yes, boss. Well, we already know where the grandparent's cabin is. We're banking on Scott taking her there. We'll organise an ART unit and surprise them in the morning. Lorne—sorry, Inspector Simpkins—is gonna feed him a line that a swap is still gonna take place. Hopefully, he won't be suspecting any movement from our end."

"What makes you so sure he'll head for the cabin?" Roberts looked angry at what had transpired, glaring at Pete.

"Seemed like it was the only place the kids felt secure and happy. That's the impression the boss got after seeing the scrapbook, anyway. You know her instincts are usually pretty good, sir."

"I've yet to see any evidence of that, Sergeant, or have you forgotten that I'm the new kid on the block?"

"I know, sir. But then it ain't the first time you've worked together, is it? She's also bloody-minded—you'll remember that trait, too. She's had that since I've known her."

"I sense you're fishing, Pete. In the past, the inspector wasn't the type to rush in and ask questions later, which is exactly what she's done here. How's Scott going to contact us? Have you thought about that? Do you know if he has a mobile? Do we have evidence of that? If he's still stuck in the seventies, I doubt he'll be up-to-date with gadgets from this century."

"Um, no, Chief. Didn't really think about that." Pete dipped his chin, embarrassed by the admission.

"Perhaps that's why I'm the DCI, and you're still a sergeant, Pete. It's my job to assess situations thoroughly before rushing in like... Oh, I don't know, amateur sleuths on a murder mystery weekend."

"Yes, Chief."

They dashed across the car park and stopped outside the chief's car.

"We'll get in touch with the armed response team and contact the local police. You better come with me. We'll leave Lorne's car here. She can drive it back to London herself if everything goes according to plan." Roberts shook his head as they both got in the car.

Chapter Fifty-One

John Scott returned to the cabin carrying half a dozen freshly cut logs for the stove. Lorne shivered but was relieved he'd thought about fighting the chill of the damp, cold cabin.

After he stuffed the wood into the stove, Lorne asked, "Why? Why now, John?" *Now will be an ideal opportunity to get a conversation going with him and hopefully gain his confidence.*

Ignoring her, he continued blowing and poking the fire.

Lorne tried again, using a much softer tone. "Why wait all these years, John?"

The fire roared into life. He closed the door and stood up. He pulled the sofa closer to the fire and sat on the edge, his elbows resting on his knees, rubbing his chilled hands together. "Why not?" He stared into the fire.

"Come on, John. Something must've triggered the feelings you'd suppressed for years. What was it?"

Still staring at the blaze, his fingers interlocked as though he was fighting something back. "Okay. If you must know, Inspector, I started working for Toni about six months ago." He fell silent again.

"And?" she prompted, quietly.

"And I picked up a fare, a woman I recognised from my *not* so happy childhood."

Lorne *knew* it. "That would be Belinda Greenaway?"

"That's right. Only I thought it was her sister, Doreen Nicholls. I picked her up from one of the ranks in town, so I didn't have a clue what her name was. Picked her up a few times after that, and the more I saw her, the more annoyed I became."

"So, when did you realise you'd made a mistake?"

"It was in the paper. I didn't know they were identical twins. I thought I was going mad. I realised I must've killed the wrong woman."

"How did that make you feel?"

"Angry. Foolish. Determined to right the wrongs."

"You took a risk turning up at Doreen's house, didn't you? You nearly got caught?"

"I did. How was I to know the old dear would be on the phone to you when I knocked on her door? That's when I realised I had to keep a close eye on you, Inspector. You're smart, I knew it wouldn't take you long to figure things out. But I threw a spanner in the works when I killed Kim Charlton, didn't I?" He turned to look at her.

"It spun the investigation in another direction, if that's what you mean. Why did you kill Kim?" she asked, her gaze searching his.

"She was a slut!" Scott screwed up his eyes and appeared to be reliving the events.

"Why did you think that?"

"I knew Wacko fancied her. We got talking one day, and he called her a prick-tease. On the odd occasion I picked her up, she used to tell me what the pair of 'em got up to. I did the world a favour getting rid of that one, believe me."

"If she disgusted you that much, why didn't you just refuse the fare? Why kill her? She was only sixteen."

Scott agitatedly wrung his hands together. "Ha! Sixteen going on bloody thirty, you mean. That night, the night I killed her, she flagged me down, said Wacko hadn't turned up. I told her he was delayed and he'd come back for her in a while. She wasn't happy about that and wanted to get home, so she opened the back door and climbed in my cab. She sat in the centre of the back seat so I could watch her in my mirror."

He fell silent again.

Lorne coaxed him further. "And, what happened then, John?"

"She was a slut. She started playing with herself—you know, down her knickers—started moaning and saying things to me, getting me going. She told me to drive down an alley and get in the back with her, *to satisfy* her, she said." His head shook from side to side as the memory played out in his mind.

"And did you, John? Did you have sex with her?"

"I started kissing her, and she tugged at my clothes, undressing me. That's when it all went wrong."

"How did it go wrong, John?" Lorne pushed for his confession.

"It just did."

"Have you ever had a girlfriend, John?"

He was silent for a long while, breathing in deep breaths, and slowly exhaling them like he was carrying out some kind of ritual. Calmer, he answered, "No."

Lorne suspected Jacques was right in his assumption Scott was impotent. "So, why did you kill her?"

"She laughed at me when I..." He stopped and ran his hands through his hair.

"When you didn't know how to respond, is that right, John?" Lorne had located a rough part of the chair, and she rubbed the rope on it.

"She...kept calling me names."

"What names?"

"Nasty, mean names. 'Johnny No Sperm', 'No-Come Johnny', things like that. I couldn't take it anymore, and I lost it. She shouldn't have teased me like that. It was her fault. She was to blame for what I did to her. I knew if I'd let her go, she would've been the type to cry rape. I didn't touch her. I couldn't." His voice trailed off.

"Did your parents abuse you as a child, John?" It surprised her, the genuine compassion she had for him.

Again, another long silence before he whispered, "Yes. They abused me for years, but when they started on Katherine, I wanted them to stop."

"Is that when you sought help, John?"

"Yeah, but they did nothing. They broke us up instead of helping us. If I'd kept my mouth shut none of this would've happened."

"Things were different in those days, John. The authorities didn't know how to handle abuse cases back then. The women you killed, they did what they could to help you. They were restricted."

Scott snarled, "That's enough. I don't want to talk about it anymore. We should get some sleep."

"I'm hungry." Lorne glanced around the cabin hoping to find signs of food. There weren't any. Her stomach groaned.

Scott turned to her and shrugged, seeming embarrassed. "I didn't think about food. Then again, it wasn't my intention to come up here. You forced this situation upon me." He ended his sentence with another sneer.

She shivered, never forgetting she was in the hands of a man who'd already abducted five women, killing four of them without a second glance. He'd shown little remorse for his actions, making Lorne fear for her safety. He'd already shown signs of being volatile, liable to snap at a moment's notice.

Before he curled up on the sofa, Scott threw a blanket over her. The gesture surprised Lorne. When he turned out the lamp, her nerves jangled. Her backside was numb, and her arms ached from hours of sitting in the same upright position.

Scott started snoring. Lorne upped her attempt to get out of her bindings.

As the sun's rays slithered through a gap in the curtain, she felt the thin rope giving way. Her heart raced. She glanced at Scott, who was still caught up in his dreams. Her ears pricked up when she thought she heard a noise outside the cabin. *Is my mind playing tricks?*

Snap. There it was again.

She moved her arms faster, yanking the rope taut. It broke. She sucked in a breath and froze as Scott stirred.

Another noise—this time it sounded as though it was just outside the window.

Scott leapt to his feet. He bolted to the window.

"Shit!" He peeked round the side of the curtain. Returning to the centre of the room, he ran frantic hands through his hair, pulling out clumps from the root. He rotated a full turn, deep in thought, his eyes scouring the room for something.

Scared by his reaction, Lorne asked, "What's going on?"

"They've found us." Scott appeared distracted for a moment but then jumped into action, stacking furniture, including the sofa, against the only door to the property. Lorne bided her time, trying to gauge what his next move would be.

"John Scott. We know you're in there. We have you surrounded. Give yourself up."

Lorne's eyes fluttered shut when she recognised Roberts' voice booming through a megaphone.

"Never. *Never!*" J.S. ducked behind the curtain where Lorne assumed the bathroom was, and came back carrying a petrol canister.

Lorne's heart leapt into her throat. *Oh, shit.* She swallowed and spoke to him in the calmest of voices. "John, give yourself up. You have my word I'll get you the help you need. None of this is your fault."

"I don't need *you* to tell me that." He tipped up the canister and emptied the contents around the room.

Tom and Charlie's faces lingered in her mind. If only she'd been a better wife and mother over the years. *Please, give me the strength and courage to get out of this.*

"Scott. You have two minutes to send Inspector Simpkins out," Roberts' voice bellowed again.

Scott moved to the kitchen area and tore around hunting for something. "There you are." He stood up. *Oh God...* Lorne fidgeted in her seat when she saw a small box of matches in his hand. *Shit. What can I do? He's blocked the door, if he sets fire to...*

"Want to say goodbye to your friends, Inspector?" Scott goaded. He took a couple of matches from the box, struck them, and held the lit flames above the sofa he'd pushed in front of the door.

"John, please don't do it. What about Katherine? She needs you. Don't you want to be with her again? She's probably out there with them now, waiting for you. Ask them?" Lorne said, grasping at straws.

He blew out the match and peeked out the window again. "I can't see her," he replied, bewildered. He paced the floor inches in front of her. "Why? Why did it have to end like this? All I did was ask for help. All I ever wanted was to protect Katherine from those bastards. I was only eight...when it started."

"Let me go, John, for both our sakes." Lorne's voice trembled as she begged him.

"Talk to them. Ask them where Katherine is?" he demanded, preparing to light another match.

She didn't need telling twice. "Sean? John wants to see his sister, is she with you?"

"She's on the way. Are you all right, Lorne?"

Searching Scott's gaze, she shouted, "John's taking good care of me. He's tired of hurting people. He just wants to be with his sister."

"He's *lying*." John bent over and shouted in her face. "She's not coming. You've all lied to me. The headmistress, the teacher, the social worker—they all lied to me. To us, they swore we'd never be parted. Five years we were forced to live apart. No one will know how much that time apart hurt Katherine and me, the damage it caused us. Damage that could've been avoided if only we'd been kept together. That wasn't too much to ask, was it? Someone had to pay for it. They all had to pay for it, in the end. They had their happy families. Mine was torn apart, destroyed. That's why I killed my parents. I took great pleasure in watching the *fuckers* burn. Now they're in hell where they belong." His eyes were wild and his tone fierce and unrelenting.

"Mistakes happen, John. No one's perfect."

"Like you, you mean? How could you carry on with the doctor like that, when you have a loving family waiting at home for you? You drove your husband and child away. People are crying out for what you've got. A happy family home... You treat them like shit, pick them up and put them down when it pleases you. You're heartless, just like the others. Family life is a hindrance to you, instead of something you should cherish." Tears sprang to his eyes.

His words hit Lorne with a powerful force. "You know *nothing* about my marriage or my family life."

"Tell me I'm wrong, but I know for a fact your husband and daughter moved out when that doc came on the scene."

Instead of placating the man, Lorne's guilt caused her to shout. "You're wrong! It's true Tom and I were having problems, but it's wrong of you to think the problems coincided with my friendship with Doctor Arnaud. For your information, I've known the doctor for quite a while. He's been kind to me. A good friend and *nothing* else." *Why am I defending my actions to a bloody murderer?*

Before Scott could respond, Roberts' voice echoed around the cabin again. "One minute, John. You have one minute left, before we come in."

Scott seemed like his nerves were in tatters. His lips pulled back, and he clenched his teeth as he lit another match. "Everyone will be better off without *us*." He threw the tiny flame onto the petrol-soaked sofa. The fire took hold instantly and spiralled out of control.

Lorne knew it was now or never. She had to fight for her life. While J.S. watched in fascination as the sofa burned and the flames sprinted across the floor in every direction. Lorne stood up, grabbed the chair she'd been tethered to and broke it over his back. Scott toppled onto the blazing sofa. Within seconds the flames were dining on his flesh. His screams followed the flames to every corner of the cabin.

Lorne was shocked when Scott refused to fight his inevitable death. His screams ceased and a smile spread across his face. Lorne felt sickened to her stomach. "*Sean*. The cabin's on fire! The door's blocked, I can't get out."

Coughing as the smoke penetrated her lungs, she watched in fear as the fire crept towards the propane gas cylinder. She ran towards the window. As the cylinder exploded, the window blew out. *Maybe there is a God, after all.*

Thick black smoke hampered her vision. Her chest tightened as she gasped for air. Her thoughts became foggy and dazed.

Lorne gripped the window's edge and threw herself through the broken glass, shards sticking into her skin, but she felt no pain. She staggered away from the cabin on to the scrubby grass as Sean Roberts dashed forwards to grab her.

Collapsing to the ground, she heard voices in the distance and then slipped into unconsciousness.

Chapter Fifty-Two

An ethereal, blurred image hovered over her. She'd arrived safely. *So this is heaven.* She'd often heard about the tunnel of light and being greeted by an angel. "What's your name?" she whispered to the angel.

A Scottish voice answered, "Lorne, I'm Doctor Collins. How are you feeling?"

Doctor, did he say? So she wasn't dead after all. "How? Where am I?" she asked, her vision clearing.

"You're in hospital. Would you like to see your family? They're waiting outside." He checked each eye with a penlight.

"Tom and Charlie are *here?*"

The doctor opened the door, and her family ran in.

"Oh, Mum. You're safe... You're safe." Charlie cried, throwing herself on the bed.

"Charlie, get off there," Tom chastised their daughter, and bent down to plant a kiss on Lorne's forehead.

"What's happened to me?" Lorne gazed at her bandaged hand as she nestled Charlie's head against her chest. "What's wrong with my hands, Tom?"

"Superficial burns and a few nasty glass cuts. The bandages are precautionary."

Holding the sheet up, she checked underneath and felt relieved to see the blue hospital gown and her bare legs.

"Can you tell me what happened?" Lorne's brow furrowed. "I have a hazy image in my head, but everything's still jumbled."

"Maybe later," Tom said, nodding towards Charlie.

"I need to know, Tom," she asked in frustration, before two more visitors entered the room.

"I'll be outside with Charlie. You've got five minutes, then I want my wife back," Tom told Pete and Chief Roberts before he left.

Pete gave Lorne a small bunch of flowers, and Sean placed a box of chocolates on the cabinet beside her.

"How're you feeling, boss?" Pete's eyes were damp.

"I wish everyone would stop asking me that and tell me what the bloody hell happened?"

Sean pulled up a chair and took a deep breath. "When the explosion blew out the window, you tumbled out. They couldn't save Scott."

Lorne was quiet for a few minutes as her brain slotted the pieces together. "That's right. I managed to untie myself, I hit him with my chair, and he tumbled onto the sofa. The crazy thing is he didn't even try to get off it. It was as if he'd accepted his death." Unexpected tears welled in her eyes.

"Perhaps he thought it was a better option than spending the rest of his life in prison," Pete suggested with a shrug.

"What about Katherine?" Lorne asked.

"We've arrested her, charged her with accessory to abduction and murder. She'll be banged up for years, if the CPS do their job properly." Roberts smiled.

Eager to go home with her family, Lorne asked, "How long do I have to stay in here?"

"I'm not really sure," Roberts said.

"Well I'm ready to go home now." Lorne pulled back the covers and tried to get out of bed.

Eyes blazing, Roberts said, "You dare, Inspector, and I'll make sure your demotion is waiting for you."

"Don't make matters worse, boss. We're already in deep shit for going it alone," her partner grumbled.

"That was all my fault. Pete was only obeying orders. Any reprimands you have to make should be aimed at me, not him." She faked a cough and patted her chest, hoping to gain some sympathy.

"Hmm... We'll see when you're back at work, Inspector. I haven't quite decided what to do with the pair of you, yet. Come on, Pete. Let's leave Lorne to reacquaint herself with her family."

As Tom and Sean Roberts walked by each other, an awkward glance passed between them.

Charlie flung herself on the bed beside Lorne again. "Is it all right if we come back home now, Mum?"

"I don't know, darling. You'd better ask your father that?"

Charlie went on to tell Lorne about her father's new job. Tom's cheeks coloured.

"I see, and your father is agreeable to you working for him again? Despite walking out on him when Charlie was born?" Lorne asked, surprised.

"Yep, he said it was time to move on. He also said I was the best mechanic he'd ever had. So…"

"That's brilliant. Maybe this means we'll be able to get our marriage back on track."

"Have I told you lately, Mrs. Simpkins, how much I love you?" Tom bent down and kissed her on the lips.

"God, you two. Get a room, will ya?" Charlie pulled a face and covered her eyes.

Lorne blushed and replied, "No, I don't believe you have, Mr. Simpkins."

* * *

The man watched the couple share a kiss through the porthole in the door, a snarl pulling up one side of his mouth. *So, you survived, did you, DI Simpkins? Maybe I'll get my wish to finish you off, after all.* The man, known as The Unicorn, turned and walked casually up the corridor, already plotting how he'd take revenge on Lorne Simpkins for costing his empire millions. *You might've nicked Gripper Jones, Inspector. But you'll never capture me…*

ABOUT THE AUTHOR

New York Times, USA Today, Amazon Top 20 bestselling author, iBooks top 5 bestselling and #2 bestselling author on Barnes and Noble. I am a British author who moved to France in 2002, and that's when I turned my hobby into a career.
I share my home with two crazy dogs that like nothing better than to drag their masterful leader (that's me) around the village.
When I'm not pounding the keys of my computer keyboard I enjoy DIY, reading, gardening and painting.

11869582R00159

Printed in Great Britain
by Amazon.co.uk, Ltd.,
Marston Gate.